First publish(
www.'

M000303173

Copyrighı   ., ~ιλυπ κeuel

*This novel is entirely a work of fiction. The names,
characters
and incidents portrayed in it are the work of the author's
imagination. Any resemblance to actual persons, living or
dead, events or localities is entirely coincidental.
Dixon Reuel asserts the moral right to be identified as the
author of this work.*

*Dixon Reuel has no responsibility for the persistence or
accuracy of URLs for external or third-party Internet
Websites referred to in this publication and does not
guarantee that any content on such Websites is, or will
remain, accurate or appropriate.*

First edition
ISBN: 978-1-8380233-2-4

This book is dedicated to 2020.

What a year.

Acknowledgements

My utter appreciation to the inner team that materialised over the years, to which I don't have enough words of thanks. To Alan, Sile, John, Geoffrey, your support is magic enough for this lifetime.

My thanks also to the fantastic team I've put together on this Blood Brute journey. For sailing the ship to shore and your technical expertise, thank you Sara, Amber, Natasha, Doreen, Mark.

To Tracy. Worlds would not exist without you. Thank you for being a constant friend.

To those from the early days, to Susan and John, and everybody in that room.

To everybody who supports me online, especially the friends I've made and have yet to meet in person. To those that have reached out and offered opportunities. To those that get the in-jokes. To those that are there no matter the hour. Thank you.

For my mother, who never lived to see this.

And especially I thank you, the reader. Without you, there'd be very little point.

Nothing would give up life:
Even the dirt kept breathing a small breath.

–Theodore Roethke, *Root Cellar*

PART 1 - AUTUMN

"We have to be careful, as those who age so slowly, not to fight upon past battlefields. In that, and maybe only in that, are we superior. To hold a grudge for a human lifespan, that is one thing. To hold a grudge throughout the whole of our lives, that would be an unlivable, untenable existence. So, we do not fight on past battlefields. We air our grievances as plainly as possible. We found, after centuries, we could live no other way."

–Salter, The Chronicler

Chapter 1

A Fresh Pulse

The outbreak began in springtime rumours. Then, the airways and cables of the world charted the outbreak and panic, as the disease overwhelmed every population. Bombs and walls of fire tried to contain it. Chemical purges charred cities indiscriminately. In all, Rise counted barely five months from the beginning of the outbreak until everything was stilled, from late spring to mid-autumn. A lone SOS in Morse code was the last they heard from the human race, before Rise and his coven packed away their broadcast equipment, their radio, computers, and TV, putting it all into the depths of the root cellar. He waited a further full month, October. Then, and only then, did Rise leave the house.

An earlier shower of hail had studded the courtyard's cobblestones. Crimson leaves brightened the hedges that Rise had planted long ago to shade the kitchen windows. Once, Rise heard birdsong and the hum of the countryside the moment he stepped from the kitchen into the yard. But today, like so many days that came before, no sound.

The rest of his coven were still on the roof, just finished with the dawn incantation. While the disease had overwhelmed all beyond Owl Court, every dawn, Rise and the two other vampires, Ogrim and Salter, spoke an incantation to conceal their little farmstead from the world. Even smoke from the nearest village of Dunsinann, or the hazy curtain on the horizon from Larnde City, never reached inside their walls. The coven always used the oldest names for such places; Ogrim joked that if they were to rename cities and towns as often as humans did, the coven would never get anything done.

Rise wanted to slip away into the world and hoped to return with good news, to return with someone still human. The coven needed a fresh pulse. If he could achieve this, Rise reasoned as he stood on the back doorstep, the residents of Owl Court would surely forgive him for leaving. Hiding indoors, they saw footage of how the human dead now rose and walked. Rise had trawled the internet, when they still had it, watching feeds from around the world of corpses alive, of terrifying creatures that knew only brute and base destruction.

"Where're you going?" Ogrim spoke from the kitchen's shade, so as not to let the weak sun touch his old body.

"To find survivors," Rise answered, as plainly as possible. He tried to appear unruffled at being followed down through the house. Usually, Rise had more time to himself after leading the incantation. *Ogrim must be faster on his walking cane,* he thought. Rise attached the crowbar to his backpack and tucked the cuffs of his leather gloves beneath the sleeves of his overcoat.

"Old man, there are always survivors after the collapse of big things," Rise said, preparing for the fight to come. Not against any zombie brutes, but against the arguments opposed to his leaving. "We need people. Cypriot will. One day, we'll look for survivors and there won't be any, only those base brutes we saw on TV. Then, what will we do for food?"

Ogrim shifted the weight on his cane and winced. The autumn weather always bothered his right knee. The centuries-old vampire glanced to the sky, as if it might finally fall around their ears. "The type of people who survive, they are not the type of people we want at Owl Court."

"Blood is blood, Ogrim. It doesn't matter where it comes from, as long as its owner still draws breath to flush it red." Rise kept his voice light and shouldered his backpack. Chocolate bars and cans of fizz rattled between his shoulders. Rise was not much for human company, save for one, but people as a whole seemed to him like any other injured animal: easily lured along by food and sweet vice.

Ogrim frowned. It seemed he might lift his clenched fist and finally, after so long, actually strike Rise. But he only smote the jam of the kitchen door and rattled its hinges. Behind Ogrim, the kettle on the hob whistled.

"There are others, you know," Ogrim said over the sound of the kettle. "Also human. Who watch this place across the ages. Who would like nothing more than to crack open our chests and let the sunlight at our hearts."

"I put on the kettle for you," Rise said, hoping the promise of tea would be enough to soften him. A palate cleanser with a drop of milk from their cow. A warm, civilized drink which they, as a coven, had grown accustomed to. *Chocolate and soda for one lot, a cup of tea for ours, and we are all equally and easily placated,* Rise told himself as he waited for Ogrim to let him leave.

"Bring back strays, then, inside these walls, when there has only been one human amongst us," Ogrim growled and waved his cane about. "But it's more likely I'll see your head on a pole outside of Dunsinann first. What'll we do if you don't return? You, Rise, are most knowledgeable about roots and boundaries. You lead our incantation every dawn. That's what protects these walls."

"I don't think people put heads on poles anymore," Rise said, as kindly as he could. But the day marched on and he chafed to leave. "I'll bring back survivors. If they come. If they listen. We need to secure our food for the long term, Ogrim. For Cypriot's sake, if nothing else. The people out there will listen to me. If they've lived this long, they'll see sense in what I propose."

"And what'll I tell our people here?" Ogrim still wore pajamas beneath his oversized wax coat, draped like a cloak around his shoulders. Ogrim always rolled out of bed and threw on the nearest thing to hand before he made his way to the roof. But now, as he stood in the kitchen, it seemed to Rise that Ogrim's clothes just made him look old and in decline. "Will I tell them what you're doing?" Ogrim added and lifted his bushy eyebrows, rage trembling in his voice.

Rise paused. He cursed Ogrim for asking the one question he didn't want to face. He took his time. Cast about for the best answer.

"Tell Salter whatever you want. But, please, don't tell Cypriot that I'm leaving." The wide step outside the back door had long been scrubbed and bleached bare. A bleak fitting for their threshold. Rise's hiking boots looked comically modern upon the old concrete.

Ogrim turned away from Rise and took the whistling kettle off the range. He paused when he noticed that Rise had also left out a teabag and spoon in his favourite mug, a deck of well-worn tarot cards alongside. Ogrim twitched his whiskery chin, as if to hide a smile, and made his tea.

"Don't tell Cypriot? Well, I suppose, if you return soon enough, Rise," Ogrim offered in kindness at last. "Then Cypriot will never know that you left at all."

Rise hesitated at Ogrim's softening. He then spoke lightly, hoping he could pull Ogrim more over to his point of view. Rise's smile didn't fade. "You may never see me again. You want these to be our last words, Ogrim? Why not wish me luck? It's for the good of us all."

Ogrim grunted as he dunked the teabag in hot water with his bare fingertips. He sucked his gums and took his time. He let Rise continue standing there expectantly on the doorstep until, crossing the kitchen with surprising speed, he kicked the back door shut in his face.

"Beware the rotting herds."

Long accustomed to Ogrim's dramatics, Rise only rolled his eyes. He lifted his scarf. Dead cattle in the surrounding fields—he could smell them now, a sick-sweet scent like clammy marbles held too long in your hand. Rise's stomach squeezed with nausea. This smell would haunt their home for several weeks more, if not months. Cypriot, the coven's lone human—he'd surely complain about the smell for just as long.

The weak sun tingled across Rise's skin, as if he had been slapped by a bunch of nettles. He covered his face, swallowed down his nausea, as he rattled one of their mountain bikes from the shed. He let himself out at the little side gate. No need to bother opening the double-doored gate alongside.

"Best to find survivors before they're turned into those wandering brutes," Rise muttered as he set off down the steep lane on Holly Hill, at the top of which Owl Court was perched. His bike wobbled with every turn of the pedal. The countryside had never been truly silent before. But now stillness across the land. Hedgerows once filled with chattering birds were silent. Even when Rise concentrated, he couldn't hear a badger in its den, not earthworms in the soil. Flies—oh yes, Rise could hear them. But it was one thing for cattle to die in their pastures after over a year with no one left to tend to them. It was quite another for bees to still and stoats and weasels to silence on the riverbanks. Leaving only masses of flies to feed on the carrion.

Rise walked his bike around a fallen tree. Its thick trunk had toppled through a low stone wall and blocked most of the road. The ripped-up roots created quite the hole and upturned rich, dark soil. Flowers grew by the trunk, the dull plum petals blending into clumps of unmelted hailstones.

"Helleborus, winter's rose," he named the flower. "A cure for madness that summons demons," Rise recounted from one of Cypriot's gardening books. He placed several flowers in a pouch beneath his coat and checked the small hand pistol stored alongside, kept well hidden from Ogrim. Rise pressed on.

As he passed through the quieted world, prickly horse chestnuts hung from branches. Some, their green outer shells cracked open, lay dark and glossy on the ground. Rise longed for spring, even if a bleak winter lay ahead first. Even his kind were of the earth and must obey its cycles. He dismounted and pushed his bike as the clutter on the road—leaves, fallen branches, abandoned things—grew denser. A countryside taking back its realm. Soon, he could walk the bike no further. Rise plunged it into a nearby ditch and made sure it was completely covered before he continued.

Trees parted in the distance where the lane from Owl Court met the main road to Dunsinann. As he approached the village, rooftops appeared like jagged black teeth out of the gloom. Bare rafters and cold chimney pots poked against the clouds. Ash from the burnt-out village still crept about in the air. Rise could smell it all, even through his scarf.

In Dunsinann stood the River Blythe, with a bridge to cross, then the village.

Low sludge lay beneath the once-pleasing arch of the bridge, between banks of exposed mud. Rise weighed his crowbar in his hands as he approached. All manner of tangled, disordered things lay between him and the bridge, as if someone had shaken Dunsinann and scattered its contents back onto its streets. What looked like jumbled grey wreckage was actually the charred remains of people amid timbers and burned-out cars. Senses pricked, the only sound he heard was his footsteps.

Rise knelt to inspect the nearest corpse.

It was hard to tell whether this person had turned into one of the brutish dead before dying, but agony all the same twisted those burnt sinews and limbs. Rise tried to recall the last time he'd watched the news and what the living dead had looked like, exactly. But that felt like a lifetime ago. However this person had died, Rise noted that we all must smile like skulls in the end. He gently touched the corpse's cheek with the curve of his crowbar, until the whole side of its face flaked away to nothing.

"Are you real?"

Rise spun around.

A lone girl stood on the other side of the bridge, so soot-covered that the whites of her eyes stood out from the rest of Dunsinann. He judged her to be no more than a teenager and, as Rise stared, she hiccupped from crying. Her dirty thumbs twisted the hem of a too-big t-shirt, worn over men's work trousers.

"Yes, I'm real," Rise called back and stood slowly, his arms open wide. He loosened the grip on his crowbar to show her that he meant no harm. They watched each other.

"Here, I have food." Rise did not look away from her as he fumbled with his backpack. He held out the first thing he found. "I have chocolate. Are you hungry?"

She sprinted across the bridge, barefoot, undeterred by all of the bones and gore and wasteland that she trampled. She flung herself across the final few feet, and Rise caught her. She tugged at him, wailing, until he realized that she wanted the rest of the food in his backpack.

"Wait, wait." Rise tried to shush her and glanced around. "Are you alone? Are there others?" He handed over several chocolate bars before he could lure her back from the bridge, into the shade of charred trees lining the road.

She ate everything Rise gave her and downed a can of fizz. She drank so quickly that most of it spilled down her sooty chin. The soda cleaned lines of white across her filthy skin. The thought flashed through his mind: *A new pulse to drink from that is not Cypriot.* Rise glanced away to compose himself.

"Oh, my god," she finally whimpered and breathlessly stopped eating. She leaned against the nearest tree, eyes closed, quiet except for an occasional cough that rattled her lungs.

"I am Rise." He offered her some water. "What's your name?"

She shook her head at the water, but did take another can of cola. After a few more gulps, she ran her tongue around her mouth. She watched him with open suspicion now, after reacting so impulsively at first. "Elaine."

14

"Elaine, is it?" Rise knew he must look crazy, wearing massive ski goggles with his face all covered. The sun was not yet too high, not yet too strong. The day was dampened by fog anyhow, along with the dull haze of soot and smoke that haunted Dunsinann. Hailstones still clung to the ground and streets and rooftops, adding to the monochrome. And, he reasoned, they were under what was left of the trees. Rise took a chance and slowly lifted his goggles onto his forehead.

"Are you alone?" He drew away his scarf a little, so that she could see his whole face. "I'm as human as you are. Are there—"

"How ... are you here? How did you survive?"

Rise smiled that she was strong enough to interrupt. As he answered, he removed some cleansing wipes from his backpack, took her nearest hand and cleaned it, turning her wrist so the underside faced up. A sinuous blue vein revealed itself to the world as he wiped.

"Elaine, I have a house a few miles away, Owl Court, on top of Holly Hill," he told her, speaking softly down at her wrist vein. "There are others there. We're all safe."

His efforts revealed more of her pale skin. It was scarred and cut and bruised in places, but considering what she must've gone through out here .... Rise only grew hungrier. He saw what might one day heal into suppleness. But he did not dwell too long on the aesthetics of veins. At the barest flicker of panic or unwillingness to come back with him, Rise would kill her. He held faith that there would be other survivors, not just this girl. *There are always others after the fall of great things.*

"Everyone in Dunsinann knows everyone else," Elaine said in a low, hoarse tone as she watched him clean her hands. Her accent was thick, local. "I've never seen you before. I've lived here my whole life. There's no house on that hill, only a ring of holly trees. Everybody knew to stay away from them."

Rise smiled, thought of the grey-green trunks that played their part in shielding his home. The sunlight was not too harsh on his face, but any more exposure would soon raise the Blaschko lines normally dormant on human skin, but activated by the sun upon a vampire's.

"That's not true," Rise countered lightly. "My home is well hidden, is all. You never wondered why there's no house with the number one in Dunsinann? That the house numbers only start at two once you get over that bridge? Well, I suppose I've always kept to myself. But I have room for others at my home." Rise ignored her suspicion and kept everything about himself upbeat and easy. "That's why I'm out searching. For people. Come back to my home. It's up the lane on that big hill, behind the holly trees, like you said."

"You have such blue eyes," Elaine murmured as she studied his face. She idly crushed the chocolate in her fist, as if to relearn the feel of food.

Rise smiled. "Many have told me that, Elaine."

"And a young face," she went on. "There are ... stripes on your skin. They weren't there before."

"We must get going." He stood and covered up again. Rise exhaled with relief when his goggles and scarf shielded his skin again. "Follow me."

"My mother!" Elaine leaped to her feet and stared over the bridge, her eyes huge and hungry. A half-melted chocolate bar still in her fist.

Rise stood with Elaine and carefully took hold of her bony elbow as he regained his grip on the crowbar.

"Your mother? She is alive, Elaine? Where is she?"

"I told her to stay inside. But she never listens. She just does what she wants, always has. I think her brain is dead already."

At those words, he shivered. Rise followed Elaine's gaze across the bridge. An old woman stood there, a slight, wan figure, all grey and dusted in soot. A long nightdress worn beneath a padded overcoat, an embroidered hem tucked into men's gumboots.

"Mammy?" Elaine whispered and held out her chocolate as she carefully crossed the bridge. Her mother watched Rise, not her daughter, as Elaine picked a path across the rubble and carcasses, this time with care.

"Mammy? Don't run. Come to me, okay?"

Rise hung back. Two people to return with. That would be all right, not too many. Especially if one of them was old and frail. Eventual company for Ogrim or, if these women didn't fall into line, someone who could be easily gotten rid of within his walls. Owl Court was such a big house, after all, mostly banisters and staircases. Even his coven had to be careful of their step. He let Elaine reach her mother and watched as they chatted softly. But after a few moments, Mammy tugged at Elaine and whispered hoarse things into her ear.

Rise stepped onto the bridge again.

This startled Elaine's mother, and she stiffened.

"She says not to trust anyone, let alone a man," Elaine called back.

He uncovered his face again and kept that light tone in his voice. "Look, I have a safe place that you both—"

Mammy screamed. A fox's wail—a sound that birthed the myth of banshees—would have sounded kinder in the burned-out village.

Rise ducked, clutched his ears, and shouted back until her scream stopped.

"What was that for?" He raced across the bridge, ready to lift his crowbar and dash in their heads. Maybe this 'Mammy' was indeed brain-dead.

The mother spoke. "They are beneath the bridge."

Rise knew words of command. Rise knew words that woke.

Slippery masses and stenches, foul and grappling things, poured into the river from beneath the arches of the bridge, like a dollop of bees dropping from the belly of a hive. The dead brutes squirmed in the river mud. Their flesh, pale and bloated, dropped in lumps from their limbs as they moved. The horde swarmed rapidly, terrifying, across the brickwork, like bees surrounding and boiling an enemy hornet, until the bridge began to crumble. Rise grabbed Elaine and her mother and hauled them back toward the line of trees just before the bridge collapsed with a tremendous crash, crushing any brute still pressed against its arches. *Destroyers of supports.* The thought flashed in Rise's mind as the trio ran. He didn't know if the brutes possessed the intelligence to do such a thing, whether this was a conscious decision by them or some kind of herd behaviour. He didn't bother with his bike, just ran full tilt towards home, pushing the two women before him. The surviving brutes weren't quick to rise out of the squelching river, but they did follow.

The trio made their way through deepening woods until they came against a stone wall, which they helped haul one another over. Elaine's mother was surprisingly nimble. They tumbled into a wide field where rotting cows were heaped in a far corner, under a clump of bare trees.

"Rest a second," Rise whispered as Elaine and her mother collapsed to the ground, gasping for breath and gagging at the stench as they huddled against the back side of the wall. For the moment, they were hidden from the brutes.

"Those monsters held that bridge for days, then wandered away. I didn't realize they were still underneath it," Elaine stammered.

Rise shushed her. He could hear brutes coming toward them, snapping through the first, thin trees, then pushing deeper into thick forest. Rise peeped over the wall, where he could see wandering shadows approaching. He couldn't quite tell if the brutes were merely following in their direction or could actually smell them out.

From where they were crouching, Rise looked across the field to judge how far they were from Owl Court. In the distance, resembling a far-off river flowing through picturesque fields along gentle curves of land, Rise saw a great herd of brutes—thousands of them, moving in silence. They produced, even to his acute hearing, only a faint, low hum. He swallowed hard, in terror that so many zombie brutes could move so sinuously through the countryside and make only the most barely discernible noise.

Then Rise saw the two hooded figures: two Warwolves, a human order of vampire hunters old as all the races of the world. They sat astride horses on a far-off ridge, swathed in heavy robes, watching the hordes too. Each carried the weapon they used across the centuries—a scythe, held with the blade curling over each one's uncovered head, as if for protection.

Squirming brutes Rise could handle. But to have Warwolves this close to his home was a whole other matter.

"I don't think they see us," Rise muttered, gesturing to the women that they needed to stand.

"The brutes don't see us, you mean?" Elaine asked, confused. "Those riders? Who are they?"

The brutes following them, though, were coming too close for comfort. Without answering Elaine's questions, Rise turned and fired his pistol into the approaching brutes. The screech of their rotting leader stilled them. They stared as he writhed frantically until he was half dug into the cold earth. Rise did not let Elaine or her mother watch. The moment he distracted the brutes, he urged them to run.

A steep and familiar hill rose from a tiny laneway. His spirits soared at seeing the way home before him. Rise urged Elaine and her mother on, through the ring of holly trees, to the walls of his compound, to the double gates. A slap of his hand on the doorframe momentarily broke the protection long enough for them to slip inside, to safety.

A great *splat* was heard behind them as dozens of pursuing brutes slapped full force against the just-shut gates.

Chapter 2

Stoat – Otter – Weasel

The scent of the house enveloped Rise on his return: Mint drying in bunches above the heaters and in window corners. The crackling fire in the drawing room. Lavender in every bedroom. Holly and pine branches brought inside and woven through the banister posts on every staircase. A pot of stew on the stove. As he passed down through the scented house, after settling Elaine and her mother in a bedroom on the second floor, Rise remembered the winter roses. He fished them out of his coat pocket, their dull plum petals all wrinkled from his adventure. Rise left the flowers next to Cypriot's tray on the kitchen's wide windowsill, where Cypriot kept his pruning shears and smaller gardening tools in neat rows. Amber glass bottles and wads of folded white cloth sat alongside. In the corner of the tray, an elegant bowl rimmed with gold housed some horse chestnuts.

Rise smiled at the tray, charmed by Cypriot's habit of bringing the outdoors inside. He stood in the kitchen's stillness, his nose filled with the pleasant fragrance of mint, watercress, thyme, from all the potted plants placed on every spare surface. Outdoors, there was only that stench.

Rise glanced out of the nearest kitchen window. The walls of Owl Court encompassed not just the house, but also a kitchen garden, several outbuildings, and paddocks for their cows, goats, and chickens. The tall pines along the northern wall stood as pillars of eternal green throughout the year. Flower beds and evidence of the coven's tolerance of Cypriot's potted plants nestled everywhere. Rise had always hoped this would be enough to keep them all safe. Rise touched the nearest branch of thyme while keeping his gaze on the high wall outside. He imagined the brutes wandering beyond. Guilt weighed on his chest, to think that he'd drawn such creatures back to his home.

"Don't think I didn't hear that racket you made just now. Don't even think, not for a moment, that I don't know what you've hidden upstairs. And also what you've brought to our walls," Ogrim complained from the drawing room.

Rise wandered towards that voice, the distance from the kitchen through the hall to the drawing room being only a few steps. He leaned against the drawing room door and found their eldest vampire standing beside the mantelpiece, inspecting a wall of shelves heaving with books. A merry fire danced in the hearth beside Ogrim's overstuffed armchair, where he kept a stack of yellowed tarot cards on the narrow table alongside.

"I returned in one piece, thank you for asking," Rise said. He could not help but smile in relief at having returned to these needling arguments that would never end. "At least I'm bringing some life into the house."

"Oh, is that what you're doing?" The insult was light but sharp. Ogrim tapped his fingers along the book spines.

"Those two women are safely upstairs, resting. I will discuss them no further until after we feed tonight." Rise ignored Ogrim's obvious pout and continued, "Just ... remind Cypriot to sweep up after himself. He has pine needles all over the kitchen."

"I shouldn't have to remind him. A pretty face shouldn't have to be reminded it's attached to a body, one that has to live with others. And that goes for you, too. Heading off into the wilds when there was never a need. Bringing those obscene dead right to our walls—what were you thinking? They're milling around out there, even now. Do I have to go out next morning and shoot those things as if they were pigeons?"

Ogrim selected a narrow title from their shelf of history books. He creaked into his armchair and wedged the book under the shaky leg on his little side table. With a nod of satisfaction, Ogrim licked a fat thumb as he reached for his tarot cards, their ink so faded and yellowed that the cards might have belonged to a child's board game.

"He ... Cypriot is our food, Ogrim," Rise spoke after a long time of standing in the doorway. Rise always felt that Cypriot could hear whatever they said in this house. Although, Rise reminded himself, if he were in Cypriot's position, he would probably cultivate a similar talent. Cypriot probably already knew about the women, if he was somewhere indoors. "So don't antagonize him."

Ogrim grunted. "You'd be better off pissing in the sink." He turned a card, the Three of Swords, on its side and used it to cut his tea leaves into tidy portions, before dumping them into the large kettle.

He's making only a cup at a time and not brewing a big pot. Rise recalled the days of rationing during the last two world wars. *So, those days are back again.*

"He's our *only* food, old man," Rise repeated softly, only for them to hear. Rise's chest burned to see Ogrim ration his tea. Such a sight should never be, that the coven should go without. The thought almost stopped his breath. It took Rise a while before he could continue. "Let Cypriot have his eccentricities. He lets us have ours."

"Until he discovers what you've brought back."

Rise said nothing as Ogrim made his tea on reduced rations. The delicate tap-tap-tap, then the scrape of the Three of Swords across the little table as Ogrim swept any remaining tea leaves back into a tin painted with garish clowns. Then Rise forced a smile. "Cypriot will see sense. He'll understand why I took in those women."

"The day will come, Rise," Ogrim said, his eyebrows lifting as he shuffled the Three of Swords back into his deck, "when Cypriot will no longer understand, when he grows too old. There'll come a day when you'll unravel us all—"

"You always think," Rise interrupted, annoyed that there would be a fight from Ogrim whenever anyone wanted to do anything, "that all we've built will come crashing down around our heads. But we've survived this far. And not just survived; thrived, even. We don't need much, we just need Cypriot. What's happened outside these walls, to the world, we will weather that, too."

Ogrim said nothing, only held up the Judgement card.

"Oh, stop." Rise rolled his eyes.

"Doom, doom and gloom," Ogrim chuckled as he shuffled the card back into the deck.

Ogrim dealt a spread.

We still hold onto the hope of finding out where we came from. Rise again felt a pang of guilt in his chest. Not knowing one's origins, being a tribeless people, they had managed to find each other: Rise, Ogrim, Salter, and Cypriot to feed on. But they had never found others like them, no other coven, not even a whisper. Rise long ago had left off the search for other vampires and instead took up the cause of ensuring that their Cypriot lived the best life possible, with everything he could ask for. Thankfully, it was neither gold or jewels that their human desired, only greenery and flattery. Ogrim, however—his search continued, rereading and redealing the tarot over and over for a possible lead. Something about foretelling the future to divine the past. Rise never really paid much attention; tarot was a meaningless pursuit to him. Rise preferred to concentrate on their future, on Cypriot. No number of cards and readings could help them there.

"Past, present and future," Ogrim muttered as he divined the tarot, echoing what weighed on Rise's mind.

Cypriot came bustling into the kitchen from the courtyard. He unrolled a large bundle of dried roses onto the kitchen table before he shrugged out of his overcoat, revealing a heavy apron that swamped his slight frame. The sleeves of his light linen shirt were rolled back to show tanned forearms and his prominent twists of veins. And the puncture marks where the coven fed from him. Lately, Cypriot had taken to unbuttoning the top of his shirt as well, so that it slipped from his shoulder beneath the gardening apron. This showed off the fine sinews of his throat, the dip of his collarbone, long black hair bundled high atop his head. Worn as badges of honour along his throat, more puncture marks, centuries old, were on display for anyone who cared to look.

A blood-hunger headache awoke in Rise's temples. Cypriot rattled about the kitchen as he hung up his overcoat and stamped feeling back into his slender-booted feet.

Rise recalled the sight of Cypriot, languid and naked on the chaise, as the three vampires fed from him. The light in Cypriot's eyes that dulled. A silence broken only by the quiet swish of clothing as they took turns upon him. Rise longed for that satisfaction, the firm and warm tension of slotting his teeth into their human. Of tasting Cypriot, as Cypriot gave of himself to keep them alive. And the satiated moments after, the puppy pile by the fire, and Rise's nose against Cypriot's scalp as they all grew sleepy, the vampires from satiation, the human from weakness and warmth. And then they would all sleep until the sun rose again and they awoke to renew their home's protection.

"We can weather it all, because we're coven," Rise said pointedly at Ogrim as that memory faded. He left Ogrim to his frowning and whining. Rise longed to feed.

Cypriot poked his head into the hall and smiled upon hearing Rise's voice. Happiness shone in that smile, and the beauty of it alone lifted Rise's spirits after Ogrim's gloom and the terrible chase home to these sacred walls.

"Thank you for my flowers," Cypriot spoke softly.

Rise ignored the last, dark glance from Ogrim and left him to his cards. He hesitated in the hall, confused for a moment at Cypriot's words, but then remembered the winter roses. Cypriot had tucked the crinkled flowers into the top pocket of his leather apron.

Cypriot didn't seem to know about the women upstairs.

Rise was happy to keep it that way for now.

"Where did you find them, Rise?" Cypriot touched the petals and beamed another grateful smile. "I haven't seen helleborus grow in any of our yards at all this year. Although I have often looked."

"Found them down by the pine trees. Out back."

Cypriot blinked a little too slowly for Rise's liking. Rise stared into Cypriot's brown eyes and became distracted by freckles across a faintly tanned nose, ruddy from just being outside. Rise cleared his throat. The door to the root cellar was sunk into the wall beside the kitchen, almost invisible as it blended into the wood panelling. Rise opened the squat door and paused at the top of the cellar's stairs.

"I thought you'd like them. Anyway, I need to speak with Salter. I'll see you tonight."

"Yes, you will." Cypriot's voice drifted after him as Rise continued down into the root cellar.

*

"I suppose it'll be nice to have something new to chronicle," Salter said as Rise descended into her lair. Salter sat at her candlelit desk, where she wrote the chronicle of their lives. The coven didn't know whether female vampires were more susceptible to daylight's sting. Ogrim and Rise could move about Owl Court comfortably once the nettings and curtains on a room's windows were at least part way drawn. But Salter, her skin darkest of the coven's, preferred to keep to dim light. She once told Rise that she liked the chill and silence of the sleeping vegetables that were stored in the root cellar, especially in the autumn after harvest. She said it helped her find words. Rise let her do as she liked, for he had long cultivated the opinion that this was how Salter sought to find the covern's meaning or purpose, just like Ogrim with his cards, or Cypriot with his plants.

"Oh yes?" Rise responded and leaned against one of the cellar's supporting beams, as if he hadn't left their house this morning at all. As if nothing had happened.

"Yes, Rise. Invoker, you should keep nothing from your Chronicler." Salter raised her dark eyebrows at him. Her pen hovered above a thick pad of lined A4 paper, fingers long and knobby-knuckled from centuries of writing.

She wrote on both sides of the page now, Rise realized. Their tea and sugar, pens, paper, even down to the rouge that Cypriot liked to use—they'd soon grow scarce after the fall of the world. As during those two world wars, lean times that Rise wished never to return to. Seeing the slight marks of Salter's penmanship press through her page from the other side, Rise winced.

"All right, then, here's the full story to put in the chronicle," Rise said, to put aside his grim train of thought. He stood from the pillar and approached her desk, always surprised that Salter's beaded, dangling scarves never caught in candles when she bent to write. "I just left Owl Court and went to Dunsinann. I returned with two survivors: two women, a mother and daughter. They're resting upstairs. They will watch us feed tonight and we shall get the proper measure of them. If they don't accept what we are, if they can't keep mum, we can kill them on the spot. I'm sure the brutes outside our walls will welcome their bodies."

Salter will not scream or throw a tantrum. She will take this well. Rise watched for her reaction.

"And ... do the women know what we are?" Salter asked in a slow, careful tone as she rolled her pen between her index finger and thumb.

"No," he answered in a short, sharp breath. "No, they do not."

"Oh, Rise! What have you done?" Salter flung her pen at him. She sank back in her chair. The candlelight threw ghostly shadows on the brick walls and across the boxes of sleeping tubers stacked all around them.

Rise did not react, only picked up her pen and handed it to her.

"Because Cypriot needs human company," he pressed. "We also need to ensure the continuity of our food. Especially if humanity has been overrun by these zombie brutes, whose dead blood we cannot—indeed should not—drink. I don't think-"

Then he saw Salter smirking. "I don't know what you find so funny."

"I am not laughing at you, Rise," she said and grew serious. "I'm laughing at your gumption. At your audacity. At your stupidity. You crazy thing, to leave these walls. And tell none of us. You, who lead our protection spell every morning. What are Ogrim, Cypriot, and I to do if a brute squeezed you to mush? Or bit and turned you into one of them?"

Rise had answered those questions thousands of times before to himself, to convince his brain, his limbs, his body to actually leave Owl Court and see what he could bring back.

Salter's smile did not return. Instead, as she took her pen back in hand, her fingers tensed as if she were eager to carve news of Rise's adventures onto the pages stacked before her. She stared into the nearest candle as if listening to the faint noises of the house: of doors opening on upper floors, the creak of someone on the stairs.

"I'm fine with whatever course of action you feel is best, Rise," she said. "It was your decision to leave and your decision to take in ... survivors. But it'll be our decision, then, to check the measure of these two women, this mother and daughter. Together, as coven, we can all see what the future brings."

Rise watched Salter. What had once been humorous exasperation had already turned into a visible tetchiness as Salter desired to write all of this down. But before he could let her return to the page, he had to make sure.

"That's your final word, then? Cypriot will be the last to know that I left and what I returned with. I'm going to tell him now. But I wanted you and Ogrim to know first. To honour the eldest members of this coven first."

"To make sure we're on your side, you mean," Salter interrupted with a knowing smile and drew a line beneath her current paragraph. She inspected the rest of the blank page to make sure it was pristine before starting. "Oh, I'm sure Ogrim was delighted indeed with your adventures."

Rise ignored her smirk. "It's not Ogrim's decision."

"No. But it is everyone's decision. It affects all of us, what you do."

"What I do to ensure our survival." Rise clenched his fist, ready for a further fight. But there was no more argument in Salter. Only, she looked at him expectantly now, obviously wanting something.

"What can I do, then, to make this up to you?" Rise had to ask in the end.

"Details." Candlelight shone and danced in Salter's dark eyes. "I want every detail of your adventures. It's hard for me to venture outside in harsh light, like you and the rest. I want what you saw."

Rise was hesitant to commit his Dunsinnan adventure to paper. But the coven lived every day with no knowledge of their past. Someone had to be the first to write things down about their kind. Someone had to build a repository for other vampires, if they ever found any.

"I will sit with you, then," he conceded.

"When?"

"Soon, when there is time and things are settled. In a few days. You can ask all you want. And I will supply every and any detail I can recall, for the chronicle," he promised, glad that Ogrim and Salter were on his side. Now, time to convince one other.

"And you're certain? This is the best way to handle matters?" Salter's voice, now that she began writing, took on a dreamlike quality. "To sneak out like a wayward maiden, tell no one, especially not the one person who should know first, most of all?"

"I'm going to speak with Cypriot right now," Rise answered, annoyed, always needled by Salter and Ogrim whenever he wanted to do anything. "He'll see sense."

"So sure of that?" Cypriot's voice sounded in the cellar, not Salter's. "Are you?"

Rise startled and turned. Cypriot stood midway down the cellar stairs, fists clenched. Tears brimmed in his eyes. In that moment, at the ring of Cypriot's voice, Rise's stomach flip-flopped. Cypriot dashed back upstairs.

"Wait," Salter commanded.

Rise paused, foot on the bottom step, hand gripping the cellar banister. His heart had already gone to the one fleeing through the hall and up through the house.

Rise had to get to Cypriot before he found the women's room. Ogrim, Salter, they all knew the lengths their Cypriot would go to if anyone dared to approach the coven. It had startled them, centuries ago, that viperous protection whenever others came too close. That was the reason he was their human. But that would have to be tempered from now on. Rise had to get to him.

"What?" he snarled.

"Rise. Did you see anyone else when you were beyond the walls?"

At this, Rise hardened his grip on the banister, wanting to be away after Cypriot before he did something crazy. But they'd vowed never to lie to their Chronicler. An account of lies helped no one. Rise answered, and answered honestly. "Three Warwolves on horseback. They didn't see us. They were far away on a rise of land, watching a huge river-like horde of those brutes move towards the city."

"But you saw them. You saw Warwolves in the lands near Owl Court?"

"Yes," Rise admitted as he thundered upstairs to find Cypriot.

"Did the women see them?" Rise heard Salter ask, but he was gone.

Chapter 3

Old Names For Nearby Places

Rise caught up with Cypriot on the second floor. Rows of terra-cotta pots perfectly lined the landing, the corridor. Even more pots of lavender clustered outside each bedroom door. All rooms empty of guests, until now. Some plants were set along the skirting boards; others were positioned right in the middle of the hall, their branches wild and sprawling. The air hung heavy, not with roots and snoozing vegetables, but with dried herbs and flowers.

Cypriot stood just outside the women's room, fists still clenched as he listened to their faint chatter. The light hurt Rise's eyes after the darkness of the root cellar. He approached Cypriot quietly, reverently, not wanting him to lash out or cause a scene. Cypriot never looked at Rise. He only stared at the delicate crystal door handle that was nearly lost amid a great mantle of dried flowers hanging over the door frame.

"Rise? What have you done?" Cypriot's usually light voice barely rasped out of his throat. He continued to stare at the door handle. "I almost don't want to know."

"Come away from the door, Cypriot," Rise whispered and called upon the favour of any god listening as he gingerly reached out and touched Cypriot's bare elbow. Cypriot didn't move. One of the fine bones of his jawline shifted. Rise realized the sheer breadth of anger that churned just below his surface.

From what he heard of the dull conversation coming from the bedroom, Elaine did most of the talking. She told her mother they were safe now. Elaine asked whether her mother wanted her hair combed out. Cypriot's lip curled. His fingers flexed toward the handle.

"Cypriot, come away. Don't open that door," Rise whispered again, coming close to, but never using, his innate tone of command, never using that against his Cypriot. "Your bedroom is just across the landing in the other wing. Let's go there. Speak alone and in private. I will explain everything."

"Why are there these women ... tell me, why are they here?"

"Cypriot," Rise warned and tightened his grip on his elbow.

Elaine must have heard them. She opened the bedroom door and stared in shock at Cypriot, wet blonde hair piled on top of her head. She wore a set of Cypriot's clothes: a faded and beyond-mending shirt and trousers. Bruises darkened the otherwise pale skin of her hands and feet.

"Elaine?" Rise stepped in front of Cypriot. Elaine was barely a teenager, far younger than he'd initially thought. He put her age at no more than fourteen. "Is everything all right?"

"I heard voices out here," Elaine stammered, looking at both of them in amazement. Then she nodded at Cypriot. "H-hello?"

"This is Cypriot, who also lives here." Rise introduced them but didn't move aside, didn't turn to see the expression that he could well imagine contorted Cypriot's stunning features.

"Why don't you go back inside?" This time, Rise lent a tone of command to his words.

Ensorcellment, Cypriot had once teased him, when Rise used that tone on a rude waiter during their travels in Andalucia. After hours, in the room above the inn, the same command came from Rise for the waiter to submit to Cypriot's seduction. The same command again so the waiter would let the rest of the coven feed from him. It was not a complete ensorcellment. Only people open and hungry to fulfil a command could obey him. Therefore, it did not surprise him when Elaine didn't pick up on his words. She merely continued to stare at Cypriot, dumbfounded.

"I'll fetch you something to eat. I'm sure you and your mum finished off the stew I gave you earlier? Must be hungry." Rise kept his grip on Cypriot's elbow, ready to turn them away from the bedroom the moment Cypriot opened his mouth to cause trouble.

"Can we not go and get it ourselves?" Elaine asked.

"I'm sorry?" Rise faltered at her seemingly innocent question.

"The food you offered? Can't we go to your kitchen and get it ourselves?" Elaine looked quizzically from Rise to Cypriot and back again.

Rise saw in her eyes fear that she and her mother were trapped inside some terrible house. That they'd never escape this crowd of suspicious people. Still, he didn't look to Cypriot, whose expression probably didn't help matters.

"Of course you can go and get your own food, of course," Rise said, to ease Elaine's worry. He backed off a step or two to give the impression that she was free to roam their home as she pleased. "I can even introduce you to the others who live here while you and your mother eat."

"Thank you," Elaine said, but did not move from the bedroom door. She patted her wet hair. "Do you have electricity? I know it's a lot to ask, after what happened and everything, but I'd like to dry my hair before I catch a chill. My mother, too." Elaine cracked the door wider to show her sitting in the tall, overstuffed armchair by the bedroom's hearth. It would be a while before the early flames of the small fire could dry anything.

That one looks even older than what I'd imagined, Rise noted about the mother.

"We have some electricity from solar panels," Cypriot answered and stepped around Rise, stepped out of his grip. "There should be a hairdryer in the bathroom adjoining your bedroom," he said with a bright, helpful smile.

Elaine's eyes widened as she took in the deep puncture marks along his throat and arms.

"Did the zombie brutes get you, too?" she asked sympathetically, and she leaned closer to Cypriot to see his wounds.

"They most certainly did not!" Cypriot's smile vanished. "These are—"

"I will bring up food," Rise interrupted and pressed his hand between Cypriot's shoulders. "Elaine, why don't you go back to your mother and dry her hair? Yours, too. I'll bring up food. Tend to your needs and your mother's first. You've all the time in the world to explore this house and the people in it. For us all to tell our stories."

Elaine stared at Rise. She didn't react to any of his suggestions. "The lines on your face, the ones that I saw earlier at the bridge. They're gone now."

"Yes, those lines come and go." Rise gritted his teeth that Cypriot had to hear this. "I'll explain all later, when everybody else is gathered and your bellies are full. How about that, Elaine?"

"Everybody else?" Elaine asked, still not closing the bedroom door.

"Yes. The other people who live here. There's myself; you've met Cypriot. There's also Ogrim, the oldest, and Salter. You'll like her. You can tell how you survived in Dunsinann and she'll write it down for perpetuity."

"Those are strange names. Are they real?"

"Does that really matter?" Cypriot snarled at her question.

"I guess not," Elaine answered, after considering his words for a moment, unfazed by his anger. She

39

continued to stare at Rise, half in, half out of the bedroom door. Her mother only had eyes for the fireplace. Pale, bare feet with yellowing toenails curled into the once-lavish rug.

"I will bring up soup and bread. We have butter, too. Maybe tomorrow in the daylight, when the sun's back again, you can meet our milking cow, Daisy? There are some ... tools on the nightstand by your beds: nail clippers, tweezers, that sort of thing, if you want to tend to your mother, Elaine? Or to yourself? I can bring you up more cola, too. We have several slabs of soda cans out in the bike shed. You'd like that, wouldn't you?" Rise blabbered as he eased Elaine into the bedroom.

"There's no mirrors in the bedroom or bathroom. Aren't there any mirrors in the house at all? My mother is asking for one." Elaine ignored all of Rise's attempts to nudge her back inside. She wasn't being deliberately dumb, Rise felt. He could sense a certain dimness, a naivety about her, that Elaine could not quite grasp social norms. Whether that was an old trait from her life before, or as a result of the plague, Rise had no idea.

But Rise remembered the mother's scream on the bridge.

"Cypriot has one. Cypriot has the only mirror in the house. You'll let Elaine and her mother use it, won't you?" Rise dug his fingers between Cypriot's shoulders until he agreed. Rise did not shut the bedroom door until Elaine nodded to everything he suggested and disappeared back inside.

Rise took a breath when the bedroom door finally closed and he rested his head against its wood. Lavender caught in his throat. He wanted to drown. Rise turned to nudge Cypriot away so that they could talk in private, but Cypriot's footsteps were already fleeing across the landing, into his bedroom, which occupied the other wing.

"So now I'm Cypriot, 'who also lives here'?" he snarled as Rise closed the bedroom door behind them and pressed the weight of his shoulder against it until it clicked. "And you're reduced to being a waiter, now, Rise?" Cypriot continued to froth and foam. "And a footman, butler and ... rescuer of wayward, wandering women? I suppose I shouldn't be too surprised at women being brought in, after all this time with just me skulking around."

Rise sensed the tantrum brewing in Cypriot's veins, and so said nothing.

One summer, their cat, Tom, had caught a red house finch and, rather than toy with the bird, crouched in the middle of the yard, yowling and caterwauling over his kill with a mouthful of feathers and blood. The others, especially Salter, who was particularly sensitive to the cat's howls, wanted to take the bird away to quiet him. But Rise knew better. This is how you handle people getting upset: You agree, tell them you'll go along with whatever they want. Let the angry wallow in their tantrums. But. You also go and take your own actions once their anger subsides; let the consequences happen. It's easier to bear a tantrum upon your return and ask forgiveness. Quicker, too.

Their tomcat, left alone long enough with his house finch, soon tired and then spent the rest of that afternoon on the sun-soaked kitchen step, cleaning his fur and nuzzling between his fat toes. As the sun set that evening, when Rise asked about the bird, their Tom only looked offended for even being spoken to.

Rise let Cypriot rant and instead eyed his jungle of a bedroom. It had originally been a drawing room, taking up an entire upper floor. Cypriot wanted all this space for his own private use, and so the coven obliged and even moved in a four-poster bed. However, as years passed, Cypriot also moved in so many plants and greenery, cuttings and manicured trees, that the room's vast size had been swallowed up in a dim indoor jungle.

"Are you proposing that I breed with those two?"

Cypriot glared at Rise and tears fell, which he quickly dabbed away. His voice was thick as he went on. "Are you proposing I progenate a new race of humans within the confines of your walls? So that, no matter what happens to the people beyond, you've a stable of blood to keep you all nourished?"

"Oh, Cypriot, stop being dramatic," Rise snapped. He left his thoughts about the bedroom aside and came back to the conversation. "It's nothing like that. I left to find survivors simply because we need them. It's the right thing to do, especially since such misfortune has befallen the world. To offer a few, and only a select few, the chance to live as you do. That can only be a good thing. For us all. You included."

Cypriot didn't answer. He wandered to one of the room's bay windows and examined its exquisite array of potted orchids. So much ivy and moss clung to the walls and windows that the room felt unbearably humid. It crawled with insects. Cypriot stood silent in the middle of it all, like a petulant elfling.

Rise let him sulk for as long as he could stand. He flicked away a bug that crawled up his arm. Then, "Cypriot?"

"It's quite a base thing you're doing, you know?" Cypriot answered coolly, his words sounding all the more aloof thanks to his haughty expression. "Creating slaves to submit to your keeping. To feed you. I'm here of my own free will. I can't even remember life before I met you all. I chose you and this coven. The giving of blood must be from choice, isn't that what you told me, when you revealed yourselves all those years ago in Shanghai?"

Even just the mention of that city flooded Rise with memories: sharp lights, sour flavours, whirlwind scents when they first found each other. Those memories would dance and dance until the end of his days. During their time in Shanghai, when he and Ogrim and Salter desperately needed a new human to feed on, they'd had to wait. It was only when Cypriot came to them that they could pull back the curtains on their existence. And their great travels together as the four journeyed across continents, back through every corner of Europe, back to this quiet rest and retirement in the English countryside.

"Shanghai, city of tailors," Rise purred, harking back to the exquisite garments the coven commissioned for their Cypriot. How Cypriot could turn the head of anybody who saw him. Silence any room he entered.

"Yes." The first hint of a smile on Cypriot's tear-stained face. His gaze drifted to the window and to the pale autumn sunlight that fought its way inside through branches and vines. Cypriot opened the shutters a little wider. The weak light fully engulfed him. On the windowsill sat the only mirror in the house. It reflected the gentle rise and fall of the breath in Cypriot's chest.

Rise took a step back from the light. He respected Cypriot's need for distance whenever he stepped into daylight to avoid the coven's touch. Although their feeding on him had lengthened Cypriot's life beyond all others, Rise could see in the stark sunlight the first faint strands of grey at Cypriot's temples. A smile line beginning where Cypriot quirked his lips. Those marks of age made no difference to Rise. You couldn't just drink the blood of a man. You had to love him, too. Rise just stood admiring Cypriot, not pressing their conversation.

"So? What are you going to make me do?" Cypriot asked in a faint tone. But his indignation had softened. Bringing up old memories, sharing remembrances—especially of their early days, before settling in Europe—was one of the best ways to calm Cypriot. Sometimes, dipping into the memories created between two people is like opening a long-forgotten pot of medicine. Once the lid is opened, arguments are softened and the arguers are on the path of healing.

"How do you mean?" Rise asked. He brushed aside a bunch of drying mint from a thickly padded leather floor cushion in the shade of the shutters. Easing down onto such a low perch, he tilted his head and pressed on softly, "Make you do what?"

Cypriot looked at him, eyebrows raised.

Rise remembered what Cypriot had first accused him of, and he laughed. "We do not expect you to sleep with Elaine or her mother, just because they're also human—"

"Good! That mother looks like she's a hundred and ten. And that daughter is a whole other story. Is she stupid? Did you see her bleached head of hair? The length of her dark roots? Skanky."

"I'm sure she'd had other things to think about during a literal apocalypse, Cypriot." Rise paced his response. If Cypriot didn't calm down, his blood tonight would taste bitter. "The daughter's name is Elaine. And that is not what I am doing here. I'm not setting up some kind of human farm or breeding institution with you as head stud." Rise chuckled, then noticed the faint crinkle of worry on Cypriot's face. He went on in a more gentle tone, wondering if he had hit upon the real reason for Cypriot's temper. "Is that what all this is about? You think I would ever mean to replace you? With what stragglers and oddballs I find in the burned-out shell of the world?"

"I won't live forever, Rise, I suppose."

"That is true. But neither will we." Then Rise raised his voice when Cypriot scoffed. "Cypriot, I only left this house without telling you because I wanted to see what was left of the world. Aren't you curious, too?"

"No."

"I think you are."

"Why?" Cypriot turned so sharply that a long, dark curl fell from the jewelled clip buried in his hair. The curl settled between his shoulders. "Because I'm human?"

Rise sighed at his insolence. It was not yet time to go to Cypriot and fix his hair or try to touch him. Cypriot needed longer. Rise felt that burn of blood-hunger in his temples again. He marshalled his breath; all such longing had to be set aside until the brim and temper went out of Cypriot.

"Well, yes," Rise continued. "Because you once lived out there, as all the other people do. Or, did. And ... I wanted to see if there was company for you. And yes, to see if our food source would last two, three hundred years from now," Rise admitted. He bore Cypriot's distrustful glance. "And," he went on, remembering the bridge, "I wanted to see their dead. The ones from the news that rose and walked as if alive."

Their gaze met and held for a long time.

"Well?" Cypriot asked in a hoarse voice. "Did you see them?"

Rise nodded.

"And?"

"And the only way I can describe them is how they did on the TV: base corpses, brutes, hungering for flesh even as they rot. I saw a great herd of zombies walking in the distance—it looked like a river, there were so many. The city is their focus—"

"For now!"

"We're safe here, Cypriot," Rise assured him. "But I had to leave Owl Court and venture out to make sure."

Then Rise saw it. The clear fear in Cypriot's eyes as he stared out of the window towards the city of Larnde. Of course. Cypriot's race had just nearly been obliterated from the world. Rise hadn't taken Cypriot's reaction to that into account.

"We are safe here," Rise repeated firmly.

"Oh yes? And yet you, who make sure that we're safe, you leave. Without telling me. Without care for what—what if something happened to you? Do you think Ogrim could invoke the dawn protection? Could Salter?" Rise realized now what was Cypriot's true fear. "I am sorry. I shouldn't have left without telling you. I won't put you in such a vulnerable position again."

"Promise me that you won't leave this house again. I don't care about the women. Bring back who you want. I can see sense in that. Just ... don't go off on silly missions into the most dangerous of places, where you could be killed and leave us all at risk of god knows what. Ogrim and Salter, they'd be fine. They could easily survive and find another me to feed on. But this world— all of it, now—it's not for my kind anymore. Not with these zombies cleaning and gobbling the land. I ... wouldn't survive."

Ignoring the sunlight, Rise rose from the leather cushion and stepped closer to Cypriot, feeling a tremor run through human muscles as Rise wrapped his arms around him. Cypriot stared into his face, then hid against Rise's shirt.

"I am sorry." Rise had to promise as his Blaschko lines appeared. He buried his nose into Cypriot's flower-scented hair and let him cry, finally. "I'll not leave the house like that again. I'll not bring back more strays, either."

"Those women will see our feeding, Rise. And what if, one day, they drink from Ogrim or Salter and they turn into your vampire kind, when I have never, could never do so, it seems?"

"I know. I know all of that. But I promise everything'll be okay. And I never have to leave again."

Rise repeated those words until Cypriot believed him. It took several more rounds of assurance and placating before Rise could ease Cypriot out of his clothes, ease him onto his four-poster bed. Amid the safest jungle in the world, Rise let their passions scour the last, lingering doubts and perceived slights from Cypriot's veins.

That's the thing about drinking another's blood, Rise told himself as he muffled Cypriot's groans of pleasure against his shoulder. You can physically feel when their doubt is overturned into genuine belief.

Chapter 4

Invoker – Seer – Chronicler

"We all decided, long ago, to eat dinner together every day." Rise smiled as he took his seat at the head of the dining table. Elaine and her mother joined them, and Rise had to hand it to Cypriot; the fare on offer was more than ample. The women's plates were piled with food, and dozens of candles were clustered down the middle of the table and arranged on nearby countertops. Even more candles were set carefully in the middle of the windowsills, mindful of the surrounding bunches of drying herbs and flowers.

"That's lovely, that you've been able to keep eating together despite what's happened," Elaine answered as she settled her mother at the table.

"You're looking better now." Rise smiled and indicated Elaine and her mother. "Both of you."

"Oh, oh, thank you." Elaine absently patted her hair, which lay long and straight between her shoulders, worlds apart from how she had looked in Dunsinann. "Your bathroom soaps are all homemade, right? They're lovely."

Cypriot seemed miffed at hearing someone's appearance being praised. *Well, about time.* Rise lifted the lid from the large stew set in the middle of the table. The rich aromas raised even his appetite.

The last time this table had stood so full of food was at last year's Yule, and, as Rise unrolled a napkin and passed his thumb over its embroidered leaves, he thought of the coming winter. It would be nice to have a full house for solstice, for the festivities, for the year end. Dark outside the windows, a merry gathering within. For the first time, Rise felt relieved that he'd left and brought back these women. They had enlivened his home, even in just the few short hours they had been here. Hope for everybody's future rose in Rise. Seeing Ogrim and Salter's secret, indulgent smiles over Cypriot's head as he ate had given Rise the idea to leave the safety of Owl Court in the first place. This scene, this together-moment at the end of every day, now with two more members ... it had to be protected. Rise just had to broach the topic of the coven with Elaine and her mother. The final hurdle before he could properly relax.

"Oh, are you three not eating?" Elaine asked, noticing that Rise, Ogrim, and Salter had barely any dishware set before them.

While they didn't really need to eat, it satisfied Cypriot for everybody to sit at table with him while he ate dinner. Rise and Ogrim would have something light, like bone broth or still-warm crackers from the oven, with sharp cheese from their goats, all topped with chives from the windowsill. Salter kept to black tea, although sometimes she would steal a cracker and let it soak until mushy upon her teaspoon. Even if nothing new happened during their days inside the walls of Owl Court, the four of them always found something to chatter about: Cypriot mostly brought news of his plants. Ogrim often joked that the dramas of orchids seemed like high drama indeed.

And so their mealtime would pass, until Cypriot finished the stew he had fussed over and mothered since breakfast, or crunched away a dinner of fat slices of bacon with buttery mashed potato and peas, all provided by their little homestead.

Rise shook his head. "We'll eat later," he explained to Elaine. "How's the stew?"

"It's quite lovely, thank you," Elaine replied awkwardly, shyly.

"All of its ingredients, everything was grown right here, from our gardens," Cypriot muttered as he sipped his stew to check the seasoning. After napping for an hour or so earlier with Rise, Cypriot had even agreed to cover up the fang marks on his wrists and neck, just for this evening, so that he would not shock their guests at the dining table. Or shake the women's faith in the good that Rise and his coven could do for them. Cypriot now wore a smart, dark polo neck beneath his usual light shirt, the black collar hiding the punctures on his neck, sleeves tucked over his wrists. After a moment's consideration, Cypriot added more pepper to his stew, then set the grinder and salt cellar in front of Elaine.

"R-really? That's ... that's fantastic, gardening and farming like that," Elaine answered, smiling at everyone around the table. "No wonder you guys were able to survive for so long. I haven't eaten a vegetable in forever. It's just been cans and packets of whatever we could find.

Honestly, we were living on liquorice and cans of dog food that I found in an old granny flat at the back of—"

When Cypriot seemed happy to receive praise about his resourcefulness and cooking, Rise stopped listening to Elaine. Instead, he stared at the small, prideful smile that pulled at Cypriot's lips. Rise took some cheese and let it melt on his tongue. It did not do much to temper the hunger that taunted him at the end of every week. But food would temper his pangs until the midnight hour. Rise let the sharp cheese dissolve in his mouth, watched Cypriot, and took his time before swallowing.

"And what might your name be?" Although Ogrim had brought his tarot cards to the table, and indeed often told a spread while Cypriot ate, his full attention was on Elaine's mother. She merely sat in her chair and otherwise followed her daughter about like a shadow.

"She is ... her name's Marnie," Elaine answered as her mother stared at Ogrim from beneath a sullen brow. Elaine lifted a spoon of stew to her mother's lips, and it took several moments before Marnie accepted the food. Not once did her gaze move from Ogrim. In turn, he held his deck and slowly turned it in his hands.

"You'll have to forgive, I mean, bear with her." Elaine waited until Marnie had chewed a little, then returned to her own food. "She became ill before all of this happened. Her doctors suspected Alzheimer's or some other dementia. But now ... I don't ... I don't know. I just make sure she's kept fed as best I can. And kept alive, I guess."

"Of course, Elaine." Rise nudged Ogrim to have some manners.

Ogrim glanced at the bottom card of his deck but otherwise left his cards alone, placing them off to one side. "After dinner," he said, leaning back in his chair. He rubbed his round stomach as if he had already eaten three stews, when he had in fact barely eaten two or three crackers. "I'm going to get one of the shotguns and pick off those brutes still milling about outside."

"You won't do anything of the sort." Rise gestured with his shoulder to the window. "It's gotten far too dark. You won't be able to see. And knowing you, with your dodgy leg, you'll fall off the wall. Leave it till tomorrow. I saw how they took out the bridge at Dunsinann. You saw it too, Elaine. I don't like the thought of having them milling around outside. Best be rid of them. But not in the dark. I'll help you in the morning."

"You can't shoot for shit," Ogrim grumbled.

"You're going to shoot them, the zombie brutes?" Elaine asked in surprise.

"Yes. They followed you back here, didn't they? And I don't need help to shoot a pig in a poke, either."

Rise smiled conspiratorially at Elaine and her mother. He winked to suggest that Ogrim was always this way. Always fighting any course of action, even a wise one.

Elaine hesitated, then smiled back, although Marnie took her daughter's hand and held it on the table between their place settings without ever dropping her scowl.

"So," Salter finally spoke. She had perched in silence on Rise's right and taken in the scene, her long, dark fingers wrapped around her steaming tea. A readiness hung about Salter, as if she wanted to be away to write all of this down. But she also looked like she wanted to question everything.

"Have you seen any other people since all of this happened? Elaine, what's your surname? Are you both local to Dunsinann?"

"Why do names matter?" Cypriot abruptly cut in. His nose wrinkled as he spoke. He took a bite of dinner and loudly scraped his spoon through the bowl. "Who does it matter to? We can call each other whatever we like now. Names don't matter anymore—"

"There's garlic in this stew." Marnie abruptly broke into the conversation and glared around accusingly.

The table silenced. The only thing Rise had heard from Elaine's mother was her scream back by the bridge. He dabbed his mouth with a stiffly laundered napkin. Cypriot knew how to set a good table. Rise wanted to lay his hands on Cypriot's shoulder, to get him to stop scowling at the two guests, but Marnie's words sunk further and further into his mind and he realized, with a glance to Ogrim, what might be troubling her.

"That's right," Rise answered. "There's garlic."

"There's carrots, too," Cypriot spoke, not quite understanding that she might be suspicious of them, as if Marnie were stupid. "Parsnips, turnips, onion, potatoes—"

"Why would it matter if garlic was in the stew?" Ogrim asked in a low tone, an eyebrow crooked high. "Does it not agree with ye?"

Elaine seemed mortified that her mother had interrupted the dinner conversation. She gently tapped their joined hands off the table, as if trying to get the attention of a naughty child to remind them to behave.

Salter carefully removed a small notebook from inside her layers of shawls. She scribbled something hastily across the first page.

"Garlic's a bulb," Cypriot went on. "Just like anything else you'd find in a stew. I personally love a strong punch of garlic in my food." He levelled a challenging look at the women and stuck the spoon into his mouth to get every drop.

This wasn't true in the slightest. The coven only tolerated Cypriot eating a small amount of garlic, for his health, lest his blood begin to taste of it.

"You couldn't cross running water at the bridge," Marnie said to Rise directly.

"Shush, mother." Elaine elbowed her mother's frail torso. "These nice people took us in. Fed us. We'd be dead if not for Rise and his—"

"Demons!" Marnie snarled and clattered her spoon onto the table.

"Mother!" Elaine caught her arm to calm her down, then explained to the table in a frantic voice, "Please don't pay any attention. She was on strong medication before everything fell. It screwed her up to suddenly have it gone, to do without. Don't listen to her, please. We're both so very glad to be here. Truly. Please."

"It's fine, Elaine." Rise forced a smile. The bitch knew all along what they were. What felt like sand beneath his feet began to crumble and slide away.

"Everything's fine, Elaine. I can see how hard all of this is for you. Please, let's just finish dinner, yes?"

"Any cure for madness can often summon a demon," Ogrim muttered as he took up his deck and shuffled it.

"How rude," Cypriot whispered theatrically at Marnie's behaviour.

Rise waited eternal minutes until dinner was over, until the women cleared their plates and a dessert of preserves and yoghurt settled into their bellies. He had no choice. Marnie already knew what they were. He had to lay out the truth, the whole truth of the coven's arrangement here. And if the women weren't willing to listen ... had he reholstered the pistol at his hip after his afternoon with Cypriot?

Before their meal, or its diners, got any more out of hand, Rise set his palms onto the table. He stood to his full height.

"Elaine? Marnie? I want you to listen carefully to what I'm about to say. You've probably realized that we ... well, we're not your average residents of this house. In fact," Rise hesitated. He hated speaking such words aloud, so blatantly, like revealing a weak poker hand. "In fact, you've been rescued by a coven of blood-drinkers, what you might consider to be vampires. The kind of old. The kind of legend." When Elaine's eyes widened, Rise kept speaking over her surprise. "Now, we mean you no harm, none in the slightest. We want to keep you both safe, and we'll protect you against what's happened to the world. We'll not feed upon you, not Ogrim or Salter or myself. You've probably guessed that Cypriot is as human as you are. We don't drink from anyone who doesn't agree with who we are or what we do. Blood like that is stale, soured, brings little nourishment. We'll not interfere with you. We only wish for company and to keep you safe. You may live with us here, unharmed and protected, for as long as you like."

"Cannibals?" Marnie shrieked, only to be shushed by an enthralled Elaine.

"N-no," Rise smiled in surprise that cannibalism was her first thought.

"Well, this one here is plump as butter," Marnie shouted. She rounded on Cypriot and glared at the soft, gawky swell of Cypriot's stomach. "Growing plump on the goody of this table."

Rise saw a black look pass across Cypriot's face and was ready to grab him before Cypriot did something stupid like diving across the table to scratch her eyes out. He'd killed for less.

"Cypriot, and Cypriot alone, is who we feed from, and we care for him above all else. Perhaps that's why he looks so plump to your eyes. Here, let me show you." Rise reached across the table and took Cypriot's arm. He pushed back the sleeve to show the twin puncture marks branded over the deep, blue vein of his wrist. Rise drifted a thumb over those marks, forever intrigued by them, forever grateful that not once did they become infected, as might a normal, open wound. Not once had Cypriot turned into one of them, either, from gaining these marks, not even when he tried drinking blood from each member of the coven. That was one of the coven's many mysteries.

"We have enemies," Rise went on, ignoring the alarm on Ogrim's face, Salter's, even Cypriot's. Rise felt that he had to tell this story and tell it in full or not at all. "We know nothing about the origins of our race, know of no other covens. Only, it seems that wherever there are vampires, there are those who hunt them. The first time we encountered Warwolves was in Transylvania. We went there to discover our origins but found only tourism and long-cold rumors. We didn't stay long, and we did not go back. But we learned just enough of the Warwolves' eternal pursuit of our kind to know there were no more left, outside of us three."

"Aren't you afraid of these Warwolves?" Elaine turned and asked Cypriot, eyes wide, a dribble of stew still on her chin.

"Cypriot has seen the Warwolves himself. They do not bother with him," Rise answered awkwardly. Of all the things Elaine chose to home in on.

"Why would they harm me?" Cypriot said, with a confident smirk. "I am as human as they are. They probably think this coven keeps me under their thumb in some kind of great, disgusting servitude. The Warwolves would probably be only too happy to 'free' me, or whatever they'd like to call it. But I feel chosen amongst all humans. It's an honour, the greatest of my life, not a servitude."

Rise had never heard Cypriot speak this way. He silently renewed his vow, made after their earlier conversation in the bedroom, to keep Cypriot safe and never leave Owl Court again.

"Trust me when I say we'll keep you safe above all else. I believe, given the world as it is now, this might be exactly what you're looking for?"

Elaine's eyes remained huge. It emboldened Rise that she didn't look to her mother or seek agreement before answering. Instead, Elaine took a breath, swallowed it down before she nodded. "Y–yes, yes I believe so. We ... we would be honoured to stay here with you, both my mother and I."

"It's time for our weekly feed. Perhaps you should watch that before you truly decide?" Ogrim chuckled, but stopped laughing when Rise glared at him.

"It ... it should be all right. I've watched plenty of movies before all this," Elaine answered, still a little unsure.

Marnie did not speak.

Chapter 5

Deep at Feed

"Thank you for dinner." Salter finally spoke. She wiped down the table and snuffed all but one candle.

Cypriot smiled at her praise, and the flame's glow flickered across his dark eyes as he took up the lone candle. He swished his hair, which had mostly fallen from its clip.

"Time for me to return the favour," he said. With a glance to Elaine and Marnie, he led the way upstairs to the upper floors of Owl Court. His candlelight disappeared into the shadows as everybody followed him up through the house. Everybody except Rise.

"Aren't you coming?" Salter asked in surprise.

Rise waited in the hall, not even with his foot planted on the bottom stair. He didn't answer Salter right away but instead waited. Ogrim's heavy step creaked the timbers as he brought up the rear and guided Elaine and Marnie upstairs. Rise inhaled deeply in the cooler, darker hall after the bustle and warmth of the kitchen. Then he smiled at Salter.

"Oh, I'm coming," he assured her. Then Rise patted the railing with the swathe of holly woven through the banister. He glanced at the cellar door. Salter had firmly shut it when she came up for dinner.

"Cypriot really does have a flair for dramatics," Salter said with an indulgent smile. Then she frowned, just a little. "Aren't you coming to feed though, Rise?"

"Yep. Coming now."

Rise wanted to see what Salter had written in the chronicle, what she had to say about Elaine and Marnie. For a moment, he wished that the tone of command worked on other vampires, too. To make Salter head up to feed so he could pop into the root cellar.

"At dinner," Salter admitted as she, too, dawdled at the bottom of the stairs, "I thought you might use your command on those two women, Rise."

"Oh yes?" Rise froze. None of them possessed telepathy. Salter could not read his mind, he was sure of that. He didn't know why she would bring up his talent for command out of nowhere.

But Salter smiled warmly at him. "What I mean is, it's good you didn't make Elaine and her mother stay here against their will. If we do ever end up feeding from them, their blood would taste the worse for it."

"Of course. Also, the command wouldn't last forever. I'd have to keep commanding them to oblige us for the rest of their days." Rise nodded half to himself, half to Salter. It was so close to the weekly feed, blood taste was all that concerned Salter. He glanced at the cellar door again. It was probably better to sneak a read from the chronicle well after tonight. Let time pass. Let Elaine and Marnie witness a coven feed. That would allow Salter to gather her thoughts and write everything down in good time. Rise would wait.

"I still need to sit down with you at some stage," he remembered. "Give you all the details you wanted about what happened at Dunsinann."

"Yes, at some stage," Salter said in a confused tone, as if moments before their feed was definitely not the right time to discuss this.

"Let's go," Rise gestured that Salter should head upstairs first.

Salter chuckled as they trooped to the second floor. "That's why I made sure you were coming. Cypriot can be an awful sulk if he's not the center of attention, or if we're late to his little performance."

After Cypriot's petulant elfling behaviour earlier, Rise could only agree. He and Salter stalked, ravenous, up through the house.

*

In order to feed, the room must be warm. They kept a room separate just for feeding, an unused bedroom at the top of the house, where heat settled beneath the well-insulated eaves.

"It's always been this way over the centuries," Rise said to Elaine and Marnie. They sat on two chairs set beside the chaise in the middle of the room. A fat candelabra that held even fatter candles sat between them.

His blood hunger maddened his temper. Rise could barely look at the women. He wanted his Cypriot. He wanted his blood.

"A warm room," he went on. "Usually candlelit, at the very least with a fire alive in the nearest hearth. Something about flame and blood-drawing. This coven learned those two things were linked, although we're cut off from the full lore of our people. That's why Salter chronicles our days, so that we, in the future, or, indeed, future generations can learn from our actions."

Ogrim bent with a crackle of his old knees to stoke the fire. He buried the poker deep into its glowing hearth. Cypriot divested his clothes. He lay on the chaise that angled towards the fireplace. The rest of the room in shadow, apart from the odd flicker and shift of flame. The women's eyes caught the firelight as they watched. Elaine appeared enthralled by it all, especially taken with the lean, smooth planes of Cypriot's body. Marnie's mouth remained a sullen, flat line, her hands clasped with Elaine's in her daughter's lap. The coven had given them an impressive silver candlestick apiece, besides the one that was set between them, so that they could illuminate the proceedings any way they wanted.

Hunger pulled at Rise's throat and innards. He didn't want to speak to the women anymore, or even look at them, or explain the ins and outs of what they were doing. He hadn't fed in a week. He was hungry.

"As a coven, we've stretched out our feeding to only once a week," Salter explained in a soothing tone, but a crackle in her voice betrayed her hunger, too. She removed her scarves and shawls, revealing a tall and rod-straight figure in a black robe of velvet and pinched lace. "With three of us feeding from one human, any more frequent feeds would weaken Cypriot. Any less often, then we would starve."

Even though his mind was on the two women and how they might react to all of this, Rise could only think of the gentle warmth that pulsed through their Cypriot as he lay splayed across the plump burgundy cushions. Rise could only think of the beautiful thick vein that wound up his throat. The slight dip in his tanned skin just beneath his ear. Rise's mouth watered as he draped a soft woolen blanket, woven throughout in bright autumn colors, over Cypriot.

"He must remain warm, even though he's close to the fire," Rise explained and watched for the barest hint of panic or disgust in the women's faces. Marnie's shriek over dinner about them being cannibals, her shriek at Dunsinann Bridge—they rang in his head. Rise lifted Cypriot's wrist and roughly worked his thumb back and forth over the joint until the deep vein there stood to prominence.

Ogrim whispered to Rise as the coven gathered tightly around the couch. "That mother, watch for her."

Rise hissed under his breath. "She's traumatized. We probably all are."

"She doesn't seem quite with it, Rise," Salter chimed in, their voices low, only for the coven to hear. Lines of spit dribbled down over their jaws. "Shellshocked, maybe?"

"The trauma of being out in the world, yeah, maybe, yeah," Rise stammered, he didn't know how loud.

Hunger befuddled him and burned in his throat. He just wanted food. He gazed upon Cypriot, ever glad, ever thankful that his human was safe inside. Maybe, by seeking Elaine and her mother this way, maybe it would convince Cypriot that Rise was correct in taking them in?

"Eldest first," Rise said in a thick, reluctant tone, his head bowed. Rise muttered a few words of thanks and prayer in the Old Language before he held out the wrist for Ogrim. Cypriot's eyes fluttered closed and Rise admired those long eyelashes.

"I accept." Ogrim drew up a short wooden stool and nuzzled his face against Cypriot's arm. Then a change came over him as Blaschko lines stood sharp on his weathered, whiskery face and trailed down his neck. Canines lengthened into fangs and curled over his lower lip.

Cypriot gave a sharp cry and jolted on the chaise when the first bite pierced his skin, reopening last week's wound.

Rise shuddered at the tantalizing cry, his own hunger nearly overwhelming him. If they hadn't always followed a feeding order, he would have shamelessly flung himself upon Cypriot to pierce and guzzle from him like a wild animal.

"Next eldest," he forced himself to speak, calling forth Salter, even though his throat ached. Salter thanked him in the Old Language before planting her exposed canines into Cypriot's other wrist. The Blaschko lines on Salter's face were like pale lines of winter frost on her dark skin.

Rise glanced at the women. Elaine watched them, leaned forwards in her chair with clear curiosity. But the mother's gaze was afar, as if she were not quite in the room anymore. Rise knew enough about humans. Some lost themselves entirely as they approached dotage. Rise touched the small pistol hidden beneath his shirt. If those two suddenly decided they didn't like what they saw, particularly when the coven was so vulnerable, Rise didn't want to be caught out.

"Now, I will feed," he told the women. "We'll not be able to speak much after, for we will be quite full. Cypriot may be weak, too. If he needs anything, please tend to him."

Rise waited.

Elaine, eyes huge and curious. Fire shadows danced across her face. Eventually she nodded, riveted at the scene that unfolded before her.

"Then last, myself," Rise knelt on the floor and knew a maddening moment when he saw Ogrim and Salter already deep at feed, heads bowed as they drank in silence. Burning seared across his skin as Rise's stripes rose. A pang in his gums as his canines grew into fangs. He parted his lips and brushed back Cypriot's dark curls to expose the side of his throat.

Then Rise became lost in the blood of their human. The trio drank until they knew every twist and turn of his veins. Knew pulse. Knew breath. Knew every corner of his heart, as all four creatures became one being, one coven, that sustained one another throughout the night.

Rise stood on the bridge at Dunsinann. "Look," he told Marnie, who stood on the far riverbank. Wind tugged at Marnie's dishevelled clothes and hair. Village ruins behind her lay still and deep with fog. The sky broiled with yellow and grey clouds. The brown river seethed with brutes. They leapt and slithered on top of one another in the frothy, muddy water, like chummed fish.

"Look," Rise repeated and held out his arms in the stiff breeze to show how he stood right in the middle of the bridge. Unafraid. Tall. "I can cross this water, no problem. Any time."

"They destroyed the bridge before you could cross to this side," Marnie answered, her voice young, unshackled of everything that had befallen her and the world about them. "The river was low and still that morning. It doesn't count."

"Then, what does?" Rise stepped towards her, advanced a few paces, crowbar heavy in his hands. The wind whipped his words away into the countryside as soon as they left his mouth. "What does count?"

Marnie stared at the street beneath her feet. The pavement and once-twee cobblework was now thick with ash, bone, trash. The bridge ended just a few feet in front of her in a set of two pillars topped with statues of pale, rearing horses. Similar statues were missing, destroyed, on Rise's side of the bridge.

"Join me on this side, then." She lifted her gaze to Rise and smirked.

He jolted at her challenge.

"I could, if I wanted to." Rise felt something creep up behind him. He turned, frantic, only to see the other riverbank empty. Only lines and lines of red and grey trees swaying, swaying.

"So, join me, then."

Rise spat at her.

"You cannot?" Marnie asked tenderly.

"I'll cross this bridge and crack your skull. As I should've done the moment I met you. Take Elaine, and Elaine only. Leave you here to rot. But, by whatever quirk of life that is in my veins since birth, I'll dash you in."

Marnie spread her arms open, mirroring Rise's earlier gesture. "You think death alone would end me, end the doubt that sits in you? And if you cross, what of those left behind?"

Rise clasped the crowbar even tighter. "I'll show you!" She didn't move as, placing one foot steadily in front of the other, Rise crossed the bridge.

Marnie still didn't move from where she stood, did not move anymore at all. When he got close, Rise saw how the paving stones beneath Marnie were prised off the road. Her bare feet were rooted deep into the earth.

Rise reached the pillars. He could go no further than the rearing horses. Could set no foot into Dunsinann proper.

Wind whipped past. Footsteps pounded the bridge behind him. Someone swept by, then hundreds more. Shadows and ghosts of long-dead people rushed past Rise, pushing at his shoulders, jostling him aside until he couldn't see Marnie any more.

"No, don't leave me!" Rise roared as every light and feeling within him followed those shadows and was sucked away into the narrow streets of Dunsinann. Brutes seethed through the waters beneath the bridge, louder now, faster. The bridge began to rumble and sink. Brutish arms flung themselves over the railings and pillars as those base creatures climbed the thing they destroyed and sank.

Behind the cavalcade of ghosts and shadows, two Warwolves, astride their horses, thundered onto the crumbling bridge. Scythes aloft, gleaming against the yellow-grey sky.

"Don't leave me all alone!" Rise called to Marnie.

A narrow Warwolf scythe passed through Rise's belly. He clutched at his middle and dropped into darkness.

Chapter 6

Lone & Lonely

When Rise awoke from his dream, the sky outside stood pale and cold. He lay alone in the feeding room, alone amid the pile of blankets. No Salter, no Ogrim. He wiped his forehead. Sweat, not blood. Carefully, Rise lifted the hem of his shirt and checked his belly, where the small pistol still lay tucked against his hip. He passed a palm across unscarred skin and exhaled a long breath of relief. He'd never dreamed so vividly, never like that, before.

A new, scraping noise jolted him into panic all over again, until Rise realized that it was only the sound of someone sweeping. Cypriot was kneeling nearby, cleaning out the empty hearth. When he noticed that Rise was awake, Cypriot gave him a small smile as he tidied away the fire poker and took up a full bucket of ashes. A fresh bandage ringed Cypriot's throat; his face was still pale and drawn from last night's feeding. The sleeves of his simple, fawn-coloured shirt hung over his hands; an apron was tightly bound around his narrow waist, apron pockets flat against his slim thighs.

"Is it morning?" Rise asked as he struggled to sit up. "You shouldn't be cleaning."

"It's nearly dawn," Cypriot answered, already leaving with the bucket and broom.

"Elaine and her mother?" Rise lifted himself out of the blanket nest and realized that he was alone in the room. Cypriot's footsteps pattered softly as he went downstairs. Rise listened to the house as he tried to wake up. The familiar shuffle of Ogrim and Salter on the roof. He realized that they would be waiting for him to lead the incantation.

"I thought you were going to sleep forever." Ogrim threw back the hood of his ancient wax overcoat and scowled when Rise arrived.

"I almost did." Rise absently rubbed his stomach as he stepped out onto a flat section of the roof. The only thing that stood taller than the points of the surrounding roofs was a lone chimney breast, shrouded in bright autumnal ivy. Rise didn't have a coat, but he'd brought a blanket from the feeding room. He'd need cover after the incantation to protect his skin from the rising sun.

As he stood outside, that silence struck Rise again. The world had quieted ever since that last signal from people. Nothing moved in the world—at least, nothing that they could see from their rooftop. The silence clung to Rise's chest. Rise remembered Cypriot at the window yesterday, when he had finally drilled down to Cypriot's greatest fear. Not a world for humanity anymore? Well, this world was never for the coven's kind, either. The world's fall levelled the playing field between Cypriot and Rise, Ogrim, and Salter. Now the world was for the brutes. The coven only had each other.

"Where's Elaine and Marnie?" Rise asked when he noticed their absence.

"I don't know." Ogrim looked at Salter, who would wear her protective scarves against the dawn until the last moment.

"Well, what did they think of the feeding?"

"Haven't seen them." Ogrim shrugged.

Rise frowned. Ogrim could complain about inconsequential things for days, but the minute something odd happened under their noses, he became so nonchalant. "Well, where are they?" Rise went on.

"Cypriot's probably giving the two women their breakfast. We'll find them. But after we do this," Salter said, trying to soothe them. She gestured for Ogrim and Rise to get into position on the flat expanse of roof, nestled between slopes of terracotta slates. Salter straightened her spine against the oncoming sun, like a dark statue against the flushed red ivy that clung to the chimney.

Rise hesitated but saw the growing strength in the dawn and felt the protection fade from the boundaries of their home, as if sand were escaping from the roots of an ill-founded castle. Uneasy, he nodded to Salter and clasped her and Ogrim's outstretched hands. Rise closed his eyes, opened his mouth, ready to dig deep within himself and begin the incantation, but Cypriot bustled onto the roof, too, interrupting them.

"Yuck. It still stinks so bad from the fields when you're down in the yard." Cypriot perched on a nearby water tank. His apron was bundled in his lap, full of fruit. He crunched on a crab apple from the pile. It was his favourite treat, although the others had no idea how he tolerated such sourness.

Ogrim took a deep sniff of the air. "At least we can't hear the brutes outside. I'd say we're too high up."

"Can you both please be quiet?" Rise tried not to snap. He resettled his grip on Salter and Ogrim's arms and closed his eyes again to gather his concentration.

"Shh," Salter shushed them. Rise wasn't sure if she had shushed Ogrim and Cypriot, or shushed him to calm down. Either way, all fell silent.

I should've made sure Elaine and her mother were okay before doing this, Rise thought as he collected himself. In some ways, the women's reaction to the coven's feed last night was more important than securing the home's walls for another day. The chant began, a call to old earth and old boundaries, deep from Rise's bones. He became the support of simple bones. His brain, the centre of all things, conjured. His heart beat for this house. It beat for its people. His tongue called and rose forth one of the lone bits of magic he, and he alone, possessed.

The coven knew nothing else of their kind, save what fiction could imagine. Some tales were pure lies, other tales became the laws they lived by. Garlic, running water, silver, crosses, mirrors, coffins. All things that should rule them tumbled through Rise's chant, until the boundary pulsed strong once again and the Warwolves, indeed all and everything else, could no longer enter Owl Court.

It was not a difficult thing to chant. But, for some reason, it only worked for Rise. Ogrim had tried the same words; Salter too, even Cypriot. But the long-salted boundary only ever responded to Rise. At dawn, they revealed themselves, bearing the brief pain of sunlight to protect their walls for another day. A coven fully revealed and trembling with power. At this moment every morning, Rise felt invincible.

As he spoke the final verse, in a tongue none understood, not even Rise, nor a tongue they could ever find any further knowledge of, something broke his attention again. Just as the incantation looped back upon itself for the final verse, Cypriot stood and threw what was left of his crab apple clear off the roof. It landed in the courtyard far below with a soft and distant thud.

Rise faltered, opened an eye and swivelled his gaze over to Cypriot. But Cypriot was neither clowning around nor being obnoxious. He stood, stiffened, and watched where the apple fell. With his tapered features and high swoop of dark hair, Cypriot looked like their tom cat when it spied a mouse.

Rise felt an odd ripple run through the circle of arms, through the boundaries of the house. As if the incantation had dipped, drooped, right when it had been called into protection for another day. He frowned, squeezed Ogrim and Salter tighter, and completed the final verse. It was as if a key clicked something closed in his chest; that was how Rise knew the incantation was in place for another day. The moment he felt that levelling-out, that slotting into place, he broke the circle of arms and rounded on Cypriot.

"Now, just what was that about?" Rise grabbed his elbow, but disturbingly, Cypriot did not look away from where he stared. Rise shook him a little. "Cypriot, answer me!"

"She's gone," he whispered.

"Who?" Ogrim asked, his cane to hand as if there would be a fight.

"In fact, they both are." A tear slid down Cypriot's pale cheek.

"What're you talking about?" Rise forcibly turned him around and stared into those brown eyes, which looked even more sunken than usual after a feed. "Elaine? Marnie? What's happened?"

Cypriot shrugged him off. He took a step away and wrapped his arms around his thin body, hugging himself around his slight pudge of stomach. "Elaine and her crazy mother," he began, but tears overwhelmed him.

"Elaine and her mother what?" Ogrim pressed, ready to let loose with his cane upon whatever foe awaited them. "Where are they? What did you do with them?"

"Easy, now," Rise switched to a softer tone. He took Cypriot into his arms and they both leaned against the water tank. He let Cypriot cry for a few moments against his shoulder. Rise glanced to Ogrim and Salter. They did not seem to have any idea what was going on, either.

"When you were feeding—" Cypriot finally pulled back and wiped his nose on his bandaged wrist. He blinked balefully around at everybody, his body wracked by shudders and sobs.

"Shh," Rise crooned. He patted his pocket for a handkerchief, but then remembered that he had given it to

Elaine—was that barely a day ago? It felt like a whole lifetime already. Salter stepped in and gave Cypriot one of her handkerchiefs.

"What happened?" Rise pressed him.

"When everybody passed out, Elaine and Marnie came at me. With one of the big candlesticks–"

Rise gripped him. "Did they hurt you?"

Cypriot loosened the bandage at his throat and revealed deep scratches made with blunt fingernails. "Last night you'd left the poker in the fire, Ogrim. I don't know if that was deliberate or not. Or was that you, Rise? But, anyway, I grabbed it when Elaine and Marnie came at me. Took out the mother. Elaine escaped. I mean, she wanted to escape. So, I helped her, just now."

"Why didn't you tell me about this the moment I woke up, Cypriot? Why wasn't it the first thing out of your mouth? Why didn't you wake us while all this happened?"

"You three are dead to the world while in your stupor! I could have been clobbered and you'd only find out when the sun rose—ow!" Cypriot squealed and jerked out of Rise's arms when he squeezed too tight.

Rise felt that draining sensation all over again, of sand escaping from beneath his feet. The growing sun tingled his skin. It was true about their vampire sleep. Even they had no idea why they slept so soundly after feeding. Ogrim's words once, that they slept like the dead, came to Rise and he shivered.

"Look, I'm sorry," Rise said to Cypriot, who had his back to him. "I didn't mean to hurt you just now. All this is ... it's shocking. When we left you, things were fine–"

"No, they weren't 'fine'," Cypriot snarled. "Anyone could've told you that. Those two weren't 'fine' at all. Not if the first thing they did, the moment all of your eyes were closed—not if the first thing on their minds was to dash me in. I think they wanted this house for themselves."

"So, what happened?" Ogrim finally found his words.

"I told you—" Cypriot began, but Ogrim held up his old, wrinkled palm.

"Tell us what happened exactly, lad. The exact events. Who did what."

Cypriot's eyes narrowed, and Rise feared he might fall into a sulk, which would only anger Ogrim more. Although she remained silent, Rise noticed that Salter was watching them all intently, like a child trying to win a sleight of hand, soaking in every moment to remember and recall and decipher. She paid no heed to the lifting sun, her Blaschko lines now white and terrifying. Rise wanted no mention of this in their chronicle.

"You all were asleep. Elaine and her mother came at me with those candlesticks that you gave them, came at me with fire and foul threats." He touched the scratches on his throat.

"Just the events, Cypriot, no embellishments," Ogrim warned.

Rise felt another wave of panic that Cypriot might sulk at this and entrench them deeper in this terrible moment. However, though his eyes had narrowed to pinpoints, Cypriot spoke in a chilling, collected voice.

"Elaine and her mother—both came at me, tried to club me with their candlesticks. In the struggle, I grabbed the poker, still red hot, then also the bigger candelabra on the coffee table behind the chaise. I ... got Marnie somehow on the side of her neck, and she just dropped."

"Dead?" Ogrim pressed.

Cypriot nodded. "Yes. Elaine, then, well, it's like she came to her senses. She fell to her knees. All fight left her. She begged me to spare her. Begged me to set her free."

"Set her free?" Rise asked in surprise.

Cypriot shrugged and sniffed back the last of his tears. He wiped his eyes one last time before he went on.

"Yes. She said she'd been trapped with her mother for over ten years, since dementia began taking Marnie from her. She'd been her caregiver all that time, throughout the fall of this world. Elaine said she'd worked so hard, done terrible things, just for both of them to last this long. That it had all nearly broken her. I thought Elaine would be grief-stricken at what I did to her mother, even if it was in self-defense. But she seemed ... not happy, only relieved. She didn't want to stay. She begged me to let her go into the world, free."

"But she wasn't a prisoner here," Rise said, frowning. Had he made a terrible mistake bringing Elaine and her mother back here? "They were free to move about this house as if it was their own."

"I think," Salter spoke for the first time. She drew her scarf around her face, Blaschko lines painfully white-hot. Her gaze met Cypriot's. "I think Elaine felt that, as long as she was caring for her mother, she would always be trapped. Always enslaved."

"Yes, that's it," Cypriot nodded. "I was in so much shock after what happened, I couldn't quite understand. But now I do. And so I agreed to bury her mother and let Elaine go."

"But couldn't you just have waited until the three of us woke up, Cypriot? You're saying Elaine has already left? When did she go? And how?" Rise wanted to shake him all over again.

"When the boundary of the house was at its lowest, just as it was being refreshed for the day," Cypriot answered and pointed out into the courtyard.

"You throwing your crab apple was a signal," Salter said.

He nodded. Then he turned to Rise. "Elaine—she didn't want to wait for you all to wake up. Not in the room where her mother was dead. She felt ashamed of their actions, of trying to kill the one thing this coven needed to survive. So, when I said she could go and be free for the first time in a decade, free to try her chances with the wilderness and the brutes, she agreed. We even shook on it."

"Where's Marnie now?" Ogrim asked as he tossed up his overcoat's hood against the sun.

Cypriot shivered and hugged himself. "In the courtyard by the pigpen. In ... in a wheelbarrow."

"How did you—" Rise began, as he realized he could bear the sun no longer and wrapped himself in the blanket he'd brought.

"I just did, Rise, all right?" Cypriot snapped. "I brought up the wheelbarrow and Elaine helped me get ... get Marnie in while you three were asleep and then down through the house again. I swore to Elaine that I would give her mother a proper burial. We don't have to do that, of course, but—"

Cypriot stopped talking when Rise shot him a dark look.

"We're hardly going to be able to leave Owl Court and dig a grave." It was Rise's turn to snarl. "The pigpen it'll have to be, hm?" Rise remembered Marnie from his dream. Let the pigs have the old crone. He spat to one side.

"I can't imagine Elaine would just leave without burying her mother," Salter wondered softly, almost to herself.

"Well, she did." Cypriot went on even more defensively. "She was sad it happened, sorry that it happened at all. Even I was sad. Then she left. Elaine got what she wanted. Freedom, although the brutes will probably get her. The end. You believe me, don't you?" He levelled this at each of them. "I let her go. She had a moment to flee, in the seconds between yesterday's incantation and us finishing today's. I had no choice. You don't know her strength, Rise. She came right at me." When nobody responded, Cypriot sighed in frustration and stamped his foot. "The three of you are all the same beast: stoat, otter, weasel!"

"I don't know if this tale is true or not," Salter said, trying to soothe Rise and Ogrim's anger. "But we have to believe Cypriot. We have no other choice."

"Why would you do such a thing?" Rise spoke slowly. Thoughts pressed inside his head, the pain in his forehead, as he tried to think through this whole mess. "Cypriot? Elaine was—"

"Oh, Elaine this, Elaine that!"

"But why, Cypriot?"

"Because, Rise," Cypriot stared right into his eyes with a challenge and a fire that surprised him. "Because you gave me no choice."

Cypriot left the roof, and the others stood listening to his footsteps as he thumped downstairs.

"We need food, Cypriot. There's not much of your lot left!" Rise called after him.

From up here, desolation surrounded them on every side, across the land, in every direction, until the hills and trees and fields met the sky.

"I'm going to check the side gate. That's the one Elaine used, wasn't it?" Ogrim clomped away awkwardly from the rooftop. "I assume so," he answered himself. "Well, let me assume nothing. I'll check all of our gates to make sure that Owl Court is actually safe. He has us by the balls." Ogrim's cane thunked as he made his way downstairs.

"Did you see the feeding room below disturbed in any way?" Salter asked from behind her scarf, as she covered her face even more with a thick, beaded veil.

Rise shook his head.

She left the roof, wincing in pain from the strong autumnal sun.

Rise was left on the rooftop. *So, we are alone all over again.* He gritted his teeth. *There are always survivors after the collapse of big things,* he reflected, remembering his words to Ogrim when he'd first wanted to leave their home.

"We ... need people," he spoke aloud to the silent landscape, to the ring of holly trees that marked their boundary. Dawn broke properly across the countryside and illuminated the underbellies of the voluminous clouds that told of coming rain.

Nothing answered him.

Rise stared at the hard little crab apples that had spilled from Cypriot's apron. Blaschko lines burned across Rise's face from the growing sun, even though most of his skin was covered with the blanket, but he paid no heed to such pain. *Seeping sands, draining sands:* the thought wound again and again around his brain.

A gunshot rang through the silence.

Rise blinked and realized that he was standing by the blood-drenched wheelbarrow. It had been covered hastily with one of the tarps from the vegetable garden. He didn't even remember leaving the roof, moving down through the house, or passing through the courtyard to their animal pens. He stared into the dark eyes of the nearest pig.

Another gunshot.

Rise looked up. High on the wall that rose above the pigpen stood Ogrim, shotgun in hand. Picking off brutes that had followed Elaine, Rise, and Marnie from Dunsinann.

"He'll frighten the animals. Daisy won't milk now, not with a warzone going off over our heads," Salter said. She sat on a bale of hay in the shadow of the stables, looking neither angry nor resigned. She only stared, like Rise, at the pigs, scarves pressed hard over her mouth with her gloved hands. Cypriot rattled about in the kitchen, humming as normal while he prepared breakfast.

"What an opportunity Elaine and Marnie had, considering the rest of the world has gone to pot," Salter whispered. "You, we, one of us needs to go out into that village again. We'll do better with introducing people to Cypriot next time. We cannot be beholden to him alone, never again. You were right all along, Rise. I know it puts what we have here in such danger, but we do need more people. To do that, one of us will have to go out again. And you cannot dump that old woman's body there outside these walls for the brutes to—"

"Don't put any of this in the chronicle," Rise interrupted. He waited through her surprise and doubt until Salter nodded.

Rise returned his attention to the gentle shuffling of the pigpen. His hands lifted and rested on the shoulder-high wall. He leaned his chin on the mossed-over concrete and let out a long sigh. The corner of the tarp lifted in the breeze that was whipping through the yard. Fingers. Marnie's squat and solid fist, attached to an arm attached to nothing much else. Only blood and bone.

Rise nodded at Salter's wisdom. Despite any promises made before this mess, he would have to leave again. Do better with Cypriot, again.

Ogrim stood on the walls for several more hours and picked off the last few brutes, until he declared there were too many stragglers, too many wanderers attracted by the gunfire. The lane and fields and the lands surrounding their home would never be free of intrusion again.

Chapter 7

Less Curious

"All we have is trust in one another," Rise said to Cypriot. Though they were alone in the kitchen, Rise spoke low, so that even the walls couldn't hear them. Rise dried the breakfast bowls and plates as Cypriot washed up. Cypriot stood in front of the sink, the full light of a soon-winter's day upon him from the kitchen window. The heavy netting had been pushed back to allow even more daylight inside. Rise remained at the far end of the draining board, out of the reach of the sun.

"Okay," Cypriot answered, neither agreeable nor annoyed.

They moved on to washing and drying cutlery. A silence fell, so still they could hear the faint crackle of the drawing room fire and Ogrim's snores. A creak from beneath their feet told of Salter working in the root cellar.

"I need to go and attend to my own tasks for the day. The roof of the timber shed needs repair," Rise tried again. He watched Cypriot. There could be no denying that he looked wretched. Rise didn't know what to believe when it came to the events of Elaine and Marnie. But he could plainly see that his Cypriot bore a deep burden, had gone through something terrible. Rise sorted soup spoons from the rest of the cutlery and dropped them into their specific home in the drawer. But then again, Rise was the one who always bore the brunt of Cypriot's tempers and tantrums. None more than Rise knew the true depth of Cypriot's manipulations, especially if his nose were out of joint over a matter so big as this.

"Don't 'okay' me," Rise could not help but snap. "There's a fresh body outside as fodder for our pigs. There was a death here at Owl Court, a murder—"

"They both came at me!" Cypriot interrupted, voice high and shrill.

"Shush, you'll wake Ogrim." Rise waved his damp tea towel.

"That crazy mother tried to kill me, and all you're worried about are the damn pigs? Unless ..." Cypriot's eyes narrowed as he pulled the plug. The sink emptied with a sickening squelch. "Unless you don't believe me?"

"Not this again," Rise responded with a sigh. He was straining to keep the conversation on track. "All I'm saying is that we, as a coven, we need to have trust in one another. Complete trust, down to our bones. We have to. Otherwise—"

"Otherwise it'll sour my blood? And I'll taste bad?" Cypriot interrupted again. His mouth puckered and he raised his delicately arching eyebrows.

Rise wanted to slap him with the tea towel. "No. Because, if we can't trust each other, what's the point in any of this? We may as well run straight out the gates and into the jaws of the nearest brute." Rise firmly shut the cutlery drawer.

Cypriot did not answer. He only gazed out the kitchen window. After a time, he closed his eyes and soaked in the sunlight. The women's scratches still fresh around his throat, marring the usually perfect punctures of his drinking wounds. When Cypriot swallowed, Rise saw the shadow of a distinct thumbprint flex right above his larynx. "Then don't you dare call it a 'murder'," Cypriot said. "If we must trust each other."

"What do you want me to say?"

"Call it an 'attempted murder' by Elaine and her crazy, crazy mother. An attempted murder that I fought off. Me, alone." Cypriot then opened one eye and glared at Rise. "Your human."

"You should've woken us—" Rise could not help but insist again. That was the most maddening part. If only Cypriot had woken them up, cried loud enough for help, tussled the women onto the sleeping vampires, something, anything, he and Salter and Ogrim would have risen. They would have.

Cypriot grabbed a cup from the draining board and smashed it on the floor. "It would have been easier to wake the dead!"

"Keep your voice down," Rise warned.

"Okay, the next time I'm being choked, I'll remember to be really, really loud and wake everybody for miles around."

Rise's skin crawled at his sarcasm. He reached into the daylight, into the sink, and popped the last soap bubble gurgling down the drain. "Did you really have to kill the mother?" Rise asked softly, deeply. He watched not Cypriot's face, nor his beginning tears, nor the flush in his cheeks. Instead, Rise watched his pulse in the great vein at his neck. Its steady flinch-thump told of Cypriot's temper.

"May nightmares plague you ..." Cypriot managed through choked-back tears. He pushed past Rise and crunched the shattered cup underfoot as he fled the kitchen.

His bare arm in the sunlight, it took Rise a long time to realize that he was in pain. Did Cypriot know about his nightmares? Rise listened to Cypriot's footsteps pound upstairs. Ogrim no longer snored in the drawing room. As he stooped to collect the broken cup fragments, Rise cradled the shards in his hand. Sand escaped from beneath his feet. Rise crouched on the kitchen floor like a caught mouse, unable to feel anything but the trap that pinned him low and choked from all sides. He squeezed his fist until the shards cut him and a trickle of blood trailed down his wrist. A line of red across his arm's Blaschko lines.

He would have to tell someone. Not just that he was leaving again, but of his dream, too.

Ogrim stood in the kitchen doorway. When Rise noticed him, he braced for the old one's temper. But Ogrim only twitched his whiskery chin and shuffled past the remains of the shattered cup.

"I think a spot of tea might be in order?" Ogrim asked lightly as he turned on the stove.

Rise stood and dumped the bloodied fragments in the bin. He stared into their refuse. Most things, they recycled. But still, there were always a few oddments of food and crockery to throw away.

"I don't know what to do," Rise admitted out loud. "If you've forgotten how to make tea, then I'll do it—"

"But—"

"Tea first. Then talk," Ogrim added with a wink. His tarot cards bulged from the pocket of his tweed waistcoat. "Maybe some cards, too? See what they say?"

Rise slumped into the nearest dining chair and listened to the water boil and the roiling squeal of the kettle. He looked at his bloodied palm, then along his arm at the deep, stinging Blaschko lines that only now began to fade.

"What do I do?" Rise asked of nobody.

"I think that you know what you must do." Ogrim set down two mugs and didn't fill his own first. A sugar bowl and milk jug followed. Freshly washed teaspoons clattered alongside.

"But can I do it?"

"Maybe," Ogrim shrugged in reply. He added a fistful of sugar into his tea as he sat opposite Rise.

Rise looked for his handkerchief once again, to clean his hand. "Oh, that's right ..." He'd given it to Elaine.

"What's lost must be recovered. Then preserved." Ogrim shuffled through his tarot.

When Ogrim fanned out the deck before him, Rise chose a random card. Ogrim looked at it and didn't say its name, only slotted it back into the deck. Kept on shuffling.

"All that's not saved will be lost," Rise agreed and watched the cards turn in Ogrim's old, weathered hands.

The sunlight turned through the kitchen, eventually moving from the sink to touch the back of Rise's chair.

PART 2 - WINTER

"A man takes his thoughts with him throughout his life. Ideas, once planted, stay growing. Often, across all time. Therefore, think with care."

—Ogrim, The Seer

Chapter 8

Of Belts & Bulls

Winter deepened. The time since the end of all things lengthened into months. Their animals made more noise now during daylight hours, gentle lows and shuffling. The odd moo from Daisy. The goats' nattering grew as sound was added back into the world. Rise took his time; said nothing, again, of his plan to leave. Salter didn't bring it up, either. Since Elaine and Marnie, members of the coven had kept steadfastly to their routines: Ogrim at cards, Salter at chronicle, Cypriot gardening, drying herbs and making preserves, puttering up and down to the root cellar and into the courtyard's sheds and barns, as if nothing had ever happened. Rise continued to tend the animals. They lost a goat or two in the winter, as they always did. He longed for the distant springtime that was dug deep into the turning of the world. More life to this house would come again soon. He just had to give it time. Rise found that time, above all else, soothed people and creatures, and his coven as well. Let enough time pass, unspoken and uncommented upon, and then you can turn around and do almost anything you please.

A snowfall had left a thick blanket on the ground, but otherwise the night stood dark. The faint curve of a new moon was almost lost against the stars, their brightness having surged back to life now that all industry and traffic had ceased. Fresh after their feed, not needing to drink from Cypriot for another week, Rise stood upon the kitchen's wide doorstep. If he could manage to find people without appearing covered up like a vagrant or rogue, like last time, his chances of success would be greater, he told himself. Again, the stillness in the world caught Rise's attention. A low hoot from an owl somewhere in the rafters of their barn broke the night's silence. Tom strutted silently across the courtyard without even a glance in Rise's direction.

Rise wondered about Elaine, even though her death was an absolute certainty beyond the walls of his home, with the world as it was now. If only she'd stayed, she would have lived.

Rise watched the stars and his breath, visible in the cold air. Orion's belt blared overhead. He followed the diagonal line made by the three stars across the sky to the glowing red star Aldebaran, in Taurus. Then he followed that ancient astronomical line on to find the Seven Sisters.

"Red eye of the bull," Rise whispered. He pulled his overcoat's lapels tighter to keep out the chill, pistol at his hip. He jogged up and down to check the weight and balance of the crowbar attached to his backpack. The first thing was to collect his bicycle from the hedge. Rise turned to close the kitchen door.

"Not this bullshit again." Ogrim's voice came from near the oven as Rise grasped the door handle.

The dark kitchen had emptied, the table been cleared, after dinner. But Ogrim now stood by the sink, leaning on his cane and dressed like Rise, face uncovered and ready to leave, ready for adventure. A sawn-off shotgun was cradled in the crook of Ogrim's elbow, barrel pointed at the floor.

"Not another word until we're outside the walls," Rise warned when he realized that Ogrim meant to come with him. He pointed to Cypriot's tray of gardening implements on the windowsill, whose blades caught the faint moonlight and snow glow. Rise touched his finger to his lips for silence, to remind Ogrim that Cypriot could probably hear everything. There was no point in arguing. They would leave together, and that was final. Before they left, Rise took a deep inhale of all the indoor greenery and the scent of his home, in case it was his last. He prayed Cypriot could forgive him. Or, even more so, that Rise could handle Cypriot's reaction, if he and Ogrim ever returned, well before dawn.

Ogrim and Rise walked across the yard, unnoticed by the world, as only their kind could move. Rise set his hand to the small side gate and broke protection for the few moments it took for them to slip outside. The brutes that had followed Rise here in the autumn were long dead, mostly thanks to Ogrim. Rise hoped stragglers would be easy to see against the snow. He expected some sort of remains—not quite corpses, but certainly a sign that brutes had been here. Like bones, scattered about. Owl Court's pigs had such trouble with Marnie's.

"The wildlife certainly benefits from all this," Ogrim said. He did not seem to need his cane at all but waved it around as he spoke. Undisturbed snow lay outside their walls. "I saw wild boar tracks from sitting up there on the wall, saw them further out, past the line of holly. There's a wolf pack about, too. Heard them howling a few nights back, at the solstice."

"Wildlife? Does that include us?" Rise muttered.

The world seemed so different since he last left Owl Court. Greenery gone, the countryside was monochrome in snow and bare trees and hedgerows of spun twigs. Even the lane through the holly trees and down the hill was nothing more than a shallow rut running along snow-covered ground. Rise took heart at the stout holly that stood dark and glossy in an otherwise desaturated world. A countryside taking back its realms. Sure, a bleak winter to get through first, but then springtime. Rise's heart lifted as he longed for brighter mornings and colourful days. In spring, this would all be green once again.

They moved around the fallen tree, where rot had long ago set in. Rise glanced to see if there were any more winter roses around its roots. But snow covered everything.

"You put us all in danger every time you leave," Ogrim began.

"Oh, I don't know." Rise swallowed down the argument brewing as they walked. "The difference between things that are life-changing and then world-changing, are they not the same?"

"Doing nothing. That's often the best way to survive," Ogrim answered, his chin in the air.

Rise changed the subject. "Let me know if you need a hand along this part. The path through here is slippery."

"Fuck off." Ogrim marched ahead.

Rise watched the wide set of Ogrim's shoulders for a couple of paces. Then he realized he was glad to be behind him. Ogrim wouldn't be able to see his face.

"Hey, Ogrim?"

"Hm?"

"Have ... you had dreams, Ogrim? When you sleep?"

"Not a one."

"No?" Rise asked, surprised. "Never? The other two seem to. Well, Cypriot does because of what he is. I think all humans dream. Salter dreams, I guess, because of the chronicle. That'd keep anyone awake, after what happened with Elaine and her mother." Rise listened to the landscape around them, never letting their chatter hide the approach of something foul. He had no idea if Salter had mentioned those two women in the chronicle or not. In his own way, Rise tested to see what Ogrim knew.

"And you? You've dreamed?" Ogrim asked after some time in thought.

"Yes. And I've wanted to speak to you about it for a good while."

"Oh yes?" Ogrim answered, sounding much like Cypriot.

Rise hesitated; eyed the back of Ogrim's head. Then he began. "I keep ... thinking about it. This same dream. Of Marnie. She is—she tells me to gather. That I cannot cross her bridge until I do."

"Well, that's plain to see what that's about."

"Really?" Rise asked in surprise. He should have told Ogrim about his dream long ago. The old coot would have torn its symbolism apart and provided an answer to Rise clearer than the sun in the sky.

"Yes," Ogrim said, and he shuffled on his stiff leg. Then he shook his foot and the limb walked properly again in full stride. "Plain to see. You need to gather more people around you because of what's happened to the world. Then you can 'cross over,' I guess. Serve your life's purpose. Gather others, set that up to flourish, no? Seems like a powerful dream."

"That's right. Maybe you're right." Rise also shifted his weight as they walked, considering this interpretation. With a dark glance to the strong slope of Ogrim's shoulders, Rise also worried that Ogrim sought to manipulate him in some way, make him think in a specific fashion about a specific interpretation.

They walked in silence as they took the lane and turned onto the main road. They passed the spot where Rise had left his bike in the hedge.

"We'll get it on the way back," Ogrim said with a shrug.

Rise took grim solace in the fact that Ogrim expected them both to return from this adventure.

As Dunsinann grew closer, they could see the snow had melted in wide dips and patches along its riverbank. Rise couldn't tell if the road had been deliberately cleared in places to make way for vehicles. No tire tracks, though, he noted, no cartwheel marks or bicycle tracks. The road seemed undisturbed, except for the patches and puddles of melted snow. He looked for animal tracks and found a few: plenty of rabbits and hare, a fox too. A wave of unease passed through Rise as the rooftops of Dunsinann stood dark against the star-studded sky. The village's narrow network of streets hugged the far riverbank. The place no longer smoked or steamed. It all stood silent now, like a stone monument uncovered in a field from a forgotten time.

A wave of déjà vu hit Rise. He hesitated, as if Warwolf riders might suddenly rush at them on the road from every angle. When Ogrim noticed him grow tense, he lifted his shotgun in readiness. Rise in turn took out his crowbar.

"It looks like those fire bombs, or whatever they were called, the ones used on the news." Ogrim eyed the line of trees behind him, gun at the ready. "It looks like they targeted even tiny places like Dunsinann. This fire damage isn't all the way from Larnde. What a pity, though. Before the world went to shit, I'd sometimes wander down here in high summer, listen to the festivals and singing. Covered and hidden, of course. It's all a graveyard now." Ogrim spoke as they grew closer to the destroyed bridge. Although ash and smoke had settled even more since Rise was last here, that dampening-down and snowing-over only made the charred corpses and burned–out cars seem even more lifeless.

"A crematorium," Rise said in a low voice.

"This is where you found the women?" Ogrim asked as they approached the bridge's collapsed pillars. They needed no torches or lamplight; their vision in the dark was as good as in day. The river remained nothing more than a trickle between two muddy banks. The water pooled and filled in odd pockets until it found a way through any blockages, around the waterlogged debris, around fallen arches and brickwork, charred cars and cadavers that had fallen into the waters with the collapse. Even thus hindered, the river slipped over brickwork and metal and bone to continue its meandering journey downstream.

"A disturbed river," Rise muttered to himself, then nodded at Ogrim's question. "I found Elaine first, as I tried to cross this bridge into the town. Then, after a bit, Marnie came out and stood over there, between the two pillars with the horse statues on the far side. Where Elaine and her mother were sheltering or living in Dunsinann, I have no idea. When I tried to cross the river and bring them home with me, the brutes hiding in the arches of the bridge awoke, somehow." The memory of Marnie's shriek pierced Rise's ears again. "The mother screamed. And the brutes were all clustered and hidden beneath the bridge. They woke at the noise and collapsed it all. As you see it now."

"Foul wretches," Ogrim spat. He leaned on his cane to peer down the riverbank at the slow, brown water. "The river is low. It must be dammed further upstream."

"Hadn't thought of that," Rise answered. He looked about for hidden brutes, but saw nothing.

"You hadn't guessed why the river was so low? What, you thought the water level was just naturally this way? In winter?" Ogrim's good eye glared at him.

Rise just shrugged and glanced behind them to watch the line of charred trees.

"What's the matter?" Ogrim asked. "You're spooked. That's not like you."

"It's a spooky place," Rise admitted. He stepped close to the beginning of the collapsed bridge and gazed across the destruction. Somehow he expected to see Marnie standing there. The pale horses still reared up on each pillar on the far side, but otherwise Dunsinann held nothing but the memory of people.

"Spooky?" Ogrim chuckled. "Our kind find things spooky?"

"This one does." Rise shook his head to rid it of his dreams. "Where's the next river crossing, then?" he asked to change the subject. Orion's belt moved through the sky as constellations turned. Soon it would set. They had to be home before dawn, whether they found survivors or not.

"Far upriver." Ogrim pointed into the dark. "Miles. Let's try walking to where the river curves out of sight over there."

Rise knew this made sense. The river could be dammed with nothing more suspicious than a fallen tree. Or, a bridge built by people. Still, Rise continued to stare at the far riverbank, where streets and cobble began. Maybe, if they went into Dunsinann, he and Ogrim could find some evidence of what Elaine and Marnie had been up to, if they ever had contact with other people. Rise narrowed his eyes. Where he'd dreamed Marnie stood, the cobblestones were indeed disturbed to show a patch of upturned dirt.

"Rise?" Ogrim's voice cut into his thoughts. Rise caught faint strains of concern as Ogrim continued. "Do not become fascinated with where you found Elaine and her mother. Let's find a new way into Dunsinann. Upriver. Come."

Rise said nothing at such a scolding, regretting a little that he had told Ogrim about his dream. Weapons now in hand and at the ready, he and Ogrim walked side by side along the riverbank road. A narrow path, one car-width wide, that drew them inland, upriver, through shallow snow.

"The waters will be narrower upstream. That's good." Ogrim pointed at the opposite bank, and already it rose much sharper on the outskirts of Dunsinann than where they had first come upon the village.

In time, they made it to the bend in the river. The water here was nothing more than a streak of thick mud smeared into the landscape. Ogrim leaned on his cane and looked across the exposed riverbed.

"I would not like to cross that mud without a bridge," Ogrim muttered.

"Someone tried." Rise pointed at scrabble marks in the mud halfway across and an odd bump of clothing. "Poor soul."

"Poor soul, indeed. Them or us, I wonder?" Ogrim led the way around the bend.

Several trees had been hacked down from the Dunsinann side and lay across the river, lashed together to create a makeshift bridge. Tree stumps on the far side of the river stood pale against the grey world, their hack marks new. The belly of the river-trickle lay far below the tree trunks, the riverbed deeper here than at the first bridge.

Rise crouched when they saw this new, makeshift bridge. He looked under the trunks that lay across the river. No brutes hid beneath. He listened to the world, but everything was silent.

"So, this bridge is recent. It's swept clear of the recent snowfall, too." Rise stood and approached the trunks on their side of the river, the entire length of wood shorn clean of branches. An easy step-up chopped into the nearest trunk. Several wet, bare footprints and prints from boot-wearers ran its length. And, surprisingly, the clear half-moon of horseshoes.

"Wide enough for horses. These prints are recent, too. That means this bridge was made after you rescued Elaine and her mother. There's more in that village than you thought, Rise."

"I suppose," Rise answered. Ogrim's mind could be so sharp at times.

"You suppose? There's no 'supposing' about it. One bridge collapsed, now a new one upstream? People settled here after the firebombs. They're probably foraging in the woods, too. I'd say that the village is long stripped of food by now. Were the waters this low last time you were here?"

Rise sighed and did not want to be needled. He didn't want to get into an argument about water levels and what the river had been like when he first met Elaine.

He'd been busy. Distracted with securing survivors. "Okay."

Ogrim frowned. "What do you mean 'okay'? That means there were more than just Elaine and Marnie in Dunsinann!"

Then someone giggled.

The next sound was the click of Rise and Ogrim's guns.

When they spun around, a gangly woman grinned at them from the branches of a nearby tree. She brought down a shower of snow as she dropped to the ground. Rise thought it was Elaine at first, or a similar teenage girl, but this woman turned out to be older, with a shock of ginger hair.

"And who you might you be, Cheshire Cat?" Ogrim growled.

Despite the frigid temperatures, she wore only a ratty, once-white t-shirt over men's jeans. A belt tight around her waist. Faded tracks and tattoos on her arms. The sight of her sallow, prominent veins turned Rise's stomach.

"Who might ya'll be, dumb and dumber?" she laughed in an American accent.

Chapter 9

Unstable Bridge

Ogrim took his time and aimed his shotgun. Her laughter stopped.

"Let's not blast the first person we meet." Rise set his hand to the barrel of Ogrim's gun. The whole point of leaving Owl Court was, well, to find other humans.

"How about we not have a repeat of last time?" Ogrim countered.

"I'm Rise," Rise said over him, so the woman wouldn't hear. He holstered his pistol but kept a grip on his crowbar. "This is Ogrim. What's your name?"

"Maxine." Her brown eyes stood huge in her head. They swivelled to take in the full measure of both Rise and Ogrim. She wasn't at all soot-stained, like Elaine and Marnie; instead, Maxine merely looked grubby, as if she had spent the day mucking out stables.

"Maxine, is it?" Rise asked. He knelt to root out soda from his backpack. "You sound American. Not from here?"

She shook her head. "I was on a package tour of this darlin' English countryside. Then everythin' fell to shit." She sniffled and rubbed the whole length of her arm under her nose. Maxine's other arm, all tattoos and veins, wrapped across her stomach.

"Are you cold, Maxine?" Rise noticed her chill. He found a chocolate bar and held it out, along with a soda. "Hungry?"

Maxine took his offering and opened the soda one-handed, as if it was a beer.

Rise got to his feet and tightened his grip on the crowbar. One fine crack to her skull was all that was needed. A terrible thing had happened to the world. The survivors, the people left behind to make it to today, were probably not in the best shape mentally, let alone physically. He wanted to get some sugar into Maxine; fluids, chocolate, caffeine. That might even her out. It had worked often enough with Cypriot, when his fussing grew too sharp. Humans, it seemed to Rise, required constant nourishment, whereas he could go at least a week, probably longer, without any sustenance at all. Rise took in the spectre of Maxine as she stood in the snow before them. He could well imagine Cypriot's reaction if they were to return with her to Owl Court.

"There was a real culture problem growing in the cities, you know? Before all this happened. Zero times," she said, then downed the soda in a few gulps.

"What on earth are you talking about, lass?" Ogrim asked after an awkward pause.

"Oh, I think you know," she said, nodding like a wise sage, cola running down her chin. Maxine looked at Ogrim, then at Rise, and studied their faces. She tilted her head and half-nodded as if deciding something. "Your skin is proof that only the pure survive. That's the rule now. That's what everybody says."

"Christ, every fucker we find out here is mad as badgers!" Ogrim shifted his feet and resettled his stance, never lowering his gun.

Rise thought the girl would freak out at such words from someone pointing a gun at her. He thought she'd run away. But Maxine only raised her eyebrows even higher. Her mouth hung open in delight. Then Maxine laughed.

"Oh wow, you're both actually out looking for people?"

"Shh, not so loud!" Rise gathered Ogrim a few steps closer when Maxine's voice boomed off the trees. He glanced over his shoulder at Dunsinann, but the village remained still and dark. "Are you alone, Maxine? Are there others?"

"Nope, just me out here." Maxine lifted and dropped her spindly arms in a shrug.

"Well, that's bullshit." Ogrim was still sighting her down his gun. "You just said 'everybody says,' so there are other people about. You're not alone. And you're talking weird about ... things."

"Oh yeah, well, there are other people around. Group of folks hold that village," Maxine chattered as she drained the soda and then giddily unwrapped the chocolate bar. "Oooh, peanut. My favourite. D'ya know how long it's been since I had peanut butter? That's what I miss. That's what I really, really miss, is peanut butter."

"We all miss a lot of things," Rise murmured, never taking his eyes off Maxine as she ate. She was too

... Rise couldn't put his finger on it. Animated? But, whoever now lived in Dunsinann, they probably slipped drugs into women's food to keep them placid and in line. Although that might have backfired with this one.

"Mm-hmm!" Maxine chirped, not appearing to notice Rise's wariness.

Ogrim glanced toward Rise and tilted his head in a way that clearly said, *Well, you found a survivor; now what are you going to do?*

Rise waited until Maxine finished eating, then took off his overcoat and offered it to her. He stood much taller than Maxine, and the coat was made of heavy, waxed leather. Its heft and volume might well impede Maxine if she decided to run, or so he hoped.

"Oh, it smells amazing," Maxine gushed as she slipped into Rise's coat and set her nose deep into the sleeve's elbow. "It's like a flower garden. Where on earth smells like this 'round here? Daisy, daisy!" Maxine sang softly to herself as she swayed about to inhale different parts of the coat. She folded the collar over her face and, with a lift of her eyebrows, mimicked how Rise wore it.

Rise didn't know what to do. He didn't want this person to come back with them. He had no qualms about killing people who were a threat, who were dangerous. But this Maxine seemed more like a junkie without her fix. Pitiful. Cast out into the snow. A survivor, albeit with a miserable life. Rise hated being far from home for so long. He had to make a decision. Had to signal to Ogrim, too, somehow, what he was about to do. At least Rise knew in his heart that Ogrim would be only delighted to be rid of this crazy girl.

"Maybe we can go into Dunsinann and meet the people living there? What're they like? How many are they?" Ogrim never dropped his shotgun, although he resettled his stance again in the snow.

"Maybe we can offer them supplies? Set up trade?" Rise asked. Ogrim's knee probably pained him, the cold eating away at the old, twisted injury he had suffered in Spain, generations ago, that never truly healed. Although, with the way Maxine acted, it seemed that she didn't even notice the shotgun or, indeed, the crowbar that Rise kept firm in his grip.

"Nah," Maxine shook her head and chewed furiously on the chocolate. "Ya won't get much from that bunch, only a punch in the jaw. Call themselves Warwolves, like it's *Mad Max* or something. Arrogant bunch of bastards."

"Okay, so maybe not," Ogrim said, catching Rise's eye at the mention of that group. They both casually took a few steps away from the bridge and drew Maxine off the road, into the shadow of the trees, lest those across the river notice them.

"Oh? Why not? D'ya know the Warwolves?" Maxine asked as she trotted after them. "They cast me out. That's why I was in the tree. I was thinking about how to sneak back in. Then you two showed up."

"They cast you out?" Rise frowned. Maxine looked so pitiful in his comically oversized coat that he could only feel sympathy towards her. But with her words, he knew what to do. She knew too much. She had to go. Rise glanced at the stars, took one last look at the line of three that glimmered in Orion's Belt, before the leaf canopy obscured the night sky. He and Ogrim kept leaning and easing, step by step, deeper into the trees.

"Oh no, wait, are you guys like the Warwolves' arch rivals or something? Like comic book villains? They're the screws and ya'll are the heroes?"

Carefully, they drew her further and further into the trees that separated Dunsinann from the countryside. When Ogrim and Rise had shuffled far enough so the noise of their guns wouldn't echo too much throughout the village, so they could turn and flee straight in the direction of home, Ogrim glanced at Rise and gave the nod. Rise looked at his overcoat. With the way the world was now, it would be such a nuisance to have to patch and repair it, to clean blood from it. Rise could only imagine how much Cypriot would fuss. And Rise really did like that coat.

Maxine continued to blabber on. She didn't even notice that they had both raised their guns and settled their aim. She twitched as she spoke and let the chocolate wrapper float out of her hand onto the snow. With another disgustingly long sniff, Maxine scratched at her wrist and poked her fingers up the sleeve of the coat, as if wanting to claw at her arm.

A branch snapped.

"Wait. You hear that?" Rise shushed Maxine when she kept talking. "You hear that?"

"Yes, I do," Ogrim whispered and swung the aim of his gun into the maze of tree trunks behind them. From the dark forest came snapping twigs and the low chatter of women's voices. The odd nicker of a horse.

"Oh, shit!" Maxine jumped. "That's Warwolves. They took their horses out hunting. Must be coming back."

"She's going to call those fuckers," Ogrim growled. "A head full of poison, that one."

"No, I'm not!" Maxine crouched into the snow and gestured that they should do the same. She began to slink back towards the road and looked over her shoulder to make sure they followed.

Rise panicked, cursed that they had not shot her just now. They couldn't take on a pack of Warwolves like this, especially not in the open, so close to the Warwolves' base in Dunsinann. They had no option but to crouch as well and copy Maxine's retreat. He gestured for Ogrim to follow, but Ogrim glared at Rise. With his unstable knee, there was no way he could crouch. For a split second, Rise thought Ogrim might turn and fire his gun into the trees. Rise gestured frantically for Ogrim to follow.

"Ogrim!" Rise hissed in a whisper. "Please!"

Maxine broke from the tree line and raced onto the road. A blur passed by Rise. For a terrifying moment he remembered the ghosts of his dream. But it was just Ogrim, who grabbed Rise's shirt as he pushed past. They hauled each other toward Maxine. The sudden smooth road camber beneath his feet sent waves of relief through Rise.

"We can move faster on a flatter surface. You guys came from this way, right?" Maxine trotted ahead, downriver, towards Dunsinann's destroyed bridge.

Despite the sound of Warwolves approaching from the forest, Ogrim gripped Rise and shook his head, to say she shouldn't come back with them.

"Yes. Let's go," Rise agreed with Maxine and hurried after her. "We can deal with her later, at any point, once we get home," he added in a low voice into that old ear, with its thick tufts of curly grey hairs. Rise put his arm across Ogrim's shoulders to offer support.

"Cypriot will, you mean," Ogrim grunted.

"We don't have much cover on this road," Rise said to Maxine as they caught up.

"Yeah, but it makes this easier," she said as she slotted herself under Ogrim's other shoulder. Rise was surprised at her strength, and it was true; together the three of them made good speed along the road. They might even make it past the curve in the river, where they would be out of view, by the time the Warwolves reached the road.

"Wow, you guys can really see in the dark. I can barely make out anything," Maxine gasped as they hurried. A disturbing wheeze rattled her lungs.

"Have they dogs?" Ogrim asked. "Will they catch our scent?"

"No," Maxine answered, eyes ahead with a determination that impressed Rise. "They don't have 'em out hunting with 'em, but the Warwolves sure are training 'em."

Rise relaxed a little when they made it to the bend in the river. He glanced over his shoulder and realized that the new bridge was now out of sight. Maxine had been right to come back to the road and follow it away.

The snow was nothing more than slush across the tarmac here. The three of them had barely left any tracks at all.

Rise heard the Warwolves step onto the road. He was surprised; their horses were shod with proper iron horseshoes.

"They must have a forge running," Rise muttered to himself as they hurried into the night. "To smelt and hammer the horseshoes. Have they an anvil?" he asked Maxine, his voice muffled against Ogrim's clothes as they carried him. "Hey, Maxine, have the Warwolves got a blacksmith?"

She looked at him as if he were crazy for asking at a time like this, as they stumbled along.

"Shut the fuck up," Ogrim wheezed.

"I was only wondering if—"

Distracted, Rise loosened his grip to turn around again, to look.

Ogrim yelped as he lost his balance between the two. He slipped and crashed onto the road. Rise and Maxine toppled onto him.

"What was that?" a Warwolf shouted from the new bridge.

As Rise helped Ogrim and Maxine to their feet, Ogrim gasped and clutched his right leg. The Warwolves could be heard gathering their horses.

"Back to the trees!" Rise insisted, voice low, as he and Maxine supported a grimacing Ogrim off the road. They returned to the maze of trees and huddled behind the first thick trunk they found, knelt into the light dusting of snow beneath the canopy. They watched the road.

"Hopefully, they'll just ride right on past," Rise whispered. "Wait, what are you doing?"

His heart jumped when Maxine dashed from their hiding place and ran onto the road. With frozen fingers and Ogrim's weight piled against him, Rise grappled for his gun. He had to take her out before she called for the Warwolves. Maxine flapped about in his oversized coat and used her bare feet and hands to smush through the slush, to hide where they'd left the road. Then Maxine paused, listening. Her red hair the only colour in the world. She did this for only a few seconds and ran back to them. When she returned to crouch at Rise's side, she blew on her purple-cold hands.

"What're they doing?" Rise asked. "Why aren't they rushing us?"

"That's not their way. They're only half mounted up." Maxine looked even more drained after hiding their trail. "But they're gearing up to hunt y'all proper. Lighting torches, redistributing arrows and ammo. They don't blindly chase nobody. I've seen 'em. They'll hunt somethin' slow. An' forever."

Rise's stomach dropped. He just wanted to be home, in the warmth of the kitchen. Never did he think he'd miss Cypriot's stupid potted plants or the thick scent of herbs and flowers that always caught in his throat. That jungle of a bedroom, swarming with insects. The warmth of tanned skin. He glanced at the top of Maxine's head as she shivered. Scents of a flower garden, indeed, Rise thought as they hid.

Chapter 10

A Cure for Madness

"I fucking hate hiding. Let them hunt us. We'll just go straight home, right now. Let them try to get past our walls. Let them just fucking try," Ogrim growled from where he rested, keeping a death-clutch on his knee.

"I'm sure by now they know where we live," Rise answered. He glanced to Maxine to see if the Warwolves had ever mentioned the vampire coven at Owl Court. She only stared at Ogrim with concern. Maxine's chest rose and fell with every shivering breath. Rise would have to question her, to see what the Warwolves knew about them. He would question her later, and question her hard. Cypriot could surely help with that.

"Lass, help me stand. We need to head for home. Not squat behind this tree as if it were a latrine!" Ogrim flapped his free hand.

Maxine nodded, apparently ready and eager for such a flight. She crouched by Ogrim and draped his heavy arm over her narrow shoulders again. Rise took up Ogrim's other shoulder and the three stood with care.

They kept to the shadows beneath the trees as they crept home, kept as much distance from the Warwolves as possible.

After what felt like the longest night march ever, exhausted, they made it to the bottom of Holly Hill, where they rested a moment by the laneway that led up to Owl Court's gates.

Now that they'd made it this close to home, everything would be okay. They'd even brought back a person with them, a survivor. Rise tightened his grip on the trio as they caught their breath. He looked about, back at the forest and along the gentle slope before them. Nothing moved. The distant hoot of one of their barn owls lifted his spirits even more. Cypriot became the next obstacle in Rise's mind. Given Maxine's character alone, Cypriot—indeed the rest of the coven, too—they'd all have a tough time getting along. But Rise had succeeded. He just had to settle Maxine in better than how it had gone with Elaine and her mother. No repeat of last time.

As they briefly caught their breath before continuing home, Rise basked in his victory. He relished reaching the humming boundary of home, just up ahead. Of striding through those double gates with his bounty.

Something moved out of the corner of Rise's eye.

Too late, he realized Ogrim's plan.

Ogrim was old, older than Rise by at least several hundred years. With such age came a deep reserve of strength that Rise was only barely aware their kind possessed. And, even though Ogrim was injured, nothing stood in the face of a vampire when flushed full of anger and determination. Upon realizing that they might just make it home, Ogrim turned and plowed all of his considerable weight onto Maxine. As he crushed her into the snowy ground, she yelped and scrabbled at Ogrim as his knobbled fingers clasped around her throat. Tarot cards scattered as she ripped the pockets of his coat in panic.

Rise just watched them struggle on the lightly snowed path that led home.

Maxine was crazy. They'd wanted to kill her at the new bridge. She'd never get on with Cypriot. But Rise also stood so close to victory. Not something he wanted to yield, yet.

He bent to haul Ogrim away, but a sudden weight hit his spine, and Rise splayed onto the struggling pair. Alien and grappling hands clawed at him. The stench of decay. A group of wandering brutes had snuck up on them. Rise was angry with himself for letting his alertness lapse. He struggled to swing his crowbar as he kicked at the attacking brutes, who were all leather-dry skin and brittle bones. The brutes' shrivelled faces blocked the stars. Their jaws chomped to bite at anything. Rise struggled to his feet and staved in the nearest undead's skull with his crowbar.

Two Warwolves on horseback broke from the tree line and galloped towards them, churning snow into dark clumps. Their scythes were sharp, steel lines against the night. Hunting bows on their saddle pommels. A ridiculous array of knives gleamed along their belts as they bore down upon the struggling pile of people and brutes. The two Warwolves attacked the zombies first—wanting a clear kill with the vampires, Rise realized.

He understood Ogrim's earlier strength now. It rose through him, too. With previously untapped resolution and power, Rise kicked the nearest brute, one on top of Maxine and Ogrim. Although Rise's boot crushed through brittle ribs and bone, his kick had enough force to fling the brute against the oncoming riders.

His senses caught the scent of fresh blood as the brutes seized upon the dark, pristinely groomed animals. Rise grasped Ogrim and Maxine as the horses toppled into the wave of grappling hands and chomping jaws. The Warwolves swung their scythes, but their reach was all wrong, their horses panicking and slipping on the snow. Rise pulled Maxine and Ogrim to their feet. He glimpsed in horror an ugly bite on Ogrim's scalp, where half of his ear had been torn away. Several brown, rotted teeth were left behind, lodged deep in Ogrim's head.

The sky crept towards dawn.

With shrieking and gut-sinking thuds, the horses collapsed onto their riders. Rise dragged Ogrim and Maxine along the final few feet of the steep laneway, to the side gate of Owl Court. A muddled gang of blood-soaked brutes and Warwolves staggered after. The only thought burning in Rise's mind was to get home. He herded the two before him like an automaton. Rise broke the wall's protection with a slap of his bloodied hand and pushed Maxine and Ogrim inside.

The rotted face of a once-young man, jaw swinging from dried tendons, eyeballs like small, rattling prunes in their sockets, appeared as Rise tried to close the gate. It attempted to force its way inside. With a final burst of anger, Rise kicked the gate shut. The flush of

Owl Court's boundary protection enveloped him once again as he, Ogrim, and Maxine collapsed in the yard. Brutes hammered on the gates. Rise lay in the dark, on the cold, slushy cobblestones of home.

Soft candlelight fell upon them when Rise and Maxine eventually pushed open the kitchen door and bundled Ogrim inside. Cypriot sat at the dining table, which was laid out and set as if for breakfast. But an open bottle of whiskey stood at his elbow, and Cypriot's expression was just as sour. He scowled at Rise, then glared in disgust at Maxine wearing Rise's overcoat, until he saw Ogrim's injury.

"Brutes got him." Rise heaved Ogrim into the large armchair that was jammed into the kitchen's corner. That rush of greenery and the floral scents of home hit him. Rise shivered at the memory of those disgusting fiends on top of them all just now.

"What happened?" Salter was seated behind the back door, where the candlelight did not reach. Now she rushed forward, tall, commanding, and tilted Ogrim's head towards the nearest candle. "For heaven's sake, Cypriot, make some more light," she snapped in panic. "I can't see."

Cypriot didn't move from the table, such was his shock.

"A brute bit him," Rise explained as Salter pulled back Ogrim's coat and opened his shirt. She checked his breath, which had lulled to nothing, as if Ogrim were in a deep sleep. His gaze had gone far away. Salter inspected the bite on his head, her long, dark fingers carefully poking at the brown teeth left behind in his skin.

"More light!" Salter barked.

Maxine jumped and grabbed the nearest candle from the dining table and brought it to the armchair. "I need water." Salter sniffed Ogrim's wound, which oozed black, old blood. She glanced up and saw Cypriot still sitting in shock at the breakfast table. Then Salter noticed Maxine. "You, girl, fetch a bowl and hot water from the kettle on the stove. Cloth, too. Clean cloth. Cypriot? Help her!"

Rise knelt on the floor before Ogrim's armchair and clasped the old vampire's knee. He'd hurt it when they slipped on the road, Rise remembered, and he rubbed the joint carefully. Rise hoped their spoiled princeling would snap out of his whiskey-sulk, all because a new person came into their midst. One of the coven was wounded. Rise needed everybody in this moment. The familiar routine of placating Cypriot could all come later.

"Cypriot?" Rise leaned a light tone of warning into his voice as Maxine obeyed Salter and grabbed the kettle. Still wearing Rise's overcoat, Maxine moved awkwardly around the new-to her kitchen.

Cypriot finally stood from his chair. A fresh pot of porridge from the stove steamed. Eventually, Cypriot stopped staring at Maxine and dutifully placed two more lamps near the armchair, though his movements were dulled by drink. Cypriot's pupils stood so dark that they seemed to swallow everything as he set down lit candles and another hurricane lamp close to Ogrim. With a nod, he indicated to Maxine where they kept their clean dishcloths and tea towels.

"Is anyone else hurt?" Salter asked as she looked around, pausing briefly to peer at Maxine again. "Is anyone else bitten?"

"No," Rise murmured as he and Maxine shook their heads. "Just him."

Ogrim made no sound, only slumped, dazed, in the armchair. His eyes showed only a heavy-lidded stare out onto the world. No words moved his lips. Even the wound on his neck was a sluggish bite, oozing oil-like blood, slow and glossy.

"What will become of him? One of our kind bitten by those base things?" Rise asked Salter, as if somehow, by writing their chronicle, she would know. As he knelt on the kitchen's flagstones and rubbed Ogrim's wounded knee, he remembered his dream from the autumn. Of Marnie on the bridge and the scythe through his belly. It had all so nearly come to pass.

"I've no idea," Salter frowned. "Someone fetch me a bowl. Hot water. Cypriot, I need your gardening tray with the pliers. And the stationery box or the first aid kit—I'll also need tape to keep his bandages in place. But first, I have to remove these teeth from his wound. They're brute teeth, right?"

Rise nodded. He watched that old, blank face while people moved about. Cypriot obeyed Salter and moved quicker now through his whiskey–haze to retrieve his gardening tray. Maxine appeared at Rise's elbow with a bowl of steaming water.

"Can he talk?" Salter checked Ogrim's eyes, which had clouded over even more. Drool formed in the corner of his mouth. She pinched his intact ear, but Ogrim did not flinch. "It's like some kind of catatonic state. I don't—I don't know what that means for us." She glanced at Maxine, but kept talking. "Our blood is not that of a human. He may not die and turn into a zombie brute, like the humans we saw on the news. A brute bite, to one of us, might have a different effect. But what that might be, I have no idea."

As the others moved and fussed around Ogrim, Rise remained at his feet. "When the outbreak first happened," he began, speaking slowly as he marshalled his thoughts and tried to remember. He didn't care if Maxine found out what they were. She would learn anyway, soon enough. "Did it happen to people like this? That they became catatonic? Did we see anything on the TV? When people were bitten? I'm trying to remember. I don't think they became like Ogrim is now, but I can't recall—"

"I've seen some people bitten. Just recently," Maxine interrupted.

"You have?" Rise pressed until she nodded, then he curled his hand tightly over Ogrim's bad knee. Never had it felt so narrow and knotted with sinews. "Was it like this? Did people become all comatose before they turned into brutes?"

"No. When people are bitten they're, like, poisoned. They thrash about. Then they die and then wake up a brute."

"So, you've never seen someone react this way to a bite?"

Maxine shook her head.

Rise sighed. "Must be just us, then," he muttered at Salter, who wiped the blood that seeped from Ogrim's neck. His blood should not be that dark, either. Rise grimaced; the oil-black blood turned his stomach.

"Why, though?" Maxine asked. "Why would you be different from anyone else?"

"Because ..." Rise trailed off. He glanced at Salter, at least wanting her permission before revealing them. Rise looked to Cypriot, too, but his face only stood pale and blank. He hoped it was a reflection of his concern for Ogrim, but Rise knew better. Rise squeezed Ogrim's knee again to draw strength. "Because we are ... we are from the folklore, Maxine. Ogrim, Salter, myself. We live here, secluded from society, as a coven. We are—"

"Vampires!" she squeaked.

Rise flinched. "Yes. We are blood drinkers," he managed with a forced smile.

He looked away as her eyebrows went high up her forehead and a huge grin pulled at her hanging mouth. How had all of this turned out to be such an utter mistake? Rise studied the lines of Ogrim's deadened face. A part of Rise wished that he'd joined Ogrim in throttling Maxine.

"So, you guys must be the ones the Warwolves are after!" Maxine exclaimed and even clapped her hands.

Salter was in the middle of lifting a tooth from Ogrim's skin. The brown shard dropped from her tweezers in surprise at Maxine's clapping and rattled across the kitchen floor.

"Oh? Yes? Is that so?" Rise stared into Ogrim's distant expression. His heart hammered at Maxine's words.

"It's growing light," Cypriot blurted into the awkward pause that followed.

Rise blinked.

"It's nearly dawn," Cypriot repeated and pointed at the window. "You need to get to the roof."

"All of us?" Salter asked in panic. "Rise, I don't think we should move Ogrim. You can try and do the incantation alone. Or, at least, I'll go up to the roof with you, if Cypriot and this new person can watch over Ogrim?"

Rise got to his feet. He did not wish to consider any of those options. His knees cracked and he could feel the toll that this whole misadventure had taken on his body. It was still a week until their next feed. They never should've stretched feeding out to seven days.

Salter frowned, as if knowing already that Rise would disagree with her suggestion. And the coven should have trained Cypriot better. Rise's thoughts ran on ahead as the pain of a bruise began between his shoulders. *I must have hit the ground harder than I thought*, one part of his mind realized, while another part chided himself on making their predicament worse. They should have trained Cypriot better, made him strong enough to suffer at least two or three feedings a week.

"Rise?" Salter asked in concern.

"All right," Rise muttered as a wave of exhaustion swept through him. He stood in the kitchen, so tired that the walls could crumble from their foundations and he wouldn't mind all that much. "It's grown too close to dawn. Let's go and conduct the incantation. We can talk then, over breakfast. We need to go to the roof. All of us."

He bore the outcry from Cypriot and Salter. Rise kept his eye on the catatonic Ogrim as they all squawked about how moving him might kill him.

"No," Rise said loudly. When he looked up at them, they fell silent. "We need to take him to the roof. All three are needed for full protection. That is what I know. Brutes and Warwolves followed us back. They bang on our gates even now." He bent by the armchair, slung Ogrim's arm over his shoulder, and drew him to a standing position. Rise wanted this heavy weight against him. It felt like the only thing grounding him to this world.

"He's right," Cypriot whispered as a tear ran down his cheek. He sniffled, wiped it away and stepped forward to sling Ogrim's other arm around his shoulders. "Rise is right."

"I'm not done bandaging him up yet!" Salter rooted around in her sleeves and slapped an embroidered handkerchief to Ogrim's neck. She hastily taped it in place as Rise and Cypriot turned Ogrim towards the kitchen door. Maxine stared at them all with huge eyes. But the smile had faded from her face. She seemed sobered by their predicament and by Cypriot's tears.

"The incantation is the most important priority. In that, we have no choice." Rise nodded to Cypriot and they both shuffled Ogrim from the kitchen. "Ogrim would have it no other way."

Chapter 11

The Dramas of Orchids

Rise cursed every step on the pilgrimage to the roof. He cursed the greenery woven through the banister that made it so difficult to grasp. Salter and Maxine followed behind and helped them along. As he bore Ogrim upstairs, taking most of his weight, Rise cursed Cypriot for being so much shorter, slighter. What had once seduced him about their human now infuriated him. Since he had first watched the stars from the kitchen door before he left, Rise had felt this whole misadventure crashing down upon him. Every step strained his thighs and ripped at his knees. Rise cursed everything and everyone about them, always in his head, never aloud, as they finally reached the top floor.

"I don't understand. What's all this about?" Maxine asked as she leaned into Ogrim's back to help tilt him up the last few steps. When everybody ignored her, she dutifully followed Salter's lead and set her hands to Ogrim's shoulders to help him.

Ogrim's exhaled breath was becoming a stench. Rise cursed again. They knew so little about the brutes; about themselves. Was Ogrim now rotting from the inside?

"Are we too late?" Salter slipped past them on the final step and opened the roof door. The morning sky beyond lay pale and bright but not yet rosy. She trotted out onto the flat section between the peaks and eaves. Salter ripped off her scarves and turned her bare face eastward.

"No, I'm not sore or scalding. Not yet." She touched her ebony cheeks.

Cypriot and Rise eased Ogrim onto the ground where the trio usually stood.

"We'll have to do it sitting," Rise said as fresh air chilled him through. There was a threat of more snow on the breeze. As he shivered, he noticed Maxine's confusion. *She's been nothing but helpful since we met,* Rise had to remind himself. "It's our morning ritual. A prayer of protection to maintain the boundaries of Owl Court," he explained, as he and Salter sat on the roof in a circle with Ogrim.

"What, every day?" Maxine asked. She watched them, especially Salter, in wonder now. Looked at Salter's discarded scarves, which lay crumpled, clinging to the orange roof tiles.

"Every day," Rise replied, with a small smile at her incredulousness. He glanced to Ogrim's dazed, slumped state and began.

"So, that's why the Warwolves never got inside this place," Maxine murmured. "And you sit here every morning to watch them, uh, incant?" she asked Cypriot, her eyes huge, incredulous, as she took in the bite marks displayed on his throat.

"Of course I do," Cypriot answered softly, inclining his head to indicate they should sit out of the way, on the nearby water tank. "Out of respect to those who keep us."

As Rise's words in the Old Language sounded across the rooftops of Owl Court, Maxine swung her legs. She watched their incantation with her eyes wide, as seemed to be her habit, as if she could devour the world by knowing and noticing all things. Cypriot stared at her dangling foot, which swung back and forth as Rise chanted. Her foot the only movement on the roof. Cypriot's lips pressed together. He inhaled deeply and fluttered his eyes closed. Cypriot wound his thumbs around each other in his lap. A bone flexed in his jaw. Despite earlier foul cursing to himself on the stairs, Rise's heart went to Cypriot. Rise hadn't meant to bring back someone like Maxine.

He's trying to be patient with her, Rise realized as he chanted. *He is trying.*

The gentle lowing from their animal sheds, the shuffle of brutes milling around their walls—everything all seemed so far away. They were safe up here, so long as he spoke the incantation. He realized now the true depth of his coven mates' fears; if something had happened to him out in the wilds of the world last night, Rise might never have returned home. And all of this would have perished.

As he spoke ancient words and felt the boundary strengthen, Rise came to a resolution deep within his soul: he would tend to Ogrim, until he healed or passed. And life within these walls would go on, survive. Rise wouldn't entertain the idea of leaving Owl Court ever again, not even to collect Ogrim's scattered tarot cards. *Leave them there, let the brutes tread on them. Let the Warwolves wonder at them.*

Cypriot is trying. Then, I shall try too. Determination to make all of this work settled in him. He gritted his jaw as the old words came. Rise leaned into the final verse with such gusto and fervour that Salter opened her eyes in surprise. If Cypriot was trying for them all to get along, then Rise could certainly try, too.

*

"No, bring him back to the kitchen." Salter gestured them away from Ogrim's bedroom on the second floor as they all left the roof. "The tweezers and bandages are still down in the kitchen. And it's probably a better place for us to keep an eye on him. Keep him sitting up, too. In the warmth of the stove and ranges."

Rise hadn't the strength to argue. He merely nodded and leaned the still-dazed Ogrim to one side so that Salter could slip his other arm across her shoulders. Carefully, the five of them picked their way downstairs.

"Oh wow, there's plants ... everywhere. It's like a jungle in here, even on all the stairs," Maxine said as they trooped through the house. She stretched and cracked her shoulders, as if she had only just now risen from a full night's sleep and was headed downstairs for a hearty breakfast. Maxine still wore Rise's overcoat but shrugged out of it when they slowed to navigate one of the landings. With care, she draped the coat across the nearest railing, the banister beneath weaved through with glossy, sharp holly branches.

Cypriot didn't answer Maxine. He kept close to Rise's side as they picked their way downstairs and into the kitchen. Relieved to be in the glow of candlelight once again, Rise eased Ogrim into the kitchen armchair.

"Now, no more moving him," Salter growled as she took a moment to finally cover her Blaschko-lined face and any of her exposed dark skin with shawls once again. Since dawn light spilled into the kitchen, she even pulled on black, fingerless gloves from her pocket. Salter's long fingernails picked at the taped handkerchief on Ogrim's neck until it peeled off. The gush of dark blood resumed. She continued to clean his wound.

Rise sank into a chair at the kitchen table and watched Ogrim's still face. Then, as if slowly coming back to himself after all of his exhaustion and temper subsided, Rise realized that Cypriot and Maxine were speaking to each other. The pair moved between the stove, the kitchen counters, and the dining table as if they were an old married couple setting their breakfast. Rise rubbed his tired face as they talked. He wished for a cup of tea.

Cypriot's eyebrows went way up his forehead as he rattled out a bowl for Maxine from the tall cupboard at the far end of the kitchen. His rosebud mouth puckered. "Are you mocking me? About all of my plants?"

"Wha?" Maxine lifted the lid on the cow-shaped butter dish, its black splotches half flaked away. She loaded an ungodly dollop of butter onto a knife. "No, I'm not. Jus' sayin', there's a lotta plants here."

"Yes, there are," Cypriot sniffed. He warmed her bowl with hot kettle water, then doled out ladles of porridge from the great pot on the stove. "It's because everything from the outside is so rotten," he said pointedly, mentally including her, as he placed a bowl on the table. Cypriot eyed the amount of butter she was about to add and turned away to tend to his own food.

"Yeah, stinks out there." Maxine slid into a chair and added sugar to her porridge, along with the butter. "I don't suppose you've got any cinnamon here? What about peanut butter?"

Rise hid a smile in his hand at how Maxine had completely missed Cypriot's snide comment. Cypriot flashed his dark eyes at Rise over Maxine's head as he brought his own porridge to the table. Maxine was probably the first person ever to call out Cypriot on his excessive gardening. Rise waited to see how they'd handle each other.

"Oh no, I'm sorry. No peanut butter." Cypriot managed to make porridge-eating appear haughty as he slid a spoon into his breakfast and brought it to his lips in a hungry, practiced motion. "Supplies are a little limited, of late."

"Aww man, plain oats, how boring!" Maxine complained into her bowl of sugar and butter.

"Tell her about your bees," Rise murmured, sleepy now and yet too amused by this unexpected conversation to excuse himself. The wound at his shoulder was nothing more than a soft throb.

"I've managed to overwinter bees." Cypriot reached into the table's centerpiece of pinecones and salt and pepper shakers. He slammed a honey jar next to Maxine's place setting and glared at the jar's dipper as if he would like to stick it somewhere else entirely.

Maxine fell silent as she ate a few more bites, did not move to touch the honey, then abruptly pushed away her bowl. "Oh wow, all this stodge is making me have to crap! I haven't eaten anything like this in months. Where's your bathroom?"

"The nearest wash closet is in the hall, two doors down," Rise answered and hid another smile at Cypriot's stunned expression. Maxine excused herself. No sooner had her shadow passed into the hall than Cypriot rounded on him.

"What the actual fuck, Rise?"

"Shh!" Salter scolded him, but soon turned back to her grim task.

Rise waited a few moments more to make sure that Maxine was truly out of earshot. "Don't have this be a repeat of Elaine and her mother. Not yet," Rise warned him, so plainly that Cypriot looked taken aback. "I realise how ... abrasive she is," Rise continued, feeling like he, too, had ripped off a bandage. "But Maxine has lived amongst the Warwolves, who've taken Dunsinann. Our time with her is limited—know that, Cypriot. We question her for now, get all the information we can. But even I know that she needs to go. At some point. Not right now, or even for a few weeks. So, just shut up and get along with her. And ... can you make me a cup of tea? Please, Cypriot. I'm ... I feel tired."

Cypriot clattered his spoon into his porridge and sat in a sulk. He eyed Maxine's bowl, then looked as if he were about to say something. But then he rose from his breakfast to oblige. He stoked the fire in their range, until the hob reddened and the kettle sang again. Cypriot remained quiet, but Rise watched the set of his shoulders, saw the sulk that brewed within him at having to put up with someone like Maxine. As he measured out tea leaves, Cypriot finally whined, "You've only rescued women so far. You realize that, Rise? Right? Can't you bring back a man for once?"

"Of course, you'd find something to complain about," Rise muttered and turned his attention back to Ogrim. At Salter dabbing the drool on his lips. She rolled her eyes at Cypriot's fussing, and Rise felt like doing the same.

"Sure thing," Rise answered Cypriot, trying not to snap at him. "I'll ask for three oiled-up party boys on my next—"

"You're never going outside again," Salter interrupted. Her hands paused over Ogrim's neck, her long fingers coated in black blood.

"Correct," Rise agreed and sank back in the dining chair. "Too bad we couldn't have kept to just Marnie and Elaine—"

"Who're they?"

Rise jumped when Maxine rejoined them. Annoyed that she'd heard those names. He took a breath as Maxine slid into her seat again and Cypriot set a cup of tea before him. One of their rare oat cakes, studded with real dark chocolate, was tucked alongside the handle and saucer. Cypriot ignored Maxine and resumed his breakfast, as if they hadn't spoken about anything of any importance.

"Maxine?" Rise quizzed as gently as he could after a few sips of tea. "In Dunsinann, had you ever met a young woman called Elaine? A teenager, short with bleach-blonde hair. Might have had an older, like an elderly woman, with her?"

Maxine dug into her porridge and shook her head.

"Did ..." he tried again and toyed with the little oatcake. It melted against his fingertips. Sometimes chocolate soothed even him. "Did the Warwolves ever say anything about someone called Elaine, or her mother, Marnie? Or, did they ever mention anything about this house on top of the hill? Anything about holly trees or the people living here?"

"This house and its small estate is called Owl Court," Salter added as she finished with Ogrim's wound. Ogrim otherwise sat in the chair, still and glassy-eyed, like one of the stuffed foxes above the piano in the drawing room. His neck was properly bandaged now, the plaster and medical tape so thick that they tilted his head slightly askew.

"What're you talking about?" Maxine half-laughed around a mouthful of sweet, buttery porridge. "Those Warwolves know exactly where you are. What's the name of this place and everything."

Rise nearly fell out of his chair. "They do?"

"Of course they do, they're not stupid. First thing they did when they claimed that village, Dun—, whatever you call it, was to spread out a huge ordnance survey map of the town. I was there when they came outta nowhere.

They came in an' cleared out every room in that little village an' herded everybody into the church hall. Took only a few hours for them to work it out, where y'all were. And man, those Warwolves are some mean bastards, let me tell you. I thought my papa was a hardass. Got nothin' on a Warwolf." Maxine shivered over a spoonful of porridge.

"But they knew about y'all living round here," she chatted on, light and airy, as if she were speaking about the weather. "They weren't sure exactly where y'all lived and how many, until they'd taken hold of Dunsinann. But they know. An' I bet they know you're vampires, too."

Rise blinked through his panic. He sat forward, pulse loud in his ears. "Then, why haven't they attacked us?"

"I dunno." Maxine shrugged. "They're a strange lot. There's only two leaders, but a few of the guys I fucked soon fell under their sway an' formed a gang with them. They're *convincing* types, as my papa would say, those Warwolves. Let me tell you that."

Cypriot's eyes were huge. Rise dropped his hand beneath the table to put his shaking palm on Cypriot's knee. A silence held the kitchen, broken only by the sound of Maxine eating.

Rise's thoughts raced. Would they be better to abandon Owl Court entirely? He took in Salter's exhaustion as she dried her hands and gazed emptily out the kitchen window onto the winter-held dawn beyond. Cypriot stared into his empty porridge bowl with a similar, blank expression. A stillness enveloped Rise, as if the shock at everything that had happened since he left this sacred kitchen finally caught up with him. Had that adventure with Ogrim only happened barely a few hours ago? Would they all be better to leave Owl Court? To move somewhere else? Do it suddenly, unnoticed, without fuss, now that the Warwolves apparently knew exactly where they lived? But where could the coven go, with the world as it was?

Beneath the table, Rise absently drifted his thumb across Cypriot's knee as they all became lost in their thoughts.

Maxine did not seem to notice the lull. She kept eating. Below the table, her legs swung back and forth.

Chapter 12

Food Want

"So, the myths aren't true," Maxine piped up. "You're not destroyed by sunlight and all that? Because the sun's up now and ya'll can sit in the kitchen, no trouble."

Rise smiled painfully as he returned from his reverie, aware now that she might be some sort of Warwolf spy. She might be testing their weaknesses and how best to kill them. Elaine, Marnie, they'd all sat around this dining table once. Memories of that evening stuck in Rise's mind. What had he gained since then? Maybe Elaine had been right to run that night? To beg Cypriot to let her go and face her fate in the world beyond their walls.

"We're not destroyed by sunlight. But we are not nourished by it, either," Rise told Maxine plainly. He recalled the sting when his skin was exposed to even dull sunshine, enough to raise his Blaschko lines, the smarting and tingling he bore every morning. How Salter suffered from even the slightest sun exposure with her darker, more sensitive skin. The kitchen was a north-facing room, as opposed to the bright, east-facing drawing room. With heavy lace netting, slightly yellowed, dressing each kitchen window, all framed with Cypriot's plants, Salter could sit in moonlit comfort during the day without wearing a scarf, so long as she sat in the dimmest spot in the kitchen, behind the back door. But as the hours ticked towards noon, especially on a summer's day, she soon would retire to the root cellar.

Not nourished, indeed. Rise shifted in his chair. The bruise between his shoulders ached, far sorer than he let on. Supporting Ogrim to the roof and down again had only worsened it. As he wondered how to keep it hidden, Rise noticed bruise marks on Maxine's neck. Made by Ogrim's hand. Rise had no idea what to say about Ogrim's attack on her, before the Warwolf and brutes appeared. For now, Rise reasoned, if Maxine wasn't going to mention anything about it, Rise was fine with not saying anything, either. Let Maxine settle into life here. He watched her swallow, and Ogrim's dark thumbprints shifted across the skin of her throat. *Let her blab and yammer on and tell us all she knows. Let Maxine see just how kind and kin the coven are.* She could be safe here, could be well looked after. Maxine might even thrive and, possibly, even heal herself after what seemed like the horror of living in Dunsinann under the Warwolves' thumb.

Rise remembered his promise to Cypriot just now, that he only had to tolerate her until they could kill her. But Rise didn't want any more killing. He wanted no more violence or death within his home.

"Well, you seem to be taking all of this in your stride, especially knowing what these three really are." Cypriot gestured to Rise, Ogrim, and Salter as he spoke to Maxine. His eyes narrowed.

She shrugged. "After the zombie brutes, after Warwolves, I could expect Bigfoot himself to live in your basement." And in the same breath, she noticed a dish set on the table's edge, piled with crusts. "You have bread? What's it made of?"

"Pea flour," Cypriot answered, unimpressed with her topic u-turns.

"Wow! You guys grow your own peas?"

"Yes."

"And, like, dry and grind them into flour."

Cypriot hesitated at her questions. "Yes."

As for having another human settled in their midst, well, that had been the whole point of Rise leaving these walls. He kept thinking with every sip of tea and nibble of oatcake. Even though Rise had just told Cypriot that they meant to do away with her, if—and only if—Maxine fell into line and stayed, she could well be a worthy addition to Owl Court. Blood was blood, after all. An extra pair of hands to muck in with the farmwork. If they had Maxine, Rise would never have to leave these walls again. *Everyone could settle into their regular old lives as before,* Rise told himself before adding to his earlier explanation. "The sun hurts us more when our Blaschko lines are raised. So, we try not to do that. Otherwise, a few brief moments in the sun won't do any harm. It is like plunging into ice water. No human should do it for long. Sunlight will kill any of us, even you, Maxine, after too much exposure. This we've learned. We're just more sensitive to light than you. Salter most of all."

"Because she's black?" Maxine spoke bluntly.

Silence gripped the kitchen again. Rise, stunned, felt all his earlier thoughts and plans slip away. Again, as if sand had shifted beneath his feet.

"No. I don't think it's to do with that ..." he began, although in truth the coven had no idea.

Maxine gave Salter a crooked look. "She's good at tending to people. Do you know first aid, Salter? Were you a nurse or something before all of this happened?"

Salter chuckled in a manner that raised the hairs on Rise's neck.

"Between farming and gardening, the three boys are forever injuring themselves. Slicing themselves open. I've learned how to stem their blood," she answered as she bent to check Ogrim's blank gaze, the curve of her tall spine towards Maxine. Salter then glared at Rise as she dragged her armchair from behind the back door to settle it beside Ogrim's. The chair legs scraped across the old kitchen tile and set his teeth on edge. Rise wondered what it cost Salter, even though she wore her shawls, to sit in the morning light. A dawn now sharp and bright through their netted windows. Ogrim did not stir. He only breathed. All Rise wanted was another cup of tea. How many oatcakes were left? Enough that he could have another?

"Stem blood? How?" Maxine pressed. "You mean stem naturally, like with a bandage? But I'd say yall's spit got some powerful juice, like, to keep blood flowing when ya'll feed? I'm guessin' that's how it works? You know, ya'll are like aliens. Not suited to this world at all."

Rise ignored her giggle. He knew Maxine was just talking aloud. Babbling. Like a junkie coming down off a high. What poisons and potions had the Warwolves filled her with to keep her in line? But still, Maxine's words stung.

"Thank you." Rise gave her a smile that he hadn't used since Elaine and her mother: his human smile. Impassive, mask-like. He'd long mastered how to soften his gaze, crinkle the corners of his eyes so they matched his smile. A smile like that could be the architecture that built bridges, helped recipients move onto their next thought. A guardrail through conversations.

"You're pretty dark–skinned too," Maxine chattered at Cypriot as she dribbled honey into her empty bowl and scooped it onto her fingertips, which she sucked with gusto. "Where're you from?"

"What on earth are you talking about?" Cypriot gave her a withering look.

"You're obviously foreign. And ya don't sound English, or American. Can't place your accent. Tryin' to work out where you're from."

"What are you saying?" Cypriot challenged Maxine. "Everything's fallen apart and you're worried about where I'm from?"

"I'm just curious!"

"Well, my mother was Scottish. Father Singaporean. That satisfy you?"

"That's quite the mix! Sheesh, I'm just askin', y'know?"

Rise let them talk, for now. All over again, he realized the danger of housing what Ogrim had called 'strays'. That doing so might accidentally put Cypriot in real danger.

Maxine soon stopped pestering Cypriot, though, and again changed topics. Rise was so busy thinking that he missed half of their conversation.

"What?" Cypriot's nose crinkled in horror. He rocked back in the dining chair. "You're asking if Rise and his ilk can shapeshift into bats?"

Although numbed by this whole predicament, Rise smiled at Maxine's innocence. "No, we do not. Some ... others might. I do not know. But not us."

"And you blood drinkers sleep in coffins?" Maxine pressed and again did not pick up on how the others were shocked by her blatant questioning.

Rise hesitated to respond to the stereotypes. "Although we do have what you'd call 'normal beds', we ... prefer the earth. Think of it like a seed hibernating over winter. We are most cosy in the ground, snugged in like worms, breathing the deep core of the earth. It's good for the soul, for our souls." Rise actually chuckled. "But most nights we're in a soft bed."

She took her time with his answer and looked around at every wall in the kitchen. Rise expected Maxine to ask about their beds and maybe to see one, and maybe even where she would sleep tonight. He wanted to suggest that they all decamp to separate rooms and take a nap.

"You have souls?" she asked.

"Don't you?" Cypriot immediately spiked right back at her, as if she could not possibly have one. He kept his face haughty, impassive, until she finally broke into her usual Cheshire-cat smile.

"How long have ya'll been living here?" Maxine laughed, apparently unfazed by, well, anything.

"Long enough," Salter muttered as she held up Ogrim's fingertips to the lamp and examined his nails.

"Oh, too long, some would say." Rise smiled painfully, and interrupted Maxine as she was asking how they'd come to own Owl Court. "Cypriot? How about some more tea, please?"

Still, Maxine chatted on, heedless. A full belly seemingly gave her all the energy in the world to pester and ask questions. "Do you need humans to drink blood from, then? Or can ya'll drink from, like, animals? Can y'all not drink from each other?"

"We only drink from Cypriot." Rise realized he must have sounded weary indeed, because Cypriot glanced at him in concern when he stood to boil more water.

"Right, right," Maxine said, not noticing much of anything. "So in order for, say, for you, Rise, to drink from Salter there, that would be tantamount to cannibalism for your kind, is that right? The blood's not the same between two vampires, or something? It's not the same, that's what the Warwolves said."

Rise gazed blankly at Ogrim. He felt that he should feel more panicked. More worried. But his leaden limbs and body only slumped in the chair like Ogrim's, so tired. When a fresh cup of tea appeared before him, Rise didn't have the strength to drink it. He hadn't even made formal introductions among them all, nor explained why he'd left Owl Court last night. Well, all in the room knew well that it was to find survivors. But, still.

"No," Rise answered her, eyelids heavy with the pressing threat of sleep. "It is not the same. Thank you, Cypriot."

"And, so, where do you guys come from? Where does a vampire come from? Are you born human and then turn? What happens if two vampires have sex?" Her legs swung even more now beneath the table.

Rise felt shock radiate from Cypriot as he moved around the kitchen and, one by one, set a cup of tea in front of each person. Rise stirred a half spoon of sugar into his cup and never took his eyes off Maxine. She didn't even seem to care that most of her questions were left unanswered. That anyone in the room who was *compos mentis* only stared at her, aghast.

"What happens if your food, Cypriot there, happens to have sex with Salter? And they have a baby? What happens then? Is that a vampire?"

Rise let the silence hang for the longest time. He stared at her as he waited for Maxine to realize her insolence. But nothing. Nothing dropped for her. She only kept glancing from Cypriot to him, over to Salter, eyebrows raised as if everybody should just break and answer her. In the end, Maxine twittered a laugh.

"Oh my god, you guys, you don't have to be so secretive. Talk about zero times! I just want to know how it all works. Ya'll said I could stay, so I'm just tryin'a find out what it's all like here. Just askin' questions to pass the time!"

"I'm sure you'll soon find some other way to entertain yourself ..." Salter murmured.

"Yeah, y'know, like a deck of cards." Maxine went on as if she had only half-heard Salter. "And there's no TV anymore, but the Warwolves would pass time by telling stories, real grim ones. So scary you'd want to throw yourself at a brute!" Maxine cackled her crazy laugh, then remembered Ogrim. "Oh, sorry." She giggled and hid her mouth behind her hand.

Cypriot left the table and lifted his gardening tray from the windowsill. He perched elegantly on the armrest of Salter's chair. After setting his tray across his lap with great care, Cypriot began the slow, deliberate process of dabbing oil from the amber bottle onto a square of cotton. Then he ran the cloth along the delicate hinges of his pruning tools. As Maxine continued to giggle, Cypriot gave Rise a meaningful look over his tray of blades.

"I'll stay down here with Ogrim for the rest of the day," Rise spoke up, his voice thick with sleep. "I don't like the idea of moving him, not to his bed, not to the sofa in the drawing room. I say we leave him in his chair. We've already moved him enough, I think." He looked to Salter for agreement.

She half-shrugged and set Ogrim's hand back into his lap after examining his nails. Salter sank into her armchair and let Cypriot lean against her shoulder. "I suppose that's the best course of action. But we'll all stay with you, Rise. In case something happens." Salter not only nodded pointedly at Ogrim, but in Maxine's direction, too. "And you look exhausted. Hey, don't wave me away like that."

But Rise felt firm in his decision. "Go about your day as normal, Salter. And you two, Cypriot, Maxine?

You two get some proper rest. There's animals and farming to tend to once you both have slept."

"You think I could sleep at a time like this?" Cypriot lifted his eyebrows. The clippers in his hands gestured unseen at Maxine's back.

"I recommend you all sleep." Salter interrupted Cypriot's silliness with a stern nudge of her shoulder. "All three of you. I'll watch over Ogrim. I want to write the chronicle, anyway." Then Salter spoke gently, as if Rise were a fussy child. "You've had a terrible adventure out there in the world, Rise. You need to rest."

Rise had to smile at Salter's choice of words. "Yes, a terrible adventure." He tried to not look at Maxine, glad Salter was not already pestering him for the chronicle details of his 'adventure'. "And I'm tired, yes. But I want to take the first watch over Ogrim. In case anything happens. Especially since it's still early. You three can rest and then get some chores done. I know there's parsnips and leeks to harvest. And I want to cloche some of the ground by the back of Daisy's barn for the early pea crop. Please, you three, go to bed for a while. Cypriot, show Maxine to a bedroom upstairs."

"Oh, you mean Elaine and Marnie's room?" he asked in an innocent tone as he worked on his tools. But his dark eyebrows lifted in challenge.

Rise nearly flinched at him speaking those names aloud, but hid his reaction. "Yes, that one, Cypriot. Thank you."

"Who're they again?" Maxine piped up. "You mentioned Elaine and Marnie earlier."

"We're not leaving you, Rise," Cypriot spoke over her. "We're staying here with you today. Ogrim is coven and we don't know what's happening with him. I'd not leave his side for all the world. Nor yours."

Rise noticed Salter's smile of pride at Cypriot's words. He sighed and fought sleep as he sipped his second cup of tea. "All right." He gave in to Cypriot's determination. "Keep watch with me."

Chapter 13

The Oldest Hunters

The worst part about nothing happening is that time still spirals onwards anyway. Before he knew it, it was Rise's third day keeping watch over Ogrim. Nothing changed about the old vampire. He sat in the kitchen's armchair, still, but breathing. Awake but nothing firing between his ears. The coven remained loath to move him and only grudgingly did so just before each dawn for the incantation. Yet, despite being brought up and down through the floors of Owl Court, despite brief exposure to the morning sunlight, Ogrim remained blank.

"Come on, old man," Rise whispered on the third night as he knelt on the kitchen floor before Ogrim's armchair. The seat began to look like part of the old vampire. Rise watched every wrinkle, knew by heart now each of Ogrim's crazy-long nose hairs, every tuft that sprouted from his ears. Rise set his hands to those withered knees. "Come on, come back. Don't leave me all alone."

A sudden impulsiveness struck Rise and made him forget all of his earlier promises to stay inside. The next time he left, he decided, it would be the last. He would bring back so many people, not just one or two, so that something like this would never, ever happen again. Rise would reclaim it all. Every nook and cranny of his home, Rise would marshal it all. Reclaim his bike. Ogrim's tarot cards. All and anything of theirs left out in the world.

With an aching head and pounding pulse, he wandered from the kitchen to the drawing room and consulted the old almanac that was tucked under the legs of a little side table.

"Why're you reading that?" Cypriot asked. He was curled up in Ogrim's old seat by the hearth, albeit uncomfortably, like when a grandparent dies and one is forced to sit and not quite fit into their favourite chair.

Rise didn't look up from the almanac. "I need to see when's the next full moon."

"Oh?" Cypriot blinked slowly and rubbed his eyes with the blanket that swaddled him. He kept his gaze dipped, as if he knew well what Rise now planned.

"Yes." Rise set his shoulder against the mantelpiece and tilted the almanac towards the almost-quenched fire. The text read so tiny, even to his eyes.

"Why d'ya need to know about moons?"

Rise ignored Cypriot's question. "You'll need to get the house ready," he told him.

"Ready for what? Solstice? For Yule?" Cypriot rubbed his face with his blanket again. He looked at the half-door set into the drawing room's wall, where they stored several boxes of decorations for their midwinter celebrations. "I suppose I could start decorating. It wouldn't be too early," he murmured, fingers toying with the hem of his blanket. "I didn't think you'd want to celebrate anything this year."

"Oh?" Rise challenged. "Why's that?"

"Well." Cypriot looked uncomfortable. "Not with all that's happened this year. What's there to celebrate?"

"You've no sympathy for Maxine, that she may want a little celebration? Even though she is one of your own?"

All expression drained from Cypriot's face. "She is nothing like me."

Rise snapped the almanac shut and pointed it at Cypriot. "That's precisely why we must decorate, must celebrate." Rise tossed the almanac aside and headed for the kitchen.

Cypriot didn't follow, or even move. "Decorating? For our latest guest, or for more new ones?" he joked in a sad voice.

When Rise paused in the hall and looked back at him, Cypriot's head had turned and he stared out of the heavily netted windows, his dark eyes watching the bleak world beyond. He wore the same expression as he did when he would stand in the full light of day, a sign he did not wish for a vampire's touch.

"There's a full moon soon enough," Rise told him, softly enough that he would not wake the house—oh, only that it woke Ogrim!—but Cypriot's hearing was particularly sharp. "Then the turn of the new year into spring. A fresh start. A new time. So, yes, with what's happening with Ogrim. You need to prepare for many, many more guests at Owl Court."

"Can I go with you?" Cypriot asked sadly. He brought his attention back inside and picked at lint on his soft, peat-colored trousers. "When you leave us again?"

Rise's face twitched. He clutched at the drawing room's door frame. "Absolutely not," he growled at him.

*

After a simple breakfast of griddle cakes and eggs on the fourth day, Rise remained at the kitchen table while Cypriot cleared it of plates and cutlery. Maxine still seemed none the wiser that nobody was interested in answering her constant questions. Rise laid his cheek on the kitchen table and wrapped his arms around his head, keeping watch over Ogrim's blank face. Overnight, in desperation, in hope, Rise's spirits had swung completely the other way. Now, he suddenly didn't want to leave Owl Court ever again.

"What god or what religion do you guys have?" Maxine asked as she sat by the sink on a tall bar stool, shelling a large bowl of peas.

Salter muttered something foul, only for Rise to hear, as she changed Ogrim's bandage with great care. The wound on Ogrim's neck hadn't stopped, but neither had it worsened.

"Oh, all of them, I suppose," Rise joked in answer and was about to change the subject when Maxine piped up again.

"Hey, can't you guys drink their blood?"

Rise frowned as Cypriot moved between their seats, rattling knives and forks. "Whose blood?"

"Those outside," she answered. "The undead."

"No, I—" he said, confused. "I shouldn't think it works that way. The blood we drink would need to be fresh, from something alive. We don't drink from the ordinary dead, anyway. I don't see how those creatures out there would be any different. And they're pretty much all dried-out, barely a drop of blood left in those brutes. You saw them that night." Rise realized that he'd come close to mentioning when Ogrim had tried to throttle Maxine. He fell silent.

"And ..." Maxine wondered, her eyes growing huge and round in that fashion that irked Rise. "What about stuff from the movies, like Dracula or Nosferatu? All that stuff? Crosses an' garlic an' coffins?"

"I've never seen someone shell more peas onto the floor," Cypriot breathed in Rise's ear as he wiped down the table. His apron was tightly wound around his waist today. Rise watched Cypriot's to-ing and fro-ing with growing hunger. Despite all of this, there went his heart.

"Necuratul nosophoros," Rise clarified to Maxine with a polite, rigid bow in his seat. "Nesuferit, the demonic, the unbearable carrier, plague. What us 'blood drinkers' have been called."

"So, you're actually the undead?" Maxine asked in a tone that suggested she might as well have asked the peas she shelled why they were green. "So, you guys are like brutes, too? Did ya bring about the zombie plague, then?"

Salter chuckled with a shake of her shawl-covered head as she dealt with Ogrim's bandages, the linen oily and heavy as she lifted them from Ogrim's throat. "We're alive, just as you are."

Maxine looked in disbelief at Salter and tilted her head to indicate Ogrim's predicament, which apparently told otherwise. Maxine wasn't silent for long. "Then, what happens if you drink each other's blood? If a blood drinker drinks from another blood drinker?" Maxine pressed.

"Well," Rise answered. Although he'd initially been irritated by Maxine, part of him strangely had started to enjoy this inane chatter. He realized that he could say any random thing to Maxine and all he would get in return was another curious question. Not judgment, suspicion, or criticism. No answers or consequences seemed to rattle about much in her head. In spite of everything, and maybe because of Ogrim's stillness and the mystery surrounding his illness, Rise found such brainless randomness from her to be quite refreshing. "Well, let me put it to you this way: what happens when humans drink human blood?"

"I have no idea." Maxine shrugged and placed her empty peapods into an enormous copper saucepan that Cypriot had scalded with boiling water. Although pungent, properly fermented peapod wine held a certain virtue. "Cannibalism? Bad things? These are the zero times, after all."

"Bad things," Salter repeated with another light laugh and shook her head.

Maxine watched Salter carefully. "And ... where d'ya get your electricity?"

"We have a stove that heats water, some solar panels; otherwise there's not much need for electricity. We've found, since all of this happened, that we never really needed electricity anyway. We were not exactly the biggest TV watchers. We've been successful in overwintering bees for beeswax, candles," Rise explained. Cypriot's tanned arms gently flexed as he weighed out sugar with their impressive copper scoop. It looked like a relic from some Victorian kitchen.

Sugar. Now, there was another item they'd soon have to ration. A flash of anger shot through him. "Hey, can we replace our sugar with something we can grow? A plant of any kind?" he asked.

Cypriot paused in weighing the sugar. As he considered Rise's question, he eyed the small library of gardening books lined between flower pots on the nearest dresser.

"I think there's a plant. Sugar beet? Beets? I've heard of it before, but I'm not sure either how to grow or even how to process sugar beet after it's harvested. Give me time. I'll look into it."

Rise nodded and had faith that Cypriot, with his extensive gardening knowledge, would find a suitable substitute. Although, where might they get seeds or sproutings for a new crop now? Rise took in the kitchen: Cypriot and Maxine with their winemaking, as Salter tidied Ogrim and changed his shirt and woolen sweater. Rise could almost see the wheels spinning in Maxine's head as she bumbled on to the next topic.

"So," she said, after Cypriot shooed her away from the copper pot when it came to a boil. Maxine slithered from the bar stool and leaned her hip against the kitchen table. "What do you guys do for fun?"

"Fun?" Cypriot lifted his eyebrows, obviously upset that Maxine did not find this to be the height of fun. He handed her the big colander to rinse.

Rise smiled through it all, lightened that there was no one to pick an argument with him, to frustrate his goals, as Ogrim had. Rise could tell Maxine anything and she would only screw up her redneck face and flitter off to chatter about something else.

"Rise?" Salter began.

"Hmm?" he murmured as he continued to enjoy the domestic scene before him. Enjoyed the cute little wrinkle of frustration between Cypriot's eyebrows as he fussed with Maxine, tried to keep her from hurting herself in the kitchen.

"Rise!" Salter barked so loud that everybody spun around.

Whatever shadow had fallen over Ogrim, it had lifted. The old vampire blinked. His face took on a new flush of life. Red in his cheeks. Brightness in his eyes.

Rise stared in shock. Then he frowned. The person looking back at him—this wasn't the Ogrim he knew, the Ogrim of old. This was someone else, entirely new.

"How long have I been out?" Ogrim's voice sounded now without his accent and, indeed, without the marks of age. But his eyes held a depth that echoed the ancient age of Rise's dawn incantations.

In the stunned silence, Rise carefully rose from his seat. As he stepped towards the armchair and this new being, he absently touched his hip. The pistol usually housed there, Rise remembered now. He'd left it in its holster on Cypriot's nightstand last night, during their briefest of breaks, before returning to the kitchen to keep watch over Ogrim. Rise's holster had been forgotten amid a sea of ivy tendrils and drying roses.

"Is that you?" Rise asked. The kitchen held plenty of knives and other pointy things if this creature was not their Ogrim. "Is that really you, old man?"

"Stop trying to find ways to kill me, lad. It doesn't become you," Ogrim snarled and then broke into a wheezing laugh on his next breath. He pounded the armrest in his usual fashion. "I seem to be awake, and it seems to be me, right?" Ogrim patted his pockets as if he'd just woken from an accidental nap. "Now, where are my tarot cards? Cypriot, make me tea."

"Don't anybody move," Rise warned. "Salter? What do you think?"

"Let the lass get back to her books and writing," Ogrim said, waving. "I wager she's not touched the ink since you and I left that night."

"So. You remember. You knew what was going on around you? You've been awake this whole time?" Rise pressed. His temperature skyrocketed. Sweat dripped from his forehead. He didn't know what to think. Of everybody in this room, Rise knew that if he moved to attack this new Ogrim, it would be Cypriot who would back him up. Salter might, too. Who knew what Maxine would do? But when Ogrim looked at him with clear eyes and a present soul, however, Rise felt only relief.

"I've not been awake. But I have not left, either," Ogrim told them.

"But, you were bitten by one of the brutes," Cypriot whispered and peeked out from where he had been hiding behind Rise.

"Oh, aye, lad. I was bitten." Without the usual creaking or cracking of his old bones, Ogrim lifted his arm and touched the fresh bandage on his neck. "But I have some unfinished business."

"Don't—" Salter gasped as Ogrim began to pick it off.

He shushed her. It was everybody's turn to gasp as Ogrim peeled off the bandage to reveal perfectly healed flesh.

"I was bitten." He spoke quietly and watched the eyes of every single one of them. "A strange dream. Like being caught in a river. Never allowed to go downstream."

A silence prevailed in the kitchen. Somewhere outside, they heard the gentle movement of their animals in their pens. Their tom cat yowled from the barn.

"How long has it been?" Ogrim asked.

"Three days have passed. This is the morning of the fourth day," Rise told him.

"Actually," Salter stood to her full height and remained still for a moment, as if listening. "Actually, it's just gone noon," she said. "With everything that's happened, I forgot to wind the clock in the hall. But I can feel it. It's just gone noon."

"You're forgetting yourself, clock keeper," Ogrim teased her, as if nothing had happened to him. He shifted in his chair. "Well, my hole certainly feels like I've been sitting here for four days. Not quite 'dead and rising on the third day,' but I can take fourth. I can take that. Even my knee has healed. How about that?"

"What's this unfinished business, Ogrim?" Cypriot whispered, still hiding.

Rise didn't know what to think. He dropped to his knees by Ogrim's chair and barked a laugh of surprise, of relief. Looking at this new Ogrim, Rise realized that if this was what a bitten vampire looked like, pierced with the teeth of the brain-dead, then that was not too awful a fate, was it? When he gripped Ogrim's knees this time, Rise could feel life in the strong tendons beneath his palms.

"It's as if," Salter murmured as she pressed a dark hand to Ogrim's forehead. He smiled up at her in a fatherly fashion, and she broke into a smile too. "It's as if the zombie blood in a blood drinker's veins needed to work its way out, like a poison." Salter dabbed her sudden tears.

"We thought you were a goner." Rise couldn't help it, his throat thickened with emotion, too. Rise absently set his hand beneath his own shirt and rubbed his stomach. Giddy with delight, he needed to feel his own breath rise and fall. "Where did you go, Ogrim? What was it like?"

Ogrim did not answer for a long time. He watched Cypriot, who eventually stepped out from behind Rise and took Ogrim's hand to squeeze. Ogrim smiled indulgently at him too, as if in relief that their human still lived.

Then Ogrim saw Maxine.

"It was like a river I couldn't cross. Nor that I could be swept away by." As Ogrim spoke, a sadness passed over him, but still he watched her. "So, because of some unfinished business, I came back, after a time."

"But what was it like?" Rise pressed him. He gazed into Ogrim's old face for any sign or clue. "How are you now?"

Ogrim finally smiled. "I am fine," he answered.

*

The crowbar, cold in his hands. Rise stood on the middle of Dunsinann's bridge again. Zombie brutes sloshed in the frantic waters below. Rise was stripped of his overcoat and wore only old jeans and a vest, his face and arms bared to the odd, yellow sky. Blaschko lines rose across his whole body, prickling and sore. Again, Elaine's mother stood on the far side of the bridge. Gaunt and straight, as if the whole scene last time had never happened. The bridge had never crumbled. Dunsinann hung like a painted backdrop to a play. The moment Rise saw Marnie, he lifted his crowbar.

"You choose death each time you stand before me." She smiled, her words clear despite the rushing wind and gushing river beneath. Then Marnie spat and several browned teeth rattled onto the cobblestones.

"I'm trying to do what's best." Rise needed to explain. He stared in disgust at her teeth. The memory of Ogrim's dark and seeping wound flashed before his eyes. Like oil seeping out of the engine of their family.

"Then gather," Marnie said, in a simple tone with a smug smile.

"Gather? Gather what?"

"More. You are in dire need of so many, many more."

"You're saying that I need to gather more people?" Rise asked, his words almost lost amid the strong wind and splashing brutes. When Marnie nodded he added, "Why? It makes sense, I suppose. But why?"

"So you won't be alone anymore."

Rise thought of his coven, of three plus one. Of his heart. "But I'm not alone."

"Try to cross this bridge, then. You will fail."

"Fail? Why? Because I am alone? I am alone right now, but Salter, Ogrim, Cypriot, they are with me, always. Summon them to my side next time."

"Those three are not with you right now. Not even the others are."

"What others?" Rise heard footsteps behind him. He turned and hundreds of shadows took form from the wind. The host began to cross the bridge. Slower now, so that Rise could make out their shapes. Some shadows bumped his shoulders as they ambled by; others wandered around him, like bumblebees. He realized then who they were. The lives, souls, echoes of everybody that he'd ever fed upon.

"All those whose life you have snuffed out since your first drink," Marnie confirmed as the shadows crossed the bridge between the rearing horses on each pillar, passing by her without a single bump.

"I was young," Rise tried to explain. "I didn't know when to stop. There was never any instruction for me. Never any guidance. Of course I've killed. Out of ignorance, out of hunger. Now that we have Cypriot, I kill only out of dire, dire need." The last of the shadows swept past and bumped him sadly.

Rise went on. "I know I'm guilty of terrible things. Things I long ago forgot, deliberately. Why must you visit me like this?"

"I was never anyone to you," Marnie said. "Just like these quenched souls that you took from the world."

"That's why I cannot cross? That's why I am alone? I'm not the only killer, the only blood drinker. There are many. I have coven."

"Three is not many. Gather so you are not alone," Marnie answered.

Rise didn't understand. "I've never found others, outside of Salter and Ogrim. And Cypriot. Anyone we've ever let drink our own blood, they've never turned into one of us."

"Then. I suppose. You really are alone."

Sudden hoofbeats behind him on the bridge. The dread tremor of the Warwolves' weight as their iron horseshoes clanged on the cobbles. Rise didn't need to look to know that their scythes were lifted against the warped sky. Rise instinctively wrapped his arms around his stomach. "But I have—" he cried.

The Warwolves thundered down upon him. His crowbar was a feeble, useless thing now. The tool of an ape. A scythe went through his throat this time, and Rise's words stilled.

Chapter 14

Unfinished Business

Rise startled awake and clutched his throat. It took a long time to trust the breath that filled his lungs, to trust that his throat was still attached to his body. That he could breathe normally, safe. He found himself on the sofa in the drawing room. Fading daylight glowed through the holly trees, as the sun put itself to bed.

That's right, Rise thought, nodding. He'd fallen asleep on the couch after such a long vigil over Ogrim. *What an awkward bed*, Rise thought as he sat in the looming dark. Blood hunger rushed upon him. Shakes rattled his body. The weekly feed was tonight. He wanted to find Cypriot, to begin that slow, silent process of pouring care and flattery upon him, so that Cypriot's blood would easily pulse through them all.

As he sat and tried to marshal his racing mind, Rise thought back over his dream. Had it been a terrible mistake to dispose of Marnie to the pigs? Her body had been consumed by them—mostly, for pigs couldn't manage every bone. But, even the femurs that remained were soon trampled deep into the mud. That also meant, however, that Marnie became part of Owl Court. Rise feared that Marnie and these dreams would haunt him forever, as long as they all remained here. Even lonelier, Rise could never tell the others about such dreams. They'd only fuss and not understand. He hoped that Ogrim had forgotten that he'd ever mentioned his dreams of Marnie.

Spooked and blood-hungry, legs still trembling from his nightmare, Rise made it to the hall. In the growing darkness, Rise kept an eye on the entrance to the root cellar. After Ogrim's return, Salter had secluded herself to fill their chronicle. Since then, not once did the lights beneath the cellar door go out: Salter's faint candlelight danced from beneath her door. He'd not read from the chronicle in such a long time. Salter was always upon it, always adding to its stories and pages. Rise could ask her for a read, of course, but that wasn't the point. He waited for Salter to leave the book alone someday, so he could read it in peace. He shouldn't need to seek permission for that.

A creak upstairs caught his attention. Rise slowly, still shaken, climbed the stairs. He let his hand drift through the fresh winter holly spun through the banister. A frown crossed his face when he passed by Ogrim's door. No usual old-man snores. He'd tried to get a moment alone with Ogrim, to ask how he really was, but it seemed that Rise never got the chance, or Ogrim never let him. Cypriot didn't help, either. He clung to Ogrim now, fussed over him as if he were his father.

Rise knocked at Ogrim's bedroom door. There was no answer.

When Rise continued upstairs towards the creaking, the holly pricked his palm with every step. The tiny snags of holly-pain made him feel alive, grounded him again in his spooked body. His throat felt as if it was gaping wide open from blood hunger.

"Gather, so that I'm not alone," he muttered.

Maxine had installed herself in an unused bedroom on the next landing, in a central enough room, as if she knew that they all wanted to keep an eye on her. Her bedroom door stood slightly ajar, as every Owl Court door required a certain knack to be properly closed. For this bedroom, the handle needed to be lifted after it was shut. Maxine did not know that yet.

Rise approached her room as he heard another creak, along with the faint slosh of water. He entered with the silence of his race and was met with a wave of warm, rose-scented air. The embers in the bedroom fireplace glowed low. Maxine sat in an old-fashioned tub set before the hearth. A single candle illuminated her wet body. She bathed, leisurely, her back to the ajar bedroom door.

He was about to make his presence known, about to make some comment on the rose soap that was Cypriot's pride. But Rise hadn't noticed something before. As Maxine squeezed a knitted washcloth at the back of her neck, suds ran between her bony shoulders, down her spine.

Two tattoos, dark, upon her pale skin.

Two large swastikas, needled on each of her scalpel-sharp shoulder blades.

"Did they drug you, Maxine?" Rise asked in a soft tone as he stepped into the candlelight and perched on the edge of her bath.

Maxine froze at his appearance.

"How ... what do you mean?" she managed to say in a croaky voice. She even blushed at her nudity as she sat in the tub, its shallow water thick with soap–scum.

He didn't answer. Rise just studied her face. He could guess now why she had been cast out by the Warwolves. A lonely death in an empty world, filled only with brutes. That was probably the best death the Warwolves could wish upon her once they were done with her. Had the Warwolves done the same to Elaine and her mother? Rise cursed, all over again, that he'd never sat down and properly questioned the pair.

"Did they drug you, Maxine?" Rise repeated as he put such thoughts aside, giving her an out regarding her tattoos, if she wanted to take it.

Maxine nodded. Then she broke down crying.

"Don't ... don't judge me for my tattoos," she sobbed. "I hid them from ya for as long as I could. That's how I survived the Warwolves, ingratiating myself with them. Following along with whatever they wanted. Whatever they demanded of me. I know. I know I'm annoying. I only ask y'all so many questions because y'all here talk to me. You're ... interested in me. The Warwolves? They didn't give a shit, only how they could torment me, only what they could get out of me." Maxine hid her face in the washcloth and cried.

"Zero times, eh?" Rise said without emotion. He just watched her bathe.

He wanted to kill her, to snuff her out. Drown her. Plunge her head of ragged hair beneath the water. Hold it there until she was no longer a threat to Cypriot, Salter, or even Ogrim, who had at least had the sense to try and throttle her before. Rise watched the soft, female body, even though everything he knew about Maxine was anything but soft. Nothing about her rose his lust, his attention, not even his nagging blood hunger.

"You're my savior, ya know that?" she went on, between sobs. "Like my chaperone in this new world. You've treated me so, so well. I'm forever grateful." Maxine smiled up at him.

Rise recognized the lift of girlish infatuation in her gaze.

"I know Ogrim hates me—" she began.

"He doesn't hate you."

"I know he does."

Rise had his mouth open to argue, but that might bring up how Ogrim had tried to strangle her before.

"You know," Maxine interrupted his thoughts. She wrung out the washcloth and dabbed her puffy eyes. "For a long time, after everything fell? I never understood why people ever insisted on surviving. Why bother, when you could just die? I wanted to die, for so long. There was never any hope, no matter where I went or who I met. But seein' y'all here care for one'nother. Sit down an' eat together ..."

Rise heard a different sort of creak out in the stairway. A creak he knew.

"Our weekly feeding is soon." He stood and left Maxine to her bath. "You can watch us, if you like. See then if you still want to be part of what we are."

As he shut the door properly behind him, Rise found Cypriot perched on the top step of the landing in the dark, like a little night elf unashamedly listening to their conversation. His long hair braided, body freshly bathed and perfumed for what was to come. When Rise gestured, Cypriot rose and followed him.

"I was just coming to find you," Rise began as they turned toward Cypriot's wing of the house. They entered Cypriot's jungle bedroom and Rise closed the door by pressing his shoulder against the wood. A single lit candle sat on the windowsill against the night world beyond. Plant shadows loomed and danced along the ceiling and walls.

"Coming to find *her*, you mean." Cypriot sulked as he flopped onto his bed, creasing the pale peach silk of the sheets. He shoved bundles of dried long-stemmed roses out of the way, towards the foot of the bed.

Rise didn't answer. A part of him just wanted the smallest sip of nourishment from Cypriot's wrist. He was tempted to tell him about Maxine's tattoos. To frighten Cypriot. To make them cling to one another in the face of the oncoming feed.

"You're planning to drink from her tonight?" Cypriot asked haughtily.

"Honestly, I hadn't thought about it," Rise admitted. Perhaps they should. Perhaps they should drink from her just that little bit too long. He recalled the dark stamp of her tattoos against her paleness. In contrast, Cypriot's skin held a tan throughout the year, sun or no sun. Although, with his parentage, freckles also dotted his nose and high cheekbones during summer, which caused no end of fussing and consternation. Maxine's tattoos spun in Rise's mind. Perhaps they should drink from her until it was a little too late?

"What if she ever had some of your blood, Rise? What if she turned into a blood drinker like the rest of you? I don't know why I cannot. I've drunk from you several times over the years. I don't know why—" His voice cracked into deep sobbing. Cypriot even looked surprised at himself; that he would have such a visceral reaction to merely discussing this. His eyes widened as he cried; his cheeks flushed with embarrassment. He grabbed for a tissue from the nightstand.

"We don't know if merely drinking our blood is enough to turn you. Or anyone," Rise said. He had remained a bit spooked ever since he woke up, as though he were still dreaming. He stood awkwardly by the door, not really knowing what to do with himself. Leave or stay. Stay or leave. "I ... any of us blood drinkers—we've no memory of what life was like before we came to be. No idea if we turned from humanity or were born this way. I can barely remember anything about my twenties and thirties. Certainly nothing of my childhood, when I—"

"Rise, do you regret that I can never turn into your kind?" Cypriot interrupted. It was something Cypriot asked every couple of weeks. Despite Rise's assurances to the contrary, Cypriot would probably ask such questions forever.

Rise was glad Cypriot had interrupted him. Whenever he dwelled on the blank gulf of his earlier life, he felt only emptiness. "If you turned into a vampire," Rise purred at Cypriot as he crossed the room and sat next to him on the bed, "we could no longer drink from you, hm? You'd no longer be the centre of our attention." Rise smiled at that tear-stained face and touched a long curl of hair, always amazed at its softness. "Shh," he went on, wiping his thumb to the corner of Cypriot's eyes. "We don't need you to turn. If you did, who would we drink from? It's never been about you 'turning' into one of us. That would make us even less of a coven. We'd have to find someone new to drink from then, yes?" He brushed back a strand of Cypriot's hair. Even with everything gone to pot around them, that strand could rival the finest silks that the world once knew.

"Ahem. Before you two get too mushy," Salter whispered as she opened the door and slipped into Cypriot's bedroom. She smiled fondly at Rise and Cypriot when she found them sitting on the bed.

"What's the matter?" Rise asked. He hadn't expected her to leave the root cellar until the last minute.

"I need to tell you both something." Salter glanced over her shoulder as if someone would appear behind her. "Well, I'm nervous about letting Ogrim drink from him." Salter nodded to Cypriot. She set her shoulders and back to the bedroom door, to keep it closed. Her hands clasped, ink-stained fingers knotting together. Salter stood without her usual shawls and coverings, now that it was night. "If Ogrim's been bitten by a brute, who knows how that's changed him?"

Rise straightened. He had not thought of that.

"You think I might be in danger?" Cypriot whispered, eyes huge and tear-filled once again.

"Could be," Salter answered. She looked about for somewhere to sit that wasn't covered with vines and greenery. "But, I don't know, Cypriot. I'm not sure. I do know that you're too precious to the coven, to all of us, to put you in any danger. Ogrim is so different since he awoke from that bite. He says he's not ill-affected. In fact, he says he's hale, hearty, unafraid of anything. But I do catch him watching Maxine, even watching us at times. He helps Maxine try and fit in, to get to know the lay of the house. But he does watch her. Us, too."

"I've kept an eye on her myself." Rise shrugged. Typical for Ogrim to get all the credit for having some semblance of caution.

"Ogrim's still a blood drinker, though. It should be okay to let him drink from me." Cypriot puffed up his chest a little. A blush of pride remained in his cheeks as he rose from the bed and cleared a low stool for Salter. She perched on it awkwardly, legs so long that her knees bunched under her chin. Rise left the bed too and checked that the door was closed tight against any potential eavesdroppers.

"I can hear Maxine in this house from a mile away. She moves like a deranged badger," Cypriot said, waving his hand dismissively. He tapped his ear, indicating his sharp hearing.

"Ogrim is a blood drinker, yes," Salter admitted reluctantly as she moved from side to side, trying to get more comfortable. "But Cypriot, even you must see how he's changed since he woke up? Ogrim seems, not worse, just—"

"Changed," Rise finished.

A silence fell over the bedroom as each became lost in their thoughts. Rise kept his gaze on Cypriot. If anything happened to him, especially something entirely preventable, Rise would never forgive himself. His stomach grumbled. The veins throughout his body tightened, as if he were beginning some medieval torture. Feeding time soon. Was Ogrim too changed to drink from Cypriot tonight?

"Speaking of worries, have either of you asked Ogrim what's his 'unfinished business'?" Cypriot broke the silence. He clambered back onto the bed and curled up with a pillow.

"Seems like this coven isn't the sole reason–" Salter began, with a wary glance to the bedroom door, indicating Maxine.

"Shh," Rise changed the subject. "None of that solves our predicament of whether to let Ogrim drink from Cypriot or not."

"I've heard it called the 'zero times' before, not just by her," said Salter. "It's a phrase used to specify a tipping point in an environment, when one species will eventually outdo another. Yet, neither senses that tipping point, until it's too late and is irreversible. I don't want that to be us. We could try and give Ogrim a warmed cup of Cypriot's blood? That's, perhaps, the best solution I can think of."

"No good," Rise dismissed Salter's suggestion. "Remember that time in Bangalore? Nearly killed us, experimenting with all the ways in which we as a coven could and could not drink." When first founded, the coven had tried all sorts of things—tricks, permutations of their need to drink. "We need to ... we need to feel your pulse in our mouths, Cypriot. It synchronizes our heartbeats. Makes your blood flow into us, accepted, in sync," Rise admitted. A blush glowed in his cheeks when he saw the surprise in Cypriot's eyes. He didn't know, Rise realized. *We'd never revealed this to him.* The light from the solitary candle caught on the planes of Cypriot's face, including the faint smile line forming beside his lip.

"Unless Ogrim should drink from Maxine tonight? Let her be the guinea pig?" Salter suggested, her callousness towards their newest houseguest surprising even Rise.

"How about no?" Ogrim's voice sounded from the other side of the door.

"Well, okay, I can't hear a vampire," Cypriot muttered as Rise let Ogrim in.

"There should always be an element of fear from the food," Ogrim went on as he stepped inside, limp-free now. He cheekily sat on the end of Cypriot's bed, uncaring for the dried roses that he crumpled or Cypriot's cry of dismay. "Not that Cypriot is afraid of us. But he knows what we are. And he respects it. His life hangs just as much in the balance as ours do with him. Oh, sure, he fusses enough about stupid things, but he respects the line." Ogrim shifted a little bit to allow Cypriot to lift away his precious flowers.

When Cypriot had set his roses aside and turned back to complain, Ogrim had stolen a rose and held it out to him by way of apology.

"I'm sorry," Ogrim admitted genuinely. "But I am so hungry. I needed to sit. And dried flowers, to me, to someone of my great age, are stupid, Cypriot."

Rise raised his eyebrows at this odd behaviour from Ogrim. Something deeply amiss with him—the honesty, the kind harshness—Rise couldn't place what it was. And he didn't know if anything that Ogrim said was true. But Rise's blood hunger pulled at his brain. He felt glad to be sitting down, too.

"This buffoon you've let in, Rise," Ogrim continued, "she's too stupid to fear anything. To her, we're not saviors, not the ones offering an opportunity for life. No. To Maxine we are freaks in a circus. To be prodded and giggled about. Questioned and questioned."

"Let me put the light of fear into her eyes. Just once," Cypriot said with eager relish. Rise could nearly see the tray of pruning tools glinting in his eyes.

"There's a queue for that," Salter joked, but there was a dark flash in her eyes, too, that told of how she would like to shake sense into their newest foundling. Or shake life out of her.

Rise frowned at them all and waved his hand to discontinue such talk. "We were thinking," Rise instead broached an earlier subject. He glanced at Salter to gauge her reaction. "Ogrim, we were thinking, what if you drank from Maxine tonight?"

"What a delicious thought."

Rise ignored his indignation. Ogrim would've normally been the first to put himself front and center of any danger. "I'm worried about you drinking from Cypriot. We don't know how that brute bite might have changed you."

"You want me to dine on that scuzz bucket?" Ogrim's voice rose and boomed.

"Oh stop, stop it," Cypriot cried, hands over his ears. He looked around nervously. "Ogrim can drink from me. No problem. Just ... stop fighting. I can't stand it when the only people in the world between me and those brutes out there start fighting!"

*

At the time for their weekly feed, with the room warm and cosy, with dim firelight flickering against shuttered windows, they gathered. Cypriot upon the chaise, Ogrim and Salter on low stools alongside. Rise stoked the fire so that the heat would stay in the room while the vampires slept. Maxine watched from a nearby dining chair, solemn and quiet since her bath. She sat by the fireside so that she would have enough light to see. Cypriot, before the coven left his bedroom, made them promise to remove any candelabras or candlestick holders near Maxine, after what had happened with Elaine and Marnie all those months ago.

His latest dream haunted his head, but Rise paid it no heed. Salter, Ogrim, especially his Cypriot—they were many, more than enough for Rise. Reminded of those two women, reminded of the disaster last time, when Rise covered Cypriot's naked body with a woolen blanket, Rise also slipped Cypriot his small pistol. A knowing glance in thanks. The blanket's warm russet and gold pattern glowed in the firelight. Then Rise almost laughed. Beneath the blanket, Cypriot had also hidden Rise's crowbar between his naked, knobbly knees, in case he'd need it, too. *Well, after what happened last time*, Rise reasoned. He ruffled Cypriot's hair.

Blood hunger thrummed in waves, pulsating between himself and Salter and Ogrim. Rise felt something slip away from his worries as he took off his winter fleece. The room was so warm. To hell with Maxine; hunger roared in his ears. Rise only wanted that pulse, to drink so deeply from Cypriot until he was satisfied for another long, whole week.

"Oldest first." Cypriot's wrist veins already bulged as Rise offered him up to Ogrim. Salter looked on hungrily, knowing she would be next. She sat beside the chaise, more uncovered and bared than at any other time in the week.

Rise was nearly driven to madness at having to wait those eternity-seconds for the rest of the coven to feed. He should be worried about the bitten Ogrim drinking from their Cypriot? Or something? Were they not all ever so worried about that just now? But his hunger overwhelmed him. In the final few moments before it was time to feed, Rise lost all sense of himself. He would've gladly thrown the entire coven away just to know that deep, primal taste of his love once more. A week was far too long between feeds.

Ogrim's Blaschko lines rose. His fangs appeared and dropped into Cypriot's wrist, eking a satisfying, age-old squeal from their human.

Maxine rose from her chair.

She leaped onto Salter. Her bony fingers dug into Salter's tightly curled hair. Looming pale and brutish, Maxine bit into Salter's throat.

"She's trying to drink!" Salter choked, terrified.

Ogrim tore himself from Cypriot's wrist and lifted Maxine bodily from Salter. With his great vampire strength, he slammed her onto the floor. Something in her back cracked mercilessly and she screamed.

Cypriot dashed past Rise—a naked, bloody figure against the firelight. The once-hidden crowbar lifted high above their heads to finish her. Cypriot's narrow chest and ribs flexed. Maxine splayed on the floor before him. She moved a little still. She reached out for Cypriot to help her, one human to another.

"I cannot!" Cypriot dropped the crowbar onto the rug with a loud clang. He clapped his hands over his mouth, smearing blood down his jaw. Cypriot shrank away into the shadows of the fireplace.

Salter's strong hand gripped Rise's and, before he realized what was happening, all three blood drinkers had descended on Maxine.

"No, wait!" Rise tried to cry, but his weak voice died in his throat.

He pulled back from Salter, head thudding with hunger, heart thudding in panic, as Salter and Ogrim tore Maxine apart. As her swastikas dislocated and broke, Maxine's blood spread across the floor. After a time of seeing only gore, Cypriot knelt before Rise and shoved his bloodied wrist, where Ogrim had just drunk, to Rise's lips. Cypriot's shocked face, pale and bloody. A pleading look in his eyes, as if, if only Rise could accept him, then everything would be okay. There'd never been force between them. Scratches and nips and occasional bruises, perhaps and only during their lovemaking, yes. But this sort of violence taking place before the fireplace? Never.

Rise lowered his head and drank from Cypriot's punctured arm.

"Too hungry for this gift." Ogrim eventually stood over Maxine's mangled body, his Blaschko lines tense and dark ridges across his wrinkled face.

"Should've done that the moment you saw her," Salter spat as she finally rocked back on her heels. She clutched her throat from Maxine's bite. Salter's blood wound down her arm and into her sleeve. She coughed and had to clear her throat a few times.

"A job well done." Ogrim poked Maxine's corpse with his boot. Then he smiled at Rise, such a kind, fatherly smile, alarming Rise as he drank deeply from Cypriot. Rise slowly began to disappear beneath a haze of sleep and fullness.

"Ogrim, what—" Rise tried to speak but only ended up talking into Cypriot's wrist.

"Don't ever get bitten by a brute, my coven," Ogrim warned them abruptly. Rise's pistol in his hands. Ogrim's eyes twitched with tears. "It is a terrible, terrible existence. I have shielded you all from what I went through, as best I could. Held on for as long as I could. I've seen this one here die. So, my job is done. Can you feel it, though? That with the fall of people, that life's just gone on too long? Life used to be sharp, brimming with passion just ready to take flight. I long for only seventeen years lived, bound in too much muscle, ready to gallop away over the hills, or laugh on horseback with friends. Knowing that maybe we marched towards death, but we were young and alive and together, so it didn't matter. Centuries later, life is too long. I want a short life, bursting night and day with passion. Not this dreariness. Anything but this."

"Ogrim, no!" Rise wrenched his fangs from Cypriot's wrist as Ogrim raised the pistol to his temple.

The gun shot one last time. Ogrim's body dropped to the floor. In the flickering firelight he still wore his sad smile.

*

The pigs the next day seemed especially hungry. Rise tipped the kitchen scraps and the rest of Maxine into their pen. He wept as he watched the animals snort and scoff their food. There was no Ogrim. Winter snow tipped down, cold on Rise's hot, tear-stained cheeks. He pulled his stupid bobble hat over his eyes as he cried, not even wanting the pigs to see his grief. Rise cried into the crudely knitted hat until he could barely breathe.

Ogrim rested now in a coffin in the root cellar. Salter promised him a proper send-off once spring came and the snow thawed. The morning prayer of protection felt so weak now.

As the pigs ate, their feet churned the mud of their pen. A pale shard of bone disappeared into the muck.

Rise had been wrong. He'd also been right. It wasn't good enough to just return with one or two people and pray they'd fall in line. Through the pain of loss, Rise saw how he could tend to many this way: within pens, within the paddocks of his home. Owl Court could host many. The odds of finding at least one or two sane people among many rescued had to exist. There had to be many,

many more rescues now, to raise and nurture. Rise wiped away his tears, but more tears came. He went to check on the chickens. Midnight passed.

"What do I have to do to secure our food? Drag people back by their hair?" he muttered, voice thick with grief as he scattered the last of the scraps from the kitchen bucket into the coop.

As the snow continued to fall, brutes shuffled outside the walls and encircled Owl Court like lonely deaths.

PART 3 - SPRING

"Survival goes not just to whoever is fittest. It also goes to those that strike down all naysayers. And pursue. And never give up. Over time, through my own idiocy, I've realized that's what being the fittest actually means. So, let us strike down. And pursue."

—Rise, The Invoker

Chapter 15

A Parade of Wolves

It wasn't good for his kind to start counting things. That led down the road of obsession. Nevertheless, Rise kept a running total of his work. He sat on the kitchen doorstep surrounded by piles of kindling. His shoulders rested against the back door, arms aching from splitting wood. He meticulously bundled and tied the kindling with twine. A glum day; the sun hid behind afternoon clouds. Rise only had to half-cover his face with an old linen scarf.

The hedges on either side of the kitchen door swelled with springtime greenery. They told of a new season. However, as Rise's piles of kindling grew, the gloom that hung over Owl Court never truly lifted.

"Not since winter," Rise muttered. It wasn't even necessary to bundle kindling like this at all. The woodshed stood just around the corner from the main house. Nipping out to replenish the drawing room's fireplace or the kitchen stove was a task of mere minutes. Really, Rise just did this for some respite. To sit quietly on the back doorstep and count pieces of wood. For nothing else to bother him.

"Did you say something?" Cypriot opened the back door, a tiny pruning tool between his slim fingers.

Rise straightened at that voice, lifted his shoulders from the door. He put down his scissors and twine.

Since Maxine, whenever they came across each other, Rise always studied Cypriot's eyes, his expression, the set of his slight shoulders. Ogrim had hidden so much, too much, to the point where Rise could barely find any forgiveness for the old vampire. And Ogrim had drunk from Cypriot that fateful night. Although that, and Ogrim's death, seemed to produce no physical ill effect on Cypriot, Rise remained vigilant. But those brown eyes only looked quizzically at him. Cypriot made an idle *snip-snip* in the air with his pruner as he waited for Rise to answer.

"Nothing. I was just talking out loud," Rise admitted. He forced a smile, to show that he wasn't moody or grumpy. But he could feel it. That forced civility that now hung between the three of the coven left behind. One day, maybe everything could be as before. For now, he bundled kindling, while Cypriot gardened, and Salter spent her days writing the chronicle.

"How's your project coming along?" Rise asked, just as Cypriot nodded and turned to go back inside. The only hungers Rise indulged in were those of the weekly feed. Even that had lost its tension and release. Although he and Cypriot still shared Rise's bed, it was just to sleep.

"Oh," Cypriot replied lightly, awkwardly, widening the door open again. "It's fine." Then, "What're you doing?"

It was obvious what Rise was doing. He didn't answer. "Your horse chestnut seeds have sprouted, right?" He tried to show that he'd paid attention. Not keeping tabs on Cypriot, no. Just attention. A flutter of longing passed through Rise's chest.

"If you plant a conker—I mean a horse chestnut seed—" A patch of paint on the door jam caught Cypriot's eye and he poked at it with the sharp tip of his pruner. "If you plant it in a plastic cup and poke holes along the side ... and if you trim the new shoots as they emerge, it produces a stunted little tree, kind of like a bonsai."

"Ah, I didn't know that."

Cypriot shrugged. "It's fun. I've always wanted to try it."

The silence between them; Rise couldn't stand it. The silence upon the courtyard, pressed up against their walls. The silence that hung over the whole world. He wanted to spring to his feet, to bellow, to rouse the countryside back to life. To take Cypriot into his arms and ignite their passion once more. But Rise just sat there, silent. The events of that winter's night had torn the fabric of Owl Court. He had no idea how to remedy it.

"Anyway ..." Cypriot disappeared inside. The back door softly clicked shut.

Rise listened to his slippered feet as they shuffled to the kitchen sink, where Cypriot pruned his little sprouting experiments upon the draining board. The wind-up radio that had once lived by the taps had long ago been stored away. When it was turned on, the radio's constant static sounded too empty, too eerie for any of them to bear. Rise listened deeper to the house, to the faint scratch and scribble of Salter at her writing desk. If she'd been diligent in her wordcraft before, Salter had now flung herself into her work. Done with transcribing the most recent events, she even created appendices to the chronicle, inscribing vast volumes detailing everything each coven member had ever done, could ever remember doing. Writing became as essential to Salter as Cypriot's blood in their veins.

Ogrim's coffin stood in the root cellar. The winter ground was too hard to bury him properly. Salter wanted Ogrim burned, though, causing more arguments there.

Rise did not listen to the house anymore.

Counting the kindling tempted him again. Rise ran his palm over the nearest bundle, liking how the snags and splinters poked his skin. At least, each day, he could still tend the plants and trees and animals of Owl Court, still provide for his coven. The only thing that got him out of bed, besides the daily incantation.

A low, bumbling hum interrupted his counting.

Rise thought at first that it was a bee inspecting the hedge's new buds and leaves. But the hum swelled. Fast, then slow, then darting fast again. Rise forgot numbers. He heard people.

He stood.

From across the fields, he heard the ragged breath of humans. Who ran in terror.

Kindling scattered as Rise raced across the courtyard and hoisted himself onto the wide, red brick wall. Holly trees rustled in the spring breeze, a breeze that tugged Rise's light scarf as he stood high above the courtyard. He lifted the sleeve of his ancient overcoat to shield his eyes against the daylight. Forced his ears to focus.

Three people. Strong individuals, their lungs and legs long used to the outdoors. Rise winced when he heard raw, horrifying fear in each of their gasping breaths. His own breath caught when he heard them trip, fall, drag each other back up. They held no weapons. No heavy belongings. Just three people, full of life and pulse, running blindly in the world. Something even further away gave them chase, but Rise couldn't work out what.

There could be no mistake, though; the three were running for Holly Hill.

"Cypriot, get Salter!" Rise shouted as he sprinted into the kitchen.

Cypriot dropped his gardening tools into the sink in shock. "What's going on?" he asked, wiping his hands on the nearest cloth.

But Rise had already made it to the root cellar door.

"Salter?" Rise called down the dark staircase. "Come quickly. You too." Rise pointed at Cypriot as he raced back through the kitchen. He grabbed Ogrim's shotgun from behind the armchair. Checked to see if it was loaded.

"What is it?" Cypriot's face paled.

Rise clicked the gun closed and grabbed a wide-brimmed khaki hat from behind the door. He mashed the hat low on his forehead, protecting his eyes in case he needed to shoot. Ready to fire on these people, ready to quench them if they posed any threat. They might be

Warwolf spies, kin to Elaine, kin to Maxine, even? But, as he opened the back door, a spark of rare and longed-for excitement ignited in Rise. Could new people just ... arrive at their front door? Could he add them to the coven's numbers, no need then for anyone to ever leave the safety of these walls ever again?

"Rise!" Cypriot stamped his foot when he got no answer.

Rise paused in the open door, his kindling discarded across the concrete step. "Survivors. Survivors are coming," he told Cypriot and tossed a coat at him.

Above the ladder to the wall, Rise had built a makeshift sunshade out of spare planks. Salter wanted to watch the spring return to the countryside. Whether that was exactly true or not, because Salter had mostly stayed at her desk while winter turned to spring, Rise obliged her. He'd built a little lean-to over the ladder just for her.

"You say there's three of them?" Salter brought a thick pile of cloaks and shawls with her when she came outside. She stood in the darkest corner of the rickety lean-to and covered her whole body, so that not a single inch of skin was visible to the gloomy sunlight. Cypriot helped smooth fabric over her head and across Salter's broad shoulders. Rise stared out of the lean-to's little window, transfixed on a point in the distance. Those breaths weakening, yet drawing closer.

"Three." He squinted, honed his hearing. Exhausted footsteps as people tramped up Holly Hill. "From this way." Rise pointed north.

"They could be running from brutes, Rise," Salter pointed out. "Can you hear what's chasing them, what's causing them to run?"

"And ... what if it's not brutes?" Cypriot asked, his voice sounding lost, scared. He held one of Salter's scarves, fiddled with its ragged threads. "What if it's those Warwolves?"

Rise almost turned to comfort him. To break that distance that had hung between them since winter. But strong legs crashed through the undergrowth. Two men and a woman appeared, all in hiking clothes. They collapsed to their knees and elbows in the tall grasses between Owl Court and the holly trees. They didn't look too filthy or worse for wear at all. Gasping for air, they gazed in shock at the red brick walls looming before them.

"What the hell is this place, Iskar?" the woman asked as they struggled to catch their breath.

Rise caught Cypriot's elbow and hid him deeper inside the lean-to, making him stand beside Salter. Nothing yet said to those below.

"I don't ... I don't know what it's supposed to be," Iskar replied and looked about, puzzled. "The OS map said there was a hill here, down south of the mines. But not that there'd be anything atop."

And then their eyes met.

Rise had experienced it once before, when the coven first came to live at Owl Court and they had met the previous owner. It had felt to Rise back then, over a hundred years ago, akin to cousins recognizing each other across a market square. As if he had found a kindred soul and recognized them, randomly, in the world. Rise felt a shocking affinity towards this Iskar person. Not as one who walked between the world's veils, as those of the coven did, as the Warwolves did. No, but certainly as one who possessed the strength, the *tuning*, to accompany one through those veils, unperturbed. Rise gripped the railing, gripped his shotgun, as he stared down at Iskar.

"H-hey!" Rise shouted to the hikers. His heart leaped. Salter and Cypriot immediately hissed and tried to drag Rise back into the cover of the lean-to. But he shook them off. He stalked away, squashed his hat down onto his head, and moved further into the daylight, down the wall.

The hikers jumped to their weary feet at his voice. They squinted up at Rise.

"What is this place?" the woman demanded, looking behind her, not forgetting their pursuers. "Who ... who are you?"

Rise ignored her as he studied Iskar: A baseball cap low on a weathered brow. Sun-lightened hair. Several fingers bulged with chilblains. Hands used to hard work. Strong lungs that hungered to survive. A pulse soon returning to normal, despite being chased.

"Be careful, Rise," Salter whispered, knowing he would hear her but the hikers couldn't. When Rise glanced at the lean-to, one of her strong, cloaked arms was draped over Cypriot's chest. She held him safe and close. Cypriot's terrified expression peeked over her arm.

Rise gave them a tiny nod and returned his concentration not just to Iskar, but to all three below.

"This is Holly Hill," he began, not revealing the house nor even his own name, yet. "Why are you here?"

The woman stepped forward to say something, her fists bunched as if ready to fight.

"Annette, no, calm down," Iskar warned her. The other hiker touched Annette's shoulder, too. She shrugged them off, much the way Rise had just done with Salter.

"We ... we were hiding in the mines." Iskar pointed vaguely north. "Then these guys ... these—"

"Those bastards!" Annette interrupted. "Get off me, Gregg," she added when the other hiker attempted to catch her by the shoulders again.

"I don't know who or what they were," Iskar went on, his blue eyes scanning the freshly trampled grass, as if remembering horrors. Eventually he looked up at Rise. "But they chased us out of the mines. Killed ... most of us. Out of nowhere. But ... they knew the exact layout of the mining facility. I-I just grabbed Annette and Gregg. And we ran."

Rise took this in. Despite his pulse leaping in time with Iskar's, he strove to think clearly. He pointed his shotgun at them, to show that he was no pushover. That they couldn't just come to the gates of his home and expect entry.

"Whatever kind of setup you've got here, we can be of use to you." Iskar held up his hands and goaded his fellow hikers to do the same the moment he saw Rise's gun. "We're ... seasoned mountaineers, outdoorsy. We were on a hiking trip round these parts when the whole world went crazy. We went to ground. Emptied the mines and its sheds of brutes. Every ... everything was fine, all this time, until those other bastards showed up, out of nowhere, and attacked us. We were outnumbered, overpowered. We just ran."

Rise glanced to the shade that held Salter and Cypriot. She shook her head, *no.*

But, curiosity ate at Rise. The last time he'd seen someone with the aura of Iskar, it was when the coven came to own Owl Court. He felt as if fate itself hung from a fine thread between them. Could Salter feel it too? From her expression, Rise guessed not. He dug deep into his mind. Remembering Ogrim. Remembering what happened each time new people were brought inside these walls. Rise lifted his gun. Annette cried out in dismay.

"Why here?" Rise growled, making his voice as menacing as he could. If the other two, Annette and Gregg, were no good, Rise could easily command them away. Iskar would probably eventually remember Rise doing such a thing, though. Rise's commands wore off and people's memory soon returned. He steadied his grip on the shotgun. Earlier, he had only vaguely heard something giving chase to these three. Now, Rise could pick out hoofbeats and the creak of saddle leather. He tried to ignore his ears, tried to appear unyielding to the newcomers.

"Why here? You're asking why we're here? I honestly don't know ..." Iskar admitted, and the other two nodded, frantic. "I ... we just ran. Blindly, from the mines. I studied the Ordnance Survey maps of this area for months now. There wasn't really much else to do. I knew of the mound of Holly Hill. I bet on there being a thicket of holly trees atop that we could hide in, until whatever danger passed. None of us knew there'd be a house here, let alone people living—" A sudden sob broke and rattled Iskar's throat and chest. Gregg and Annette comforted him, draped their arms over his shoulders and chest, rubbed his back.

But Rise could feel Salter's reluctance. He could nearly taste Cypriot's fear on the air. Rise lifted his attention away from the new people and instead watched the horizon line. Horses and riders fiercely chased the hiker's trail. Warwolves, no mistake.

"And, if you were to be let inside our walls," Rise began, but Salter dashed from the lean-to and grabbed his elbow. The hikers were startled at her odd appearance; at Cypriot, too, when he stepped into the sunlight.

"Rise, what do you think you're doing?" Salter hissed in his ear, giving no more attention to the people below than she would to an ant on the ground. She squeezed his arm, reinforcing his aim. "You can't possibly be serious about letting these people inside? Haven't you learned from what happened in the autumn? In the winter just past?"

Even she would not speak the names of Elaine or Maxine or Marnie aloud. Rise mulled Salter's admittedly valid points. He sought Cypriot's opinion, too, with a glance, but Cypriot only looked pale and lost.

"I don't ... I don't know ..." Cypriot shrugged his slight shoulders.

"It's obvious what to do," Salter spoke over him harshly. "Command them to go away. Or shoot them. Just see them off, Rise. What good are they to us? It's as if you haven't learned anything from the last two times we took people in."

"We must gather, so that we are not alone," Rise pointed out with a weary sigh. The phrase from his dreams tumbled from his mouth. He didn't know what would happen if Salter and Cypriot completely refused to let these people inside. What sort of divisions or conflicts would occur.

But that tug towards Iskar. Rise wished for Ogrim's guidance. He'd have known what to do. "When before has anyone of worth ever come to these walls unprompted, Salter?" Rise said as he tried to puzzle out what to do. The hoofbeats neared, distant no longer. A challenge to goad horses up the sharp slope of Holly Hill, but the Warwolves would do it. Rise remembered the night in the lane, when the Warwolves and brutes had attacked him and Ogrim and Maxine. Those horses would be goaded to the edge of endurance.

"Hey!" Iskar interrupted, his arms lifting high to show they meant no harm. "Again, I don't know what kind of setup you've got going on in there. But you need to know that ... we don't care. We just ... we just want to survive. We have skills. We'll be of huge help to whatever way of life you have in there. We won't judge, whatever's going on. But ... please, don't—" Iskar's voice broke again, and he dissolved into tears.

"Please don't leave us out here to die," Gregg finished, his sandy hair dripping sweat onto his t-shirt, arms deeply tanned and weathered from a life of outdoor work.

"Rise. You can't just do as you want."

Rise had never heard such a hard tone in Salter's voice. She had never revealed that she had the gift of command. Rise didn't know if she could command vampires, too, different from the way that Rise could only command human minds. But something in her voice set his teeth on edge. A finality to her tone, like the click of a lock.

"So, you don't want to save them?" Rise let Salter cast her final vote in the matter. Not once did his gaze leave Iskar. Rise longed to speak with him, to suss out his strange and rare aura hanging, like taut, plucked strings, between them.

"I do not," Salter said firmly. Before she returned to the shade of the lean-to, she added, "and I say that because of our past experiences with letting people in. I mean no offence to you, Cypriot, or your race."

Cypriot nodded as she walked away. Today he'd shadowed his eyes in faint traces of kohl. It only enhanced his look of wide-eyed fear. "I don't want them in here, either, Rise," Cypriot admitted as he joined Salter in the lean-to. "Even though they are my ... race, as Salter put it. I don't care. I don't want them in Owl Court. It's been far too awful, everything that's happened before. I can ... barely get through a day as it is—"

"You bastards!" Annette shouted. "Our lives are in your hands!"

The ringing of her voice turned the hooves of the Warwolves' mounts. Rise caught the shift in how the horses pounded the earth as they now angled directly towards Holly Hill. The Warwolves were close enough to hear her. Close enough to bring them right to the gates of Owl Court.

Always, in the background, in the shadows and shades of the coven's lives, the threat of the Warwolves had followed them. Throughout time, wherever the coven moved or relocated. Once Rise had safely installed everybody at Owl Court and sealed the boundary, he'd hoped that the Warwolves would be kept at bay forever. Let them have Dunsinann. Let them have the surrounding countryside, the cities. As long as Rise had Owl Court and this hill, he didn't care. But now the vampire hunters wheeled and tore towards the coven's walls.

Outnumbered, outvoted, a streak of stubbornness flashed through Rise. Like the first autumn morning when he first left Owl Court. Ogrim had been against that, too. Everybody here, always against every little thing that Rise tried. All he ever wanted was to strengthen their position. The literal dead walked the earth. The crabs around Rise just wanted to haul him right back into their bucket.

He gritted his jaw. Lifted away the shotgun from the railings, as if to give up on the hikers.

"Oh, thank goodness—" Cypriot began in relief. He sagged into Salter's shoulder.

But Rise flung the shotgun aside and raced down the ladder. Feet sure upon the courtyard's stones, Rise could move faster than the other two. Salter, weighed down in her protective shawls, was no match for him as he raced towards the double gates. Cypriot and Salter shouted, but for once he would not listen. Something whizzed past Rise's head as Salter threw something at him. But he did not stop.

It would be the fastest transaction of his life. Rise smacked his hand off the narrow door alongside the double gates, breaking Owl Court's protection. Iskar's startled face appeared in the barely open door. Rise grabbed his shirt and dragged Iskar inside. As Rise reached for Annette, as she sprinted towards them, shadows broke from the holly trees. Glossy, strong horses thundered through the ring of grey tree trunks. Glinting scythes raised above wild manes. Riders' faces hidden behind deep hoods. Far more than three individuals now, the Warwolves had increased their numbers at least tenfold.

Rise hauled Annette inside. Iskar tried to dart back out again as Gregg stumbled, terrified by the approaching marauders. But Rise held Iskar back and instead reached to his belt for his pistol.

A Warwolf blade passed through Gregg. One moment he was a blinking, breathing being. Next, his head separated and thudded to the ground. His body dropped. Annette screamed.

It was the last thing Rise saw as he slammed the gates closed. Protection rippled strong throughout again. Unearthly sounds, then, as the Warwolves hissed and shrieked. They could do nothing before the protected walls of Owl Court, not even scale its heights. Rise took a shaky breath. For a long time, he just stared at the wooden door before his nose and listened to the terrible noises. Iskar and Annette wailed as they knelt before the door, their faces contorted in shock and grief. Their cries just as terrible as the Warwolves' beyond. At least the boundary held. Rise pressed his palm against the red bricks. The boundary would protect them all.

Only when the two hikers ran out of tears and breath and could only kneel in numbed sorrow, only when the Warwolves dismounted and circled their horses beneath the shade of their holly trees, did Rise look over his shoulder.

In the courtyard, near the well, Salter held a sobbing Cypriot against her chest. Her expression grim, she took Cypriot inside, scattering the kindling even more with a kick from her strong leg. The back door slammed.

Chapter 16

The Desolate Green

After a few days of curious observation, the coven could only call it a sentinel. A permanent presence left by the departing Warwolves. A hooded figure stood outside Owl Court's walls. The Warwolves did not rally or converge in great numbers to overwhelm them after the encounter with the hikers, as Rise first feared. Instead, a lone figure, a scout, stood watch in the grasses beneath the holly trees. A scarecrow in their wildflowers.

When two weeks, three weeks passed and the sentinel continued its watch, Rise gave up on throwing the odd brick or log of wood at it. Instead, he reached for his pistol and took pot shots at the cloaked, hooded figure. Rise listened keenly to its breath. He blamed his poor aim on stress, on lack of sleep. He blamed a whole host of things, even declaring the sentinel to be bulletproof. If he came close to hitting it, it would slip into the shade of the trees, only to reappear at another part of the wall a few hours later. Addressing the sentinel, shouting at it, brought no answer. Whoever stood there was indeed alive, though. Bait, perhaps, to draw them out.

Gregg's body softened, then hardened, as it decayed into the earth. Eventually, over the course of those odd weeks, Salter convinced Annette and Iskar not to mourn Gregg's remains any longer. At least, not to mourn from the height of Owl Court's walls, where the sentinel could easily see and study them.

Across the courtyard, almost a month after their arrival, Annette helped Salter muck out the cowshed. Annette, it turned out, was quite the artist. Her borrowing of charcoal and paper from Salter had kicked off an unlikely friendship. Rise listened to their idle conversation that drifted across the courtyard, as he still bundled kindling at the back door. Iskar helped him. Silently they worked, in unspoken agreement not to interrupt the chatter of women. Too weak to cast any shadows, the afternoon's sun hid behind thick clouds. Rise, along with a wide-brimmed hat, needed only a light scarf over his nose and throat.

Inside the house, in the kitchen, Cypriot curled up in the armchair with Tom, reading a gardening book. Rise eavesdropped on Cypriot to hear his soft lips move, hear him murmur how to correctly plant root vegetables inside, in large containers. Of late, Cypriot had turned towards gardening inside, as if he didn't want to have anything to do with life even beyond the house anymore.

"Not that the shed you've allotted us is uncomfortable ..." Iskar said. They lugged kindling, side by side, from the back doorstep to the woodshed that was tucked behind the stables. Iskar's smile was hopeful, lopsided from beneath the too-low cap of his baseball hat. "But. Do you ever think we could sleep inside?"

The kindling weighed against the old wound in Rise's shoulder. Neither of the hikers had witnessed the coven feeding yet. Neither knew what the residents of Owl Court really were. Yet. And Rise was no closer to getting to the bottom of that enticing draw towards Iskar, either. Even Salter felt nothing strange from him.

Before Rise answered, he surveyed the courtyard, feeling the presence of the sentinel beyond, listening to Annette and Salter's easy conversation, Cypriot's murmurs. Rise wished for Ogrim's hunched and limping figure to cross the yard, just once. For the old vampire to shout at the pigs. The spell of protection had weakened so much since Ogrim's death. Ogrim would have known exactly how to handle the hikers and, especially, the sentinel.

"To eat and bathe, you and Annette come into the house." Rise glanced from the weathered toe caps of Iskar's hiking boots to the hope and edge of fear in those bright blue eyes. Eyes not so dissimilar from Rise's own. "But to sleep? No."

Meals in the kitchen? Fine. Storytime and tales of life before? Not at the kitchen table, like others before. Not on the drawing room's fireside rug. But Rise allowed such things to happen outside. He allowed a sizable bonfire to be built beside the well. At night, Rise sat on the kitchen doorstep and listened to the previous lives of Annette and Iskar, as Salter wrote everything in the chronicle. Firelight flickered in the hikers' tear-filled eyes.

"Oh, okay." Iskar sounded disappointed as they reached the woodshed. A low and well-hidden building, covered outside and in with stacks of logs left to season. He gestured Rise inside first. "It's just ... the roof repairs on our little shed went well. It's watertight. And comfortable. We were just hoping, Annette and I, that if we completed those repairs, that we might be allowed to sleep inside the actual house at some stage. I know we're coming into the middle of spring. Then it'll be summer. But, spring and summer around these parts are no guarantee of good weather."

Rise couldn't fault the truth in that as he ducked inside. "It must be odd," he admitted, hearing only honesty in Iskar's question. "To come into the kitchen to eat. To pick your way to a bathroom to wash. Then be booted out for the night."

"Your cat, Tom, he's treated better." Iskar chuckled.

Rise had to smile at the joke. But his heart still hung sore in his chest. As they stood in cramped darkness and inhaled the scent of timber, Rise wanted only one thing. He closed his eyes and drew away his scarf. The air was thick with tree-smell, as if they had delved into the dim, green heart of a forest.

To take Cypriot away from all this. Go somewhere else. Be alone, together. Rekindle the early days, when they could barely be separated, barely stand to be apart. Back to early days, when they were more often than not one creature upon the bedsheets, rather than two lone and clothed idiots, apart.

"Never mind. Sorry I asked," Iskar piped up. He packed his large bundle into place among the rest of the kindling; tidied up the sacks of sawdust alongside. "Let me change the topic. Um, I did want to ask you ... if you ever knew what happened? With the virus, and how the brutes came about?"

"The now is the now." Rise could express it no more simply. "How the world got into this mess has nothing to do with me, personally. All I care about? What's inside these walls." He delicately put aside the presence of the sentinel and his futile efforts to kill it.

"You know what, Rise?" Iskar considered this for a few moments. "I thought I wanted to know how all of this happened. For a long time, I'd try and find out. But, really, it was useless. How could I, a mere coffee server who loved hiking and camping every spare moment, possibly find out anything close to the truth? You're right, Rise. The now is the now."

Loose threads hung from Iskar's fingerless gloves. They caught on the last of the sticks that he stored away.

"You're missing some fingernails," Rise noted, still trying to puzzle him out.

"Oh, these? Lost three nails on this hand over the winter. It was ... it was rough out there. Thank God we found the mines. Even though we had to get rid of a lot of zombie brutes from the facility and even down in the tunnels, they were old miners, you know? My hiking group, though? For the short time we lived there, since the end of the world, we'd never been happier," Iskar admitted with a sad smile. He showed his nailless fingers to Rise.

Rise's sore heart went out to him. "For a time," Rise wanted to agree, "we too, we'd never been happier." But Rise cleared his throat and glanced away, wishing he had a similar baseball cap that he could pull low over his eyes. When he found his voice, Rise moved on. "We're lucky to be protected here with physical walls and ... other things. To have enough food. Raise enough chickens, pigs, goats. I'd always hoped that there were survivors out there, that I could integrate you all into life here at Owl Court. Have Holly Hill as a bustling ... well, as a beacon. I always hoped that life here could continue, no matter what went on outside the walls. That's why I prepared."

"I'm glad you did!" Iskar said, laughing.

Rise faltered; watched his head on the low ceiling. That lone Warwolf outside lodged as a splinter in Rise's mind, preventing him from laughing, too. If only the world could be rid of them entirely. The Warwolves, the final obstacle to them all surviving in peace. An obstacle, too, to Rise's dreams of overseeing a bustling community.

"You both still mourn Gregg and mourn all of those you once knew. Time, more time, needs to pass," Rise pointed out to Iskar. "But you are right. It is spring and there's green on the branches once again." He allowed himself a small smile. Even Cypriot had fallen into line since they'd taken in the hikers, cooking for the extra mouths like a mother hen.

What more could I ask for? Rise thought.

"Then, let it pass." When Iskar spoke, it was in a slow, deliberate tone.

"Hmm?" Rise came back to the conversation.

There was barely any light in the little woodshed, save for what dullness spilled in from the door left ajar. Awareness passed between them. Then Iskar lifted his hand. For a moment, Rise thought that Iskar would try something. An attack. A move of seduction.

"You can't be suspicious of the whole world, Rise. You've taken us in. Given Annette and I ... you've literally given us our lives. Why don't you give us time to show you how grateful we both are? We can all make it in the world, even with whatever that thing is outside, watching us. We can, together." Iskar's hand paused, half-lifted between their bodies. Blue veins beneath ruddy, chapped skin.

Rise stood stuck to the ground. His heart hammered. Iskar's blood would taste of wild things. Of hiking under midnight skies. Of teamwork, friendship. Perhaps notes of Iskar's childhood, of the kindness that surely ran within him. Maybe even a memory of a grandmother's Yorkshire puddings swimming in rich beef gravy. He might taste of so many slants of life that Rise had never experienced in Cypriot's pulse.

"I don't claim to understand everything about you, Rise, or the people you live with." Iskar spoke softly and he stepped back, respectfully. He sat on a nearby barrel, knees cracking. "But, Annette and I, we're more than happy to help you all survive. In whatever shape that takes."

Iskar's rolled-back sleeves exposed a slab of forearm between the cuff of his shirt and the frayed rib of his gloves. A deep pulse siren-called to Rise. Iskar would be hale and hearty. Rise sank to his knees before the barrel. He gingerly touched the nearest vein. Prominent upon Iskar's skin, like a raised road welcoming travelers.

Iskar didn't seem to intuit what was about to happen. He kept talking.

"All I can do is repeat myself, Rise. You ... rescued Annette and I, and Gregg too, almost, when those freaks chased us. That's ... that's more than enough to tolerate whatever it is that goes on here—"

Iskar's voice cut off in a sharp yelp when Rise's fangs dropped into his wrist. Hot blood spurted into Rise's mouth. He ignored the burn of his Blaschko lines searing into life. The pulse of a tall, fit body, slowly regaining its strength from weeks of Cypriot's meals, it all flowed into Rise. Bonfires. Friendship. Rise clamped his eyes shut as he Iskar's blood drowned him to the world. All sound slipped away. He drank in secret, on his knees in the woodshed, surrounded by stockpiles of logs and kindling. Rise drank, gulped down, drank more until Iskar shifted and leaned his shoulder against the nearest wall.

He's not learned how to be drunk from properly. Not yet trained. But, one day, perhaps even Salter could drink from Iskar, too? Recognizing that possible future, Rise dug deep into his resolve and forced his fangs to withdraw. He did not wish to drain Iskar, or anyone, to the point of death, not even to the point of weakness. He remembered those on Marnie's bridge. A sip like this from another, between the weekly feeds, though, that would hurt no one. Not even Cypriot, not that he needed to know.

"I am sorry," Rise managed to say, although his tongue and throat were drenched in such delicious blood. He sat back on his heels and wiped his mouth with his scarf. Rise quickly split the scarf in two, lifted Iskar's arm above heart-level and bound the cloth around the twin punctures on Iskar's wrist. Rise expected horror, or shock, or panic. But Iskar only watched him curiously with heavy-lidded eyes, his face ashen and cap askew.

Rise retreated further and set his back to the wall of kindling to catch his breath. Everything about Iskar thumped through him. Rise knew what he was now, something Rise had never known could even exist: a blood match. Rise could explain it no other way. Iskar's blood dovetailed with his own. Different from Cypriot's, whose blood pulsed alongside. This was different, a deep primal matching, previously unknown to Rise. He sat in awe, realizing this was why he was so drawn to Iskar.

Iskar, though, looked pale.

"I shouldn't have gone for your wrist," Rise apologized. The cautious part of his brain told him to check the distance between the barrel that Iskar sat on and the door, in case Iskar tried to make a run for it. One of the nearby logs would have to be grabbed to dash in his skull if things went sour. But, as more of Iskar seeped into his veins, Rise knew that would never happen.

"That'll be a nuisance for you to keep hidden," he went on, speaking to Iskar in a calm and measured tone, as if he were a frightened dog. "I should have ... I should've drunk from your upper arm, or the top of your shoulder. Somewhere more hidden, easier for you to hide." At least Rise had not drunk from Iskar long enough for his bitemarks to deepen and become permanent, like Cypriot's. Despite his babbling, a luscious satiety spread through Rise. He just wanted to curl up and sleep. Then wake, full and ready to keep order once again.

Iskar blinked hard several times, then shushed Rise. He resettled his baseball cap, lifting the peak in a kind gesture. That lopsided smile returned.

"If this is the sole payment for living here." Iskar inhaled a deep breath and let it out slowly. "Then I will pay it, any time." Then Iskar opened his mouth to say more, lips pallid, wrinkled.

"We are the blood drinkers of lore. Of fiction," Rise admitted before Iskar could even ask. He studied Iskar's reaction to this with great care. It would do no good for Iskar to freak out and have a repeat of the last times they'd brought in survivors. Rise could hear Iskar's heart quicken to resupply lost blood, all while Rise's own heart leaped with new blood. "We're not so different from how our kind is often portrayed. In other ways, we are quite different indeed from what people imagine. But, by being what we are, a coven, it's how Owl Court has stood strong against the outbreak and everything that's happened to the world."

Finally, Iskar nodded. He seemed more awed than terrified or shocked.

"I ... we ... usually only drink from Cypriot. It's ... quite the thrill to drink from another," Rise explained, trying to lighten the conversation.

"I won't tell him." Iskar touched the scarf on his wrist, marvelling at it. "He's been so good to Annette and I. He is like us, though, isn't he? He's human. I suspect it's you and Salter who are ... so different?"

Rise nodded, through a pang of guilt. But fresh blood thumped through him, cleansing away memories of Maxine and Elaine and Marnie. Once he slept off this feed, Rise would control himself better around Iskar.

"Have there been others?" Iskar asked in the cozy silence as he peeked inside the scarf to check his wound. Already, the bleeding had stopped. The twin holes were just pinpricks now. "Other people here, before you took us in?"

Whoever asked it of him, this question would have to be answered one day. Rise could not lie. Nor did he have any inclination to, not to Iskar. No lies between them. In the dim light of the woodshed, all close and satiated, Rise studied the outline of Iskar's face. The revelation of Rise's race only made Iskar curious, not afraid. Rise took great comfort in that.

"Yes, there have been others." The rich tang of Iskar faded from his mouth. Rise ran his tongue around his teeth to make it last. "First, I found a mother and daughter near what we call Dunsinann. The little village down the road. The mother, Marnie, she was ... traumatized. Had dementia long before the brute outbreak. They couldn't accept what we were. I don't think there was anything that any of us could have done, for either of them." His nightmares—thankfully none had haunted him since winter. Rise fought sleep.

"They left here?" Iskar asked in surprise.

Rise couldn't figure out any other way to explain their departure without sullying Cypriot. So he just nodded. "Then, a few months later, we found a young woman, Maxine. She was ... she ..." Rise wondered how to explain Maxine as he yawned.

"She didn't work out?" Iskar offered, as if he understood. When Rise nodded, Iskar added, "We found some people like that. A husband and wife. Just ... couldn't fit in with how the rest of us were trying to survive in the mines. Missed internet and electricity and hot water. Can you imagine? The rest of us, we ate whatever. Worms, grass, bats, tree sap. Anything."

Rise shook his head to clear the last trace of his Blaschko lines. "Maxine didn't work out."

"It's for the best, then. Let the world deal with people like that," Iskar said after a moment's reflection. "Life is ... different now. We all have to pull together. There's no time for, no tolerance for ... for people who can't get along."

Rise thought of the pigpen. He clicked his tongue, always liking that final tang of blood.

"Well, I'm glad to have four walls around me and a roof over mine and Annette's heads. Whatever this is, Rise," Iskar said, indicating the handkerchief on his wrist, "it is a small price to pay for your hospitality."

"I have longed to have many people live here. To keep them safe," Rise admitted. He met Iskar's gaze, and they both smiled. "As regards Cypriot, it would hurt him so much that he alone couldn't keep Salter and I satisfied. Even with Ogrim's loss, he would—"

"This is a secret I gladly keep," Iskar interrupted. He pulled off the scarf to reveal his bite mark again. The veins around the tiny twin holes were barely puffy or swollen.

Rise stared at those marks, praying that everything wouldn't end as before. Twice before. He looked at Iskar's wrist, until he realized that Iskar was staring at something.

Glancing over his shoulder, Cypriot stood in the woodshed's door. Rise's stomach dropped at those dark and widened eyes. A rosebud mouth parted in shock. Rise darted to his feet, caught Cypriot by the collar of his soft shirt, and pinned him against a wall of kindling, lest he run. He felt the sharp ridge of Cypriot's collarbone, like a rod in a birdcage, beneath his forearm. Rise's mind scrambled for something to say, to explain all of this.

"I told you, ages ago," Cypriot said, voice cold, cheeks darkened red, as he shoved Rise away. He tossed back strands of his long hair and smoothed down his rumpled shirt over his slight swell of stomach. Eyes downcast, he muttered, "That I didn't care, Rise. Bring in who you need to. Do with them whatever you want. Whatever you deem fit. I told you then that I didn't care. I still don't."

Cypriot didn't lift his gaze, even after he spoke. Iskar quickly bound up his wrist and cleared his throat, as if to say something. Rise lifted a hand and gestured for Iskar to keep quiet.

"Anyway," Cypriot sighed, quick and sharp, as if impatient to get back to his day. "I just came in here to get another sack of sawdust for—"

"Cypriot." Rise spoke his name clearly, coming close to using a tone of command. "Salter does not know anything about this. I had to see ..." Rise glanced at Iskar and saw his concern, his face still pale from blood-drinking. "You need to understand, Cypriot, that I had to see if this man was trustworthy enough. Promise me that you won't run and tattle to Salter—"

"As if I would ever, ever betray us? After Ogrim held on so long in a tortured body, just so he could see us safe from Maxine?"

Rise flinched at Cypriot's words. Now he'd have to explain even more about their race, more about blood drinking, to Iskar. They, as a coven, barely knew anything about such things to begin with.

Before he could form something convincing to say, Cypriot snorted. "Oh, forget it." He turned and fled the cramped woodshed.

Rise stood in the doorway and watched him sprint around the corner of the stables, heard him cross the yard. After a moment, Cypriot slammed the kitchen door. In the stables, Annette and Salter fell silent.

"He's been weird since Maxine. Since Ogrim died," Rise muttered. At the thought of having to sort all of this out with Cypriot, Rise just wanted to go straight to sleep. "Since, really since, ever since I brought anyone new inside our walls."

"You told me about Ogrim the first night we came." Iskar's hand fell on Rise's shoulder as he joined him at the door. "It's not hard to see why Cypriot's been so upset. Will I speak to him?" Iskar offered. When Rise turned and looked at him in surprise, Iskar added, "Well, what should we do?"

"We?" Iskar's hand felt warm where it rested close to Rise's old wound.

Iskar raised his eyebrows, also surprised. "Unless ... Cypriot catching us just now, what he said to you, unless that changes things ... changes this?" He lifted his wrist.

Rise shook his head furiously. Pride fluttered in his chest that, whatever in the world had brought Iskar to his gates, that they had chosen so well. "No, nothing changes for me. So long as you are still willing to-?"

"Good." Iskar tipped his cap in a friendly goodbye and left the woodshed. "I won't tell Annette until you say so. If there's anything I can do to help, just ask."

Rise did not move. He heard Iskar enter the stables to grab a yard brush. To sweep the step at the back door, Iskar told Annette and Salter. No, he didn't know what had gotten into Cypriot.

Rise played back what just happened. He savoured the lingering taste of Iskar in his mouth and Iskar's warm palm against his shoulder.

*

That night, the clouds cleared and they lit another bonfire. Cypriot brought dinner outside and served everybody stew in deep, earthenware bowls. Tom joined them and was rewarded with a small bowl of his own. Even Salter took a serving, as she angled her body and writing paper towards the fire for better light. That night, Cypriot sat across from Rise, at Salter's elbow. He neither ignored Rise nor entertained him. Iskar sat between the two women and looked a little relieved to do so.

Salter's first duty, once the hikers had settled after the horror of their chase, was to question them thoroughly about every person they'd encountered since the brute outbreak. Annette and Iskar recounted tragic tales, often through tears. Everybody bore a constant burden since the outbreak of feeling that they had no right to breathe while others around them rotted. Annette and Iskar had no new information about the Warwolves, but they told the coven about clashing gangs of humans, other survivors, who had also appeared in the past few months. Neither Iskar nor Annette had ever seen anyone resembling Elaine, her mother, not even Maxine. Nobody knew of them. Nobody missed them.

"And you say your uncle was a butcher, Annette?" Salter asked, pen held enthusiastically above her paper as everybody ate. Covered in long, draped scarves with her hood thrown back, Salter cut quite the dramatic figure. When Annette nodded, Salter looked across their little picnic. "I was thinking, Rise, that Annette here could illustrate scenes from the chronicle. What do you think?"

Rise poked at his stew. He didn't like the sound of that one bit. Cypriot didn't pay attention to anybody. He ate his stew and shared it with Tom. Otherwise, Cypriot stayed silent.

"I've seen Annette's drawings. You're talented," Rise complimented Salter's new best friend. "The fact that everything is in charcoal, in black and white, it reminds me of what the world looked like the day I first left this place to find survivors. Almost grey, colourless." Rise thought of Maxine. He didn't ever want to see those broken shoulder blades again. "It's a lovely idea," he settled on at last. "Just run by me what scenes she's illustrating."

"What?" Salter laughed. "Why?"

Rise didn't answer.

"H-hey," Annette piped up, glancing nervously between them. "Let me tell you more about my uncle, yeah?"

Rise ate alone, listened to the conversation, then stopped listening for a while. He perked up again when Iskar and Annette spoke about the early days of the outbreak.

"We only saw it happen on TV," Cypriot said, enthralled by Annette's tale of having to set someone's broken leg when the hikers escaped into the mines. "There's so much that we, in here, only saw from behind a camera lens."

"I remember the first time a brute came to these walls," Rise offered. "It looked like such a frail thing. Lonely. Not like how the news reported at all."

"That's when brutes are by themselves, Rise," Salter pointed out. It seemed that she couldn't keep the sharp tone from her voice. "They're quite another matter when they're in a horde."

"Yes. I know," Rise answered, just as testily. "I've literally had them on top of me."

"And dragged them back to our gates."

Again, Rise didn't answer. He grew uncomfortable sitting on the stout logs arranged around the bonfire. Put out at being spoken to in such a manner, he shifted his weight.

"You're too used to playing the gentleman, Rise," Salter chuckled when she noticed him move about. Her laugh held a hard edge.

Rise froze at her tone. "Oh?" He glanced to Cypriot, who didn't seem to be listening at all.

Salter addressed Iskar and Annette when she went on. "When the world was right, the rest of us never had such freedom from class, from skin color, from our backgrounds, until we all came here to Owl Court. The people out there, they tolerated Cypriot being with Rise in, say, a first-class train carriage. Because Rise could play debonair and eccentric wealth so well. Even Ogrim could get away with a decent second-class ticket, because of his Greek looks. But ... not me, though, I'm afraid."

"That sounds like it happened a long time ago," Rise said in a way that warned Salter to keep their cover in front of Annette. But a lump of meat caught in his throat as he glimpsed the sudden, deep sorrow in Salter's eyes. He swallowed deeply. "I ... I had no idea, Salter. You should have told me, back then. I would have done something about your treatment."

Annette and Salter shared a knowing glance. Salter didn't continue. The conversation soon pointedly turned back to Annette's uncle and butchery. The only thing keeping Rise from wanting to sink into the earth was Iskar's blood steeling his pulse.

The stars glinted. He turned his attention to the night sky and picked out several constellations, mourning the loss of Orion until next winter. Salter had never said anything to him about her treatment, back when the world was whole. How was Rise supposed to know?

"Don't speak too loudly," he warned the lot of them as he slurped back the last of his stew and got to his feet. Rise pointed at the far-off wall as he opened the back door. "That sentinel thing outside can probably hear us all."

He let the door slam and went upstairs to an empty bed.

Chapter 17

To Draw Blood

The next morning, Rise woke to the muggy light of a new dawn. As he shouldered into his overcoat and hurried to the roof, he noticed the banisters. The ivy hung all scraggly and overgrown. Usually, Cypriot was so meticulous about pruning any vine out of place, no matter where in the house. But each one that Rise passed instead hung untended.

A layer of dew lay on the patchwork fields surrounding Holly Hill. The oncoming dawn struggled against heavy-bellied clouds. Rise took a deep inhale of the countryside as he stepped onto the roof. He dug his hands into his pockets, cursing that he'd forgotten his gloves. Salter already waited on the rooftop. She leaned against the great chimney that led to the drawing room, her face hidden beneath the deep hood of her cowl. But Rise saw her eyes, tired and red from lingering too late at the bonfire.

"You can feel spring in the air," Rise said to test her mood.

"Have you checked to see if that sentinel is still out there?" Salter asked, from the chimney breast.

Rise hesitated at her tone. He opened his mouth to ask what was really bothering her.

"Where's Cypriot?" she instead asked as she glanced about the roof. Then Salter chuckled. "Is there trouble in paradise?"

Rise gritted his jaw. He didn't see why the fact that he'd not slept with Cypriot last night should be cause for commentary. Even when Ogrim was still with them, there was never a moment's thought given to people's private lives in this house.

"Oh, sorry, so sorry I'm late." Cypriot's sleepy voice came muffled from inside the house. Then he stepped onto the roof. He half-wore a huge rain jacket over his white nightshirt, hands hidden beneath too-long sleeves. His bare feet scurried to his usual seat on the water tank. Cypriot flopped onto the mottled plastic with a big yawn.

Despite everything, Rise couldn't help it. His heart thumped at how cute he looked.

"Cypriot, are you all right?" Salter trotted over and pressed her gloved hand to his forehead. Then she took off her black cotton gloves and tried again. When she tilted his head, Cypriot's hood fell back. His usually manicured hair hung tangled and rumpled. Cypriot's dark eyes, rimmed in red, nearly fell into purple hollows beneath. He yawned right into Salter's face.

"Too long at the bonfires?" She smiled, apparently just as tired.

"Jus' sleepy." Cypriot rubbed his eyes. "I couldn't nod off at all last night. The thought of that creepy sentinel thing watching us kept me awake. When I got to my bed, it was so strange, too. I kept hearing ... hearing, like the sound of a passing train. You know, when it pulls out of a station? A steam train screaming its horn—that's what I heard. Kept screaming at me all night."

Salter brushed some hair out of his haggard face. "No trains run anymore, Cypriot. They never ran near here, anyway, not close enough to hear. You're probably remembering Shanghai, when—"

"Sun's nearly up." Rise had to interrupt. Although he was about to go to Cypriot, too, just as Salter had, to soothe him. Rise knew all about plaguing dreams. And he wanted to talk to Cypriot, properly, about what happened yesterday in the woodshed. But with a warning twinge from the horizon, Rise snapped back to why they were on the roof in the first place. He stood opposite Salter when she left Cypriot to his yawning. If Ogrim were here, the trio would have formed a circle. Their group now stood smaller. The prayer of protection weaker.

By the time the last of the incantation left Rise's throat, Cypriot had curled up on the water tank, fast asleep. Snores came from beneath the hood pulled over his eyes.

"Oh my," Salter whispered as she covered herself after the incantation. Then she selected one of her thicker cloaks and wrapped it around Cypriot. Salter stepped back and gestured for Rise to carry him.

"Something's bothering our Cypriot," Salter said, worry in her voice, as Rise dutifully obliged and lifted Cypriot into his arms. Rise had almost forgotten the light heft of his body.

"If Cypriot's dreams disturb him so, there must be something really bothering him," Salter went on, holding the attic door as they stepped inside. They descended the stairs, banister ribboned with untended greenery. Rise led the way, carrying Cypriot.

"Rise, go easy on him. Those new hikers are lovely and all, but Cypriot is still our Cypriot."

"Cheer him up—or he'll be too tired to feed from?" Rise asked. They crossed the wide landing, its ceiling-high windows shaded against the morning light.

She paused when they reached the top of the next set of stairs. Salter frowned. She'd never confronted Rise since he'd taken in the hikers. "No. Because Cypriot's obviously upset about something, Rise. It might still be at the fact that you allowed those hikers in at all. It might be that sentinel. It could be all of that, or any number of things. But you need to figure it out, Rise. Make things right. You're closest to him."

"It's just not good enough anymore to fuss over Cypriot and placate him," Rise said firmly, checking to see if he was still asleep. "That approach only ever worked for a short time, Salter. Until the next perceived slight came up and upset him all over again. It only worked while there was just the coven of us, a full coven at that, at Owl Court." Rise steadied his foot on the next step before descending the final flight of stairs into the hall. He eyed the banister's overgrown ivy. Deep down, Rise agreed with her. He would have to nip this in the bud, this sort of—any sort of—angst weighing upon any of them. There could be no more of it.

Salter didn't answer him. But she did sigh loudly.

"What are you going to do now?" Rise asked her when they made it to the hall. He hoped that Salter might be away from her writing desk for a while, that she might instead fuss over Cypriot.

"I want to check the chronicle," she said. "When we first came here, we were told that dreams were important in this place, right? I want to read back, see exactly what was said. The summer of 1914, I think?"

"August, 1914," Rise agreed wearily as Salter disappeared into the root cellar.

When he entered the kitchen, Rise settled Cypriot into the armchair. Cypriot continued to sleep and curled into a tight ball of folded limbs. Rise tucked Cypriot's feet beneath the huge overcoat, hiding the chipped ruby varnish on his toenails.

Then, Rise just listened to the house. He breathed in the greenery that hung and bulged from every surface. The scent of green was so much stronger in the kitchen than even outdoors. Had Maxine once stood by that stove? Had Elaine and her mother really once sat at that dining table? Once people are gone, you can write them entirely from your life, as if they never existed at all. Who would counter Rise right now if he wanted to carry on as if those three women had never come to his home? The others—Salter, even Cypriot—they did not seem to ever care about the bones of those once-people that were trampled into the pigpen. None seemed to worry over Elaine's fate abroad in the world. It was an easy thing to forget people once they were gone. An easy thing, too, to act like they never existed at all.

The only movement came from the drip of the tap. A stubborn leak that refused every attempt at repair.

From the kitchen window above the sink, in the dawn light, the courtyard stirred. The hikers gathered fresh water from the well to start their day. Iskar and Annette washed their faces and hands with bars of Cypriot's rose-scented soap. When Cypriot had made last night's dinner, some porridge was also made and left out, alongside his bonsai tree project. Rise filled the kettle. Warmed the stove.

It seems like I've done nothing but think. For over a year.

Rise caught the kettle before it whistled and woke Cypriot. He handed out bowls of porridge to Annette and Iskar at the back door, showed them the still-sleeping Cypriot and asked that they dine outside that morning. Annette seemed too sleepy to care and accepted the food gladly as she wandered away to their shed. Iskar lifted his eyebrows as he took and held the porridge, but Rise shook his head, even though blood-longing spiked his veins.

For the rest of the morning, Cypriot slept in Ogrim's armchair. When the hikers finished their morning chores and drew more water from the well, Rise hesitated. It was nearly midday. Cypriot needed something to eat.

"Oh, there you are." Salter emerged from the root cellar and startled to see Rise just standing in the kitchen. Without another word, she caught his elbow and steered him towards the cellar. For a terrible moment, Rise thought that he was in for another round of scolding about how he needed to placate Cypriot. Or that Salter knew about him and Iskar. Rise's heart leaped. Had Cypriot spoken to her last night at the bonfire after he'd left?

"What is it?" Rise pressed. He'd avoided the root cellar since Ogrim's death. There was nowhere else to put Ogrim's body, not in the middle of winter and not now, with the months of spring barely upon them. It had been hard enough for Rise to sneak out before the hikers came to drag in fallen logs for timber. So, they'd kept Ogrim safe underground, in the cold and dark that was best for their kind. Kept Ogrim safe until the world softened towards summer once again. Then, and only then, would Rise bury Ogrim beneath the holly trees.

Candlelight flickered as Salter brought him downstairs. With a sinking sensation, Rise felt that his life with the coven was nothing more than shuffling between its members, from one problem to another. At least Iskar had the presence of mind, the kindness, to make life a bit more enjoyable for Rise.

"Salter?" He finally wrenched his arm from hers at the bottom of the stairs. "What's all this about?"

"Shh!"

Rise noticed that the whole cellar was in disarray. Salter's usually neat desk and chair were pulled back from the brick walls. Papers, including some of Annette's charcoal drawings, were scattered across the floor and also covered the vegetable crates. Salter's large, lone candlestick sat in the middle of the mess, its flame casting ghostly shadows. Their packed-away broadcast equipment, their radio, computers and TV, shimmered in the dark. Ogrim's broad coffin rested in the corner, unperturbed by Salter's mess.

"Salter, what the—?"

"I can hear things, Rise," Salter said in a hoarse whisper. She tiptoed to the candlestick and lifted it high, showing him the underside of the strong ceiling beams and all along the brickwork walls. Salter pushed aside another tidy pile of papers, the great big cellar broomstick, and ignored how they all scattered to the floor. "I hear ... I can hear scratching. Scraping. Behind the walls. As if someone—brutes, I don't know—are digging to the root cellar. But then, Rise ..." Salter faltered. She set a hand to her forehead and her candlestick shook. "But then, I don't know. I'm not so sure. What if I'm dreaming it all? I probably, I probably am."

"Digging to the root cellar?" Rise shivered at the idea. Even he feared that, especially when they stood by the light of a solitary candle. The weakening in the protection prayer, in the boundary, played on his mind. But Rise could not allow himself any panic. What solution was there to solve the boundary's protection? Find another Ogrim?

"I've had a deep listen; I can't hear anything." Rise shook his head at Salter's dramatics. "There's no way what you're describing could happen. Now, I don't doubt that you hear something. But the vegetables stored down here do creak and shift from time to time. You've said so yourself, Salter. There's too much protection, even beyond what we invoke, around the whole of Holly Hill for anything to dig inside Owl Court's walls. Do you think, for example, that the tree roots would allow it? And you were there the day I marked the boundary of this house with the whitest salt—"

"Yes, I know," Salter cut him off. Her gaze roved about, eyes wild in the candle flame. A sheen of sweat across her dark skin. "I'll also ask Cypriot to come down and listen, too. Although our hearing should be better than his ... he really is the oddest little creature ..." As she trailed off, Salter's fingers flexed every now and then from beneath her velvet sleeves.

While Rise could only grimly agree with her on that point, he suspected that whatever ailed Salter had nothing to do with noises or digging. He certainly couldn't hear anything. No, something else surely bothered her. Change could make a person act so differently. Rise perched against her flung-aside desk and casually folded his arms.

"Has something happened with Annette? Or ... with both hikers?" he asked, sounding concerned without naming Iskar. Maybe Cypriot had told her how he'd found them in the wood shed?

Salter made a noise as if to dismiss his concerns.

"Did someone say something?" Rise pressed. "Did Annette pass a comment on you or ... any of us?"

"No, nothing like that." Salter still held her candlestick and inspected the ceiling. Then she noticed how Rise leaned against her desk. Salter sighed out a small laugh and shook her head as she joined him. She perched on the desk's edge and set the candle between them.

"Nothing like that at all," she repeated. "I do worry though, Rise. About Warwolves. About that sentinel. About marauding gangs of people, those out in the wilds, that Annette and Iskar reported. About brutes. Then, I come down here ..." Salter stared at her mess in shock, as if seeing it for the first time. "I come to the root cellar and try to record it all as best I can, to fill my days. Fill the chronicle. Fulfil the duty of setting down our history, as it stands."

"I'd wager that there's a lot the chronicle can't record, though. That it doesn't know," Rise muttered, then regretted it. He glanced at Salter, but she wasn't listening.

She scanned the floor, brown eyes usually hidden whenever she walked outside. Salter looked at the walls, the rafters. "It's as if this whole place is going to crumble right onto our heads, Rise."

Rise idly tapped his knuckle on the desk, happy that she only half-listened. "I think Cypriot shares your concerns?"

"I'm sure he does. Put yourself in his shoes. He was never the best at getting along with others, even when the world was right. There's been too much change for him lately. For us all."

Rise couldn't deny that. He might've taken things a bit too far with Iskar. His attention not entirely on his coven-mates. But it had deeply annoyed Rise that he hadn't known why he was so drawn to Iskar in the first place. And now that he knew Iskar's taste, the matching and dovetailing of their blood, Rise had solved that mystery.

"Well, then, I guess I do need to have it out with Cypriot," he said.

Salter turned to Rise, the candlelight illuminating her face. "You never offer an apology, do you, Rise?"

He hid his surprise at her abruptness. "Not if it's unwarranted, no."

She laughed, exasperated. "The third time we allowed new people in here, Rise, you asked no one. Again. No permission sought. Again. Just our gates thrown open—"

"The third time seems to be working out," Rise bristled.

"And now we are outnumbered in our own home," Salter said lightly, as if Rise couldn't possibly understand. "You and I and Ogrim, as blood drinkers, outnumbered Cypriot, at first. That worked until the world fell. But now people, humans, they outnumber us here. At Owl Court. Do you realize that one bad apple among their ranks, a deliberate incitement—even an accident—and they might rush down upon us both? And they'd wipe us out, Rise. Easily."

Rise said what she probably wanted to hear: "Just having Cypriot alone as our source of blood was stupid of us. Always was."

"When we could've had many?" Salter asked.

She did not have the power to read minds, Rise told himself, nor the power to read dreams. How Salter could know that the word 'many' was so marked for him, Rise had no idea. He could only put it down to chance.

"Ogrim, he kept you inside, Rise. You know that, don't you?" Salter glanced at the coffin in the corner of the disarrayed cellar. "He kept you as close to his tea kettle and books as possible, using those tarot cards to manipulate you. Stay within the walls. Keep us protected. That insularity came with Ogrim's ancient age. Did you know he rode with the great Dionysius of Syracuse? Ogrim lived to a great, great age. But that's ... also kind of why I want his body burned, not buried. As if to burn away the last of him, release him from the earth. But Ogrim was wrong to do that to you, Rise. I hope you know that."

Rise hesitated. Salter wasn't wrong. But Ogrim's coffin stood nearby. He didn't like how she hopped from topic to topic, either. Bringing up old things, old names. Too much chatting to Annette, with her long, auburn hair. "I wasn't manipulated," he countered. "Staying inside has kept us safe. This far."

"This far, Rise, yes. But just because——"

"Is all of this from what the chronicle told you?" Rise interrupted, having had enough of Salter's whinging and needling. What was he supposed to do? Turn back time and undo every move and choice made before the outbreak? Rise thought of Iskar, of the future. There, at least, lay hope.

Salter sighed, as if she'd had enough, too. She shrugged simply and returned to eyeing the walls with great suspicion. "Well, treat those hikers and Cypriot a bit better than you did last night, snarling at us over the fire. It would seem they are our masters now."

Rise wanted to roll his eyes at such talk.

The chronicle nestled at the side of Salter's desk, not far from his foot. Out of her line of sight. Since the autumn, since before Elaine and her mother, he'd never caught Salter away from the book long enough to read it himself. Rise untucked his shirt but made it look like he had just readjusted his seat upon the desk.

"Numbers matter to us, Rise. They always have," Salter went on. "That's why living with only one, perhaps two, people that we feed on is best. That is manageable. To reach further, to reach for more, I don't think that is how a coven should work. Perhaps ... perhaps that's why we've never found huge groups of our kind? We might work best—thrive, even—in small numbers? Do not long for masses of people at your feet, Rise. It will only spell our downfall."

He waited until she seemed particularly distracted. When Salter's gaze flickered to the ceiling beams again, he tilted to one side as if stretching his hip. Rise clasped the chronicle from where it lay against her desk and slid it under his shirt in a smooth motion. The leather cover frigid against his stomach.

"Is that what the chronicle tells you?" Rise repeated, so that it seemed he was listening.

"Of course it does. I doubt we'll ever meet more of our kind, not with the way the world is now."

"That feels like a lonely future," he admitted, making the noises he thought she wanted to hear.

"It's the future that's been put before us," Salter sighed. "We've no choice but to live it. In this beautiful house that has only ever been a home, Rise. Never a prison. Until the world changed. Months ago, when the first brute approached the walls of Owl Court, Rise. You told me afterwards, for the chronicle, that you held such pity for that creature. The zombie was just an unfortunate human, mangled by disease. Forced to rise and walk the earth, even in death."

Rise remembered back to that night, before finding Elaine, many months ago. He remembered too the blast that had followed, when whatever government that had been left firebombed the distant city of Larnde. Necessary to wipe out the nest of brutes, the TV had said, back when there was still electricity. That enormous river of brutes he'd seen that day with Elaine and Marnie in tow, like a seething scatter of ants—it was still out there, Rise realized. The whole firebombing of great cities, all the way down to little spots like Dunsinann, hadn't worked. The brutes still clumped together and gathered, even in death.

"What of it?" Rise asked, unsure why they were even talking about this.

"You still have that sympathy? For a brute?"

"Why are you asking me this, Salter? I've no pity for brutes anymore. Only disgust. The thought of their bite runs shivers through me. To have your blood, your life, tainted by brutes—I can see why Ogrim chose to end his life."

Rise spoke no more of hopeless things, of things he couldn't possibly change. He had the chronicle to read. He let Salter talk on for as long as she wanted. Then he left the root cellar.

Cypriot had just woken as Rise entered the kitchen. When Cypriot stretched and his coat's hood dropped down over his eyes, Rise quickly took the chronicle from under his shirt and hid it in the double-deep rows of gardening books on the nearest windowsill.

"Rise, I know that I asked you to bring back a man the next time we encountered people." Cypriot's voice croaked. He smacked his lips, righted his hood out of his eyes, didn't notice what Rise had done. "But, I never expected it'd be like this," he joked sadly. He curled his arms and legs around him on the old armchair.

Rise didn't know how to answer. He didn't want to discuss Iskar at all. Salter had already worn him out. He brought Cypriot a glass of water, poured fresh from the sink.

"I noticed that the banisters are looking a bit overgrown," Rise began when he handed him the glass. "I can't imagine that you're deliberately neglecting your plants. Do you want any help trimming them?"

But Cypriot wasn't listening. He stared at Tom, who had curled up on the kitchen table in the empty fruit basket. "You know," he said, idly rolling the glass of water between his hands, condensation smearing his palms, "I'd leave here, if I could."

"What?" Rise jolted in shock. "Why are you saying that?"

"But I can't leave, can I?"

Rise frowned, wanted to pour the water over his head to make Cypriot talk sense. "Now listen here, Cypriot, I'll hear none of that. You'd leave me, leave the coven? All because you found Iskar and I—"

Cypriot shook his head. "That's not the—"

"Then why?" Rise shouted.

In the silence that followed, the windows began to shudder. A deep rumbling came from outside. Rise barely remembered grabbing Ogrim's shotgun from behind the door as he and Cypriot raced from the kitchen. Hauling himself onto the wall, Rise looked for the sentinel first. But it was gone.

Hordes of scythe-wielding horseback riders and packs of dogs crashed through the holly trees. They wheeled about and formed a seething circle around the whole of Owl Court. Rise grabbed Cypriot and ducked out of sight into the lean-to.

Guns discharged in the air. Horses thundered, trampling the narrow strip of grass surrounding the red brick walls, the riders riling their huge, muscle-bound dogs to bay and howl. Daisies and dandelions were crushed in miserable patches of yellow and white. The Warwolves gathered in huge numbers. They threw down tarps, long rods. At first Rise panicked, thinking that they meant to build ladders to try to get inside. But then he saw what they were really up to. Once the grasses were trampled, they all dismounted. Pitched tents, hammered home stakes, built campfires.

Rise stepped out of the lean-to and discharged Ogrim's shotgun at the nearest figure. One of the people below dropped their scythe and slumped dead, but those around the body just burst out laughing. They returned fire at Rise from sleek automatic weapons, but returned fire idly, as if it didn't matter whether they hit him or not, nor if any or all of the people below and around them lived or died.

Iskar and Annette climbed onto the wall, crouched beside Rise's shoulder in the lean-to. Horrified by the hordes pitching camp below.

"I guess we're really sealed inside now," Cypriot murmured, oddly resigned, as he pulled away from Rise.

Rise could only stare in shock at the audacity of the Warwolves. He didn't even realize that Cypriot had crept back inside until he heard *snip, snip, snip* coming from the house, as Cypriot trimmed the vines along the banisters.

Chapter 18

A Fine Crack of Thunder

"I've no idea what they're up to," Rise growled at Salter. She'd made her way up from the root cellar and now stood beneath the lean-to as well. Rise had banished Cypriot to stay inside the house and was rewarded with a snarl about having to trim all of the banisters anyway. Annette and Iskar hauled up an old tin bath and spare sheets of corrugated roofing to line the lean-to's walls. The Warwolves below occasionally discharged shots at the house, at the walls, at the trees. But other than that, the huge, well-equipped group only concentrated on making camp.

"They're digging in," Salter said at first, her voice distant and afraid as she watched the bustling activity. Then she shook her head. "I mean, they're pitching camp, as if to stay down there. Do you recognize anybody?" she asked Iskar and Annette.

Annette had come to Owl Court with a tiny pair of binoculars stashed in the pockets of her cargo shorts. She used them to survey the people below.

"It's hard to tell. They're all wearing hoods and masks. I can't see anyone's faces. What about you, Iskar?" She handed her binoculars to him.

Rise felt the minutes pass torturously slowly as he waited for a response.

Then, finally, Iskar straightened from where he had peeked around the lean-to's walls. "No, I don't know anybody down there. Not that we got a good look at them, either, back at the mines. Their horses are enormous, though. Well-fed and well-shod. Dogs look in their prime. Their camping gear is top-class, too."

"It's those weapons that scare me," Salter pointed out. "Very different from what we have."

Rise glanced at Ogrim's shotgun in his hands. Very different indeed. Dread fell upon him. Was his coven supposed to have done things differently all along? It seemed as if the Warwolves had fallen in with army types, or gangs of some sort, to have automatic weapons. Must've raided goods stores for their camping equipment and everything else that their animals needed. Everybody beyond the wall seemed sturdy and strong, too, no trace of malnourishment.

"And we just stayed inside, all the while," Rise murmured beneath his breath. He caught Iskar looking at him, but Rise just shook his head.

"So," Salter said pointedly to Rise. "What do we do?"

Rise set the shotgun against the lean-to's archway. "Try and speak to them, I guess? See what they want."

"It's obvious what they want, Rise!" Salter snapped. "They want us all dead."

"Well. Then. We need to see if we can come to some kind of compromise, right?" Rise tempered his desire to really snarl at her. That would do no good. "Or, I could command them away, over and over, until they grow tired of it?"

"C-command them away?" Annette asked, looking, terrified, from Rise to Iskar. She stood close by Salter, as if in the protection of her taller height. "What does that mean?"

Rise waved his hand at such questions. "We need to open communications with them first."

"Do we?" Salter asked, surprised. "Shouldn't we make plans to get away, to escape?"

"And where are we going?" Rise snapped this time as he stepped onto the wall, arms wide to show the Warwolves that he held no weapons. His heart pounded harder when he saw the full size and scale of the camp nestled at their walls. Like a medieval army about to storm a castle. As he stood alone, an easy target upon the wall, Rise saw his future: of issuing a tone of command, of the camp all leaving. Then, either days or weeks later, the Warwolves would remember life before his command. They would return. Rise had to prepare to keep a constant watch, ready to repeat his command again and again, loud enough, perhaps for the rest of his days, all to keep Owl Court safe.

He recognized the two original Warwolves from the day he'd rescued Elaine and Marnie. That duo sat around the nearest campfire with another who was small, slight. The sentinel.

Rise tried listening to them, to catch what they said to one another, even to hear the collective pound of their pulses. But the Warwolves sounded strange to his ears. Rise assumed it was due to drugs or alcohol, some kind of stimulant that they all had taken before converging here. Rise couldn't pick apart their words, nor even what was in their hearts.

Several Warwolves noticed him, and silence soon spread throughout the camp. One of the original duo, dressed in deep red, face hidden beneath a hood, stood some distance from the campfire. That one took up an impressive scythe and approached the walls of Owl Court imperiously and, with a flick of the wrist, indicated that the sentinel should come too.

Out in the daylight, Rise tossed up his hood as he felt his Blaschko lines develop. He could be just as dramatic.

"What is the meaning of this?" he shouted down.

A twitter of laughter from the entire camp.

Cursing that he couldn't see anybody's faces, nor make out their words, Rise swallowed his temper. He didn't look to the lean-to, to the terrified eyes he knew were watching. Rise could still hear the *snip, snip, snip* of Cypriot trimming the ivy. He didn't care if Cypriot hated him, wanted to leave, even if none of them could. So long as Cypriot was safe. That was all Rise cared about.

"I said—" he tried again.

"Your question is meaningless." The Warwolf dressed in wine red spoke with a woman's voice, in a neutral, practiced accent that Rise couldn't place.

"He was always great at asking questions, that one," said the sentinel.

Now, there was a voice that Rise recognized.

"Elaine!" he gasped as she threw back her hood.

Elaine looked so different. Confidence shone not just in her gaze, but throughout her whole body. Her cheeks were full and plump. Fingers strong and composed upon the automatic weapon that she held. Taller now, somehow, too. Rise opened his mouth to shout a command. She pointed to neon earplugs that were jammed in tight. Her eyebrows raised in a 'how about that?' gesture. Frustrated beyond words, Rise banged his fist on the wall.

"But he's never any good at answering," Elaine went on, telling the red-robed figure. When she glanced at him again, her arms went wide in a smug gesture. "But surely you know who these people are, Rise? Didn't I tell you that everybody in Dunsinann knows everybody else?" Elaine asked, smarmy, faking innocence.

Her words brought Rise right back to the day he found her on the bridge. He glared at Elaine, wishing that Cypriot had cracked her skull along with her mother's that fateful night. Everything she knew about the coven, everything that the coven had revealed to her, she'd undoubtedly revealed to the Warwolves. The sheer damage that those Warwolves could wreak upon not just their home, but the whole coven itself, struck Rise. Not just destruction or a complete wiping-out, but base and drawn-out torture for their kind.

"So, this must be his latest obsession?"

Rise realized that Elaine was speaking of Iskar, who now stood in the doorway of the lean-to, shotgun in hand. Rise waved him back, but instead Iskar shook his head.

"Was the brown boy not good enough?" Elaine laughed, dragging Rise's attention back to her. "Too much of a pampered princess for you, Rise? Or too much of a right little savage? What has Rise told you, hm?" Elaine asked Iskar. "Did he tell you how his coven murdered my mother? How he and his freaks took us in under false pretenses and, once we were witnesses to their depravity, once we tried to escape, did Rise here ever tell you what happened? I'm sure my mother's bones are in that pigpen of yours. That little princess never had any intention of burying her honorably."

"Rise, hurry up and command them away," Salter hissed from the depths of the lean-to. Her dark hands cupped Annette's ears, so that she wouldn't be affected. "Do the same for him." Salter gestured at Iskar, for Annette to pull him inside and cover his ears, too. Iskar obeyed, but his angst-ridden gaze remained on Rise as he stepped back into the lean-to.

"I never died out here, Rise," Elaine went on. "Out in the world. But. I ran from your horror show of a house. If only my mother could've too."

Rise remained silent. He hadn't known Elaine to be so talkative. Gone was the slightly dim and unsure girl. No point in explaining to every ear listening what had actually happened that night. That Cypriot had let her go willingly. That Cypriot had thought he'd done a kindness in releasing Elaine from being her mother's eternal caregiver. But then he remembered that conversation on the rooftop, right before the dawn incantation. Cypriot had seemed so shifty, squirming when he talked. A long-hidden wave of doubt hit Rise.

"The Warwolves watch all places now. Like the mines," Elaine sneered. "Like Dunsinann. In fact, I'm surprised you didn't hear us moving about. Usually you, Rise, with your great hearing, I'm told, must've wondered what the noises were? I guess you were just too charmed by that little brown boy to think straight."

Rise thought of Salter's worry, down in the root cellar. And he could see it now, where he'd failed. He hadn't given Elaine a purpose outside of her mother. But the Warwolves had. He studied their hooded faces, trying to figure out if there were any sort of weakness he could exploit. If he jumped down from the wall into their midst, if he drew on his deep well of strength, Rise might take out Elaine and at least two or three others. But, everybody below was so heavily armed ...

"So, they did what a Warwolf does best," Elaine went on, to the audience of the camp. "They waited for you, Rise. They watched and waited, and yet also acted and built and conquered in the background. Something you should learn, hm?"

Rise waited until Elaine was finished, until her smugness crescendoed and she ended such talk. He didn't care if his command didn't work on her. He would send the rest of the entire camp of Warwolves away, for they were people, just like anybody else. Rise wagered that they couldn't all be wearing earplugs. Then he would jump down and take out Elaine.

Despite everything, he took heart in the fact that the walls of Owl Court were protected by his incantation, even if weakened by Ogrim's passing. After tasting Iskar's blood, Rise understood now why the hikers had come and not other bands of people. Owl Court's walls would hold against anything the Warwolves could throw at them.

Rise took heart in the fact that Elaine had not been turned into a vampire by the Warwolves, if they knew how to perform such a process. Rise could not imagine the cocky young woman, so different from the meek soul he'd poured cans of soda into, would not want such a transformation.

He opened his mouth and, drawing upon the deep tone of command sleeping within his vampire veins, Rise ordered the camp to flee.

That should see them off.

Rise indulged in smugness and readied himself to take on Elaine.

But another chuckle rippled through the camp. The sound nearly froze Rise. The people below weren't commanded to do anything at all. The red-robed one standing alongside Elaine tossed back her hood to reveal a pale, almost lead-white, face. As they stared at one another, Blaschko lines rose across her skin.

Stars blinded his vision as he realized the truth: the command only bent the ears and will of humans. It had never worked on his coven. It had never worked on—

"Vampires," he gasped. Rise wanted to vomit. Then, almost as if he had forgotten the red brick walls beneath him, something deep within his heart went to the Warwolves below.

"You're ... you're coven, too?" Rise asked. He couldn't help it. His voice broke and squeaked.

The woman laughed. Her lines rose more; beautiful, rose-red stripes against the paleness of her face.

"No, please," Rise, desperate, pleaded. He forgot everything else that stood around him. "We've never found any of our kind, never found any other vampires at all. Only dead rumors and tourist traps. Tell me, please, tell me more about our kind. Please." He knew he was begging, in ignorance and darkness, like an animal destined for slaughter, but Rise didn't care. That his coven's eternal watchers were vampires too—it was too huge an opportunity not to at least try to ask. "There was only ever a coven of four here. Now there are others? Please, tell me about us. Something, anything!"

"Rise!" Salter shouted at him.

"Why?" Rise ignored her. "Why do you want to kill us, your own kind? There's so few, so few of us in the world."

"No, Rise." The vampire spoke. She pointed at her camp. "There are not few at all. We are many."

One by one, the Warwolves got to their feet and removed their hoods. It took only a few seconds for all of their Blaschko lines to sear into life across the many different hues of their skin. Their faces displayed a huge array of colours, Blaschko lines ranging from brown to pale blue-frost, like new stretch marks, to pretty, rosy pink. Despite everything, Rise couldn't help but find them stunning, beautiful, as he saw the true blend of his kin for the first time.

"Then," Rise could barely ask, voice caught thick in his throat. "Then why not make contact with us here at

Owl Court? We could have joined together years ago, or pulled together now against the zombie outbreak."

Elaine laughed. "Catabar," she named the red-robed vampire. "I told you what he's like. All questions, no answers or apologies. He hasn't changed, I see."

"Fight the outbreak, you say?" Catabar laughed at him, on and on. "Why would we do that? Who knows what fucked-up science the human-people did to cause this plague? But. It has wiped clear the earth of those same human-people for us." She paused. A smile grew across Catabar's lips. Her voice carried without her having to shout. "Since the outbreak was nothing but a tiny rumour to the world, we acted. And what have you done, Vampire Rise? Looks like you've sat at home and grown flowers. Well. You've been observed by us. Judged unworthy by us. It's your fault that we've come here. It seems that you don't properly understand time, Rise, not as one of our kind should. The moment the outbreak began, the Warwolves too began. We experimented with what these new zombie brutes could do for us. We can't eat them, and there's too many to completely kill off. But. They do have their uses."

"Myopic Rise." The other vampire from Catabar's campfire approached, taller, tan-skinned, with cropped black hair. Blaschko lines deep and dark across her long face. This one wore rich royal blue, in contrast to Catabar's red. "I am Menelos," she announced with pride, and then she scolded him like a great aunt. "That's your greatest failing, I'm told, Rise. To never see what's happening right in front of you. We have always, always watched Owl Court. The apocalypse was just our long-awaited opportunity to act."

"What failed your sight?" Catabar took up the scolding. "What failed the deep feelings from the earth beneath your feet? Distracted elsewhere? Too taken with soft flesh and warm beds to see what was going on outside your walls? You didn't help when the world was ending," Catabar finished, wrinkling her nose at him. "No, you all stayed inside."

"What?" Rise asked in confusion, mindful of just how long they were able to stand the sun while uncovered. *Arrogant fuckers.* "What could I have done?"

"Helped? Perhaps?" Catabar suggested in a calm voice, as if all of this was quite obvious. "Made yourself known to us? Something, anything, besides nothing. You protected a single boundary. But you could have done so much more."

"Doing nothing is often the best way to survive," Rise answered, digging deep into his resolve, remembering Ogrim's words from what felt like centuries ago.

"Oh? And how's that working out for you?" Menelos asked. Catabar chuckled. "You know," Menelos went on, "we hold warehouses and postal sorting offices. We hold a whole distribution center now. After this, after Owl Court, the Warwolves are looking at taking regional airports. Those who don't submit to our spread will be destroyed, either by us, or by the brutes. Tell me, Rise, what do you hold? What did you reach for when everything else fell—just these four walls?"

"And you won't have those for much longer," Catabar pointed out.

Menelos inclined her head, gave Catabar a desirous look. Then she continued. "We saw you leave here once. Then twice. Then you opened your door a third time. But. We only struck when it suited us. And that's despite Elaine's report of the savagery you laid upon her and her mother. Showing them how we feed. Disgraceful!"

"One day, Rise," Catabar said, "you'll have to answer to a god who won't be as merciful as us."

"I've never believed in any religion," Rise spat, scowling at them. He felt as if he was now inhabiting a different body entirely. That he was no longer Rise of Owl Court of Holly Hill at all. But someone else. Just caught out here upon a wall.

"Well," Menelos said. "Not believing has kept you separated from your own race—"

"We tried," Rise interrupted, already feeling defeat arrive at his gates. "Despite our best efforts, we tried. We offered humans the best deal possible, the best opportunity to survive. Considering that the rest of the world is gone. Yet, they betrayed us. And that one," Rise pointed at Elaine. "She will betray you, too. So, why do you come here to destroy my home?"

Catabar frowned at Rise's interruption while Menelos was speaking. Her Blaschko lines were far more ornate than anything Rise had ever seen. They unfurled elegantly down Catabar's throat, across her collarbone to where her embroidered coat met a red velvet hood.

Neither Menelos nor Catabar answered Rise. But they looked at one another and, after a time, chuckled again.

"Why? Why not, Rise?" Menelos asked, her dark eyebrows high up her forehead, her tone fake and incredulous. "Have you, by any chance, ever heard of the Warwolf trebuchet? Do you know what it is?"

Mystified, Rise only shook his head.

"None of you deserve grace." Catabar laughed at his ignorance. "Not you, Invoker. Not your Chronicler. Not your Sustenance." Catabar tossed up her hood and, touching Elaine on the shoulder, they all spoke no more and returned to their campfire.

Chapter 19

Beyond the Holly Trees

A glowing moon rose in the night sky. The silence of the world was broken only by the occasional low hoot, as if the owls were disgusted by the intruders.

"You know, they haven't made any demands, Rise. Not really. Those creatures out there ..." Iskar told him as they sat on the floor of the lean-to, one of Cypriot's squat candles illuminating the dark. "They must have something up their sleeves. And, I think I know what it is, with their cryptic talk about trebuchets and destruction. The Warwolves, they probably have explosives."

"Explosives?" Rise blinked out of his idle thoughts. The revelation of Catabar had wiped clean anything and everything he thought he knew about his life. As if a giant practical joke had been played on him and his coven, over hundreds of years. A joke that everybody else was in on, yet he'd had no idea.

Iskar nodded and slurped back some stew. Cypriot had brought them up dinner and blankets, and merely peeked at the camp beyond the walls, before silently returning inside. As if none of it mattered. In the courtyard, Salter and Annette sat together. Earlier, Salter had taken her into the root cellar to explain what the coven truly were here at Owl Court. No bonfire, not tonight.

"I didn't realize it at first," Iskar went on. "But that's probably why the Warwolves flushed us out of the mines. There's a warren of old coal seams behind the newer ones, in the hills. One corridor of the complex where we stayed opened out into a new section. Where someone—I'm guessing like the local council or some blasting company—were readying to begin mining again, and were storing supplies there. We found crates and crates of plans, detonators, explosives ... all to make new tunnels, just left there from before the brute outbreak."

"Explosives ... like dynamite?" Rise asked, his stomach twitching as if hungry for the next blood feed that normally would have been days away. But he wasn't hungry. Neither did he truly experience the terror he felt he ought to. Rise just felt blank, mystified.

From beneath the peak of his baseball cap, Iskar levelled his gaze at Rise. "I mean, like lots and lots of dynamite."

Rise thanked him with a touch to his arm. But all Rise could think of was the bricks and ceiling beams of the root cellar. Salter's concern. Of scratching noises heard through the walls. Of the brutes digging in.

"What are we to do?" Rise asked of the world, of no one. They had no real defensive weapons to hand, save farming equipment. Were they all just to sit and wait for the end to crash in on them?

"If there's nothing that can be done, then let's change the subject," Iskar suggested with an ironic grin, as if their deaths didn't await them all on the other side of the red bricks. He went to chew on his thumbnail, but winced when he realized it hadn't grown back yet. "You know, Annette's uncle used to be a butcher. She wanted me to ask Cypriot about the pigs you're raising, how you're slaughtering them. But, she was way too intimidated by Cypriot to ask him herself. He's a formidable fellow to try to talk to. I told Annette, though, that she should at least try."

Rise lifted an eyebrow. Iskar spoke so normally, unfazed by everything that had happened. Rise admired such steadiness. He'd rather not mull on the ins and outs of Cypriot's character, though. He decided to change the topic himself. "They were in the church, weren't they? The Warwolves, at Dunsinann?"

"I think so. I've never met one. Until now. But I've heard that many of the gangs in the world, that they're starting to raid—what did you call the place?"

"Dunsinann."

"That some raid Dunsinann. Others use it as a base, or as a trading post. It's a small little village, out of the way, low population. Not many brutes wander so far upriver from the bigger cities. Horses and dogs, like those out there, would be easily kept in the surrounding fields, especially on the far side of Dunsinann. That town is small enough for a clan of people to keep under control. With control over the bridges in and out, Dunsinann might be quite the little hub of civilization now." Iskar then shook his head. "I'm not from these parts. But I never thought I'd say something like that about Dunsinann. But there you go."

"There you go," Rise repeated as he became lost in his thoughts.

"It's cool, though, how you guys have your own names for places."

"Mm-hmm."

Rise missed walking. Even clomping along on stiff and ill-used legs, it helped him think. He remembered his first trip to the village to find survivors. He'd hoped to find people there, not just a mass of brutish zombies. Instead, Rise had found so much more.

"I always thought," Rise began with a little clearing of his throat. "That my kind, that we were some kind of sub-race. A withered branch of people that fed on wrong and dead things. I've carried that shame, knowing—or at least thinking, until just now—that we were the last. Nothing more than a dying line that probably deserved to be extinguished. But in light of Elaine out there, of this Catabar vampire, Menelos, and all the others, it came to me. What if it was the other way around? What if we were the new, all those around us the old? What, then, would that be like?"

Rise glanced at Iskar to see his reaction.

Iskar didn't look at him. He seemed nervous. "Realizing there's more of your kind gives you options, surely. Perhaps protection, too, if you can bargain with them all out there. Maybe even a future, Rise."

"I wonder what Ogrim would've made of all this?" Rise went on.

"I didn't know Ogrim," Iskar said. "But I do get the feeling, Rise, from talking with Salter and Cypriot—who are terribly worried about you, by the way, not that it's my place to tell you—that Ogrim meant more to you than you realized."

"You never met Ogrim, but he would have liked you," Rise admitted, a flush of pride, of companionship, rising in his cheeks. He ignored Iskar's mention of Salter and Cypriot.

"Then, I am honoured. Ogrim seems to have been highly respected." Iskar's voice was thick with respect. He stretched and cracked the deep joints along his back.

"He was," Rise said. "He was."

Their pigs' hungry squeals interrupted his and Iskar's talk. *No Ogrim*, Rise thought as Salter and Annette crossed to the pigpen. *No Ogrim anymore to witness this day.*

"I ... have an idea," Rise announced wearily. He got to his feet, patted Iskar on the shoulder.

"Okay. You'll let me know what it is, I'm sure. Until then, I'll keep watch," Iskar whispered as Rise handed him the last of his stew and descended the ladder.

Rise went to the drawing room, but not without pausing in the kitchen first. The house smelled of rich, simmering meat. Cypriot was nowhere to be seen or heard. The thick bulge of the chronicle was still hidden amongst the gardening books.

"No time for that right now," he said to himself, with a regretful shake of his head. There was never time for anything, it seemed. Not even to breathe. Not even to satisfy his months-old curiosity as to what Salter might have written. Rise had no time to stop and indulge himself. It was probably best, before Salter realized that her book was missing, to find some sneaky way of returning it to her. No time even for that.

Instead, Rise hurried to Ogrim's old armchair and the rickety table alongside. From a hidden drawer beneath the lamp, Rise took out a spare deck of tarot cards. Ogrim had never shown him how to make a spread or read them. Rise had some knowledge of tarot, but not much. Not enough to be a seer like Ogrim. *Foretelling the future to divine the past*, that was what Ogrim had tried to explain to him. Hate roiled in Rise's stomach that the old vampire had left right when they needed him most. He shuffled the cards, crinkled and yellow from disuse. Rise thought of Ogrim's true deck, now scattered over the lane and indeed probably across the whole landscape. Or maybe each card had merely rotted away in the winter snows and spring's thawings. Rise drew a card.

Judgement.

"Great, thanks," Rise muttered, feeling judged by the entire universe as he slotted the card back into the deck. He'd always preferred to concentrate on the future, on keeping Cypriot well and whole, of having lots of survivors around to ensure the coven's long-term survival. For doing this, he was instead to witness it all being swept away? He shuffled some more, then tried again.

Judgement.

He sighed sharply and threw the whole deck on the floor. It wasn't even that Rise didn't understand the point that the tarot made, but there was no way he could learn what that specific card truly meant and symbolized, outside of its name. Ogrim never kept any books about tarot, so confident that he already knew everything. The internet was long gone. Rise stared at the scattered cards that littered the fireside rug. He expected that the only card to face upward would be Judgement. But no. A different card, out of all the others, lay face-up.

The eyes of an owl gazed at him.

"The Ten of Swords," Rise murmured as he bent to pick it up. He didn't know what it meant. But it gave him an idea. He tucked the card into his shirt pocket. "It's not called Owl Court for nothing," he murmured.

Before going outside, Rise instead went upstairs. Landing after landing, flight after flight, he listened for Cypriot. Rise couldn't hear him. As he turned into a tiny, unused bedroom on the third floor, Rise paused. Listened hard. Cypriot was crossing the yard to the animal sheds, light-footed as always. Rise could make out the flutter in Cypriot's heartbeat, the panic that constricted his veins. With no time to go to Cypriot, either, Rise entered the bedroom and opened the lone wardrobe. Mothballs stung his nose. A lone rosary hung from a hook inside. In truth, its crucifix burned his palm the whole way down through the house as Rise made for the lean-to. But he didn't care.

Iskar hadn't moved from his vigil, from where he peeked at the camp. His baseball cap tumbled off when Rise suddenly climbed the ladder.

"I thought—" Rise stuck out his hand. The corpse attached to the cross gleamed in the candlelight. It mystified Rise how anyone could find hope in such a symbol. Worshipping a vampire made more sense. "I thought," he went on, showing Iskar what he'd brought, "that this might bring you comfort?"

"Oh." Iskar looked embarrassed.

Rise snapped his fingers closed around the beads. "Unless, they're of no use to you?"

Despite everything, Iskar chuckled. He knelt and prised open Rise's fingers. "No, I'll take any comfort that I can get. You just surprised me. I thought these things hurt your kind?"

Rise shrugged, although he was glad when Iskar lifted the rosary out of his hand. "I just wondered if you or Annette needed spiritual aids. At a time like this."

"At a time like this," Iskar repeated. He held the beads to the candle and they shone glossy and green, as if carved from polished emeralds. Iskar had grown strong and hearty from just the past few weeks at Owl Court. His blood would taste of good sleep, of warm wood timbers and nighttime bonfires. Rise felt the pull to drink from him again. "I didn't mean to offend," Rise carried on. "Just with everything that's ... well, going on outside, I thought—"

"Thank you." Iskar smiled at him. He even stood and kissed Rise's cheek. "I thank you. For thinking of Annette and I at a time like this, when you've your own to think about, too. I'm not particularly religious. But I'll see if Annette wants this. Not right now, though, I don't want to interrupt her and Salter. But I'll ask her later."

If there is a later, Rise didn't say aloud. Here, though, in front of him stood his blood match. One that kept pace with him, even now, throughout the night. Iskar understood. He understood the world beyond the walls in ways that Cypriot never could. Iskar could steer this ship with him, to the bitter and unknown end.

"Is there a name that you have for the people you drink from, Rise?" Iskar asked curiously as he examined the beads. Some had little carved faces. "Does Cypriot, apart from his own name, have a special term amongst you and Salter, like a title?"

Rise was touched by his question. He answered truthfully and, despite everything, he allowed himself a small, wry smile. "I call Cypriot my own heart," Rise replied.

Iskar nodded and glanced out of the lean-to, at the campfires below studding the dark. A fine bone moved in his temple.

"What is it?" Rise softly encouraged him.

"W-what might, in circumstances like these, what might my name be, then?"

Rise had to smile. Iskar's simple, human need for company, to fit and be named as belonging, touched Rise. "How about 'the best,' then?" he asked with an even wider smile and tilt of his head. "That's always how I've thought of you, ever since you ran to my gates for shelter."

"The best?"

Rise nodded but said no more.

"This place—Owl Court, I mean—has a weird protection over it, right? Like, it's not quite hidden from the world, but it's not advertising itself, either."

Rise had been in the middle of nodding in agreement. Then, with a dog barking beyond the wall, he realized that the night grew late and he'd dallied too long here with Iskar. There was no good in answering questions about protection when all of Owl Court was in jeopardy. He recalled the eyes of that lone owl, staring at Rise from the drawing room floor. The card still nestled in his pocket.

"Say one for me," Rise curled Iskar's fingers over the rosary beads and hurried down the lean-to's ladder.

Rise usually had little reason to enter the barn, other than to drop off or store the smallholding's produce. Tonight, he went to see the owls. But, instead, Rise found Cypriot. Cypriot stood in the middle of the barn, so enervated that he leaned against one of the stout wooden pillars, a feed bucket barely gripped in his fingers. He yawned loudly, looking as if he'd never slept at all.

"You've grown distant from me," he said, without turning around.

"Have I?" Rise was about to dismiss Cypriot's concerns so that he could climb the long ladder into the loft, where the owls nested. But then he relented, straightened and allowed the conversation to unfold. Maybe, if they all lived to see another sunrise, maybe he could get Cypriot to return the chronicle to Salter, who either hadn't noticed it missing or was keeping mum about the whole thing. So. Rise paused. He stretched out his arms, indicating the dire state of the world. "Is it any wonder, considering all that's happened?"

"Why don't you come to my room for a while?" Cypriot still hadn't turned around. But his voice deepened with an unmistakable tone of promise.

Rise had lost so many days of his life to that voice and to that swathe of warm, velvet skin. But now, no more. "You know that Annette and Iskar are afraid to talk to you?"

"Good. I don't want to talk to them. They keep smiling at me. Trying to be all buddy-buddy. I hate it." Then Cypriot let out a short, sharp sigh, as if it pained him to remain on his feet.

"What did you think of Elaine?" Rise asked, as curiosity about that particular lady bubbled to the surface. "What did you think about everything she said?"

"The coven secrets, they were never for her. Unless you'd told that Iskar fellow all about her already?"

Rise shook his head.

Cypriot finally turned around. His haggard face streamed with tears. "Come to my room," he pressed, as if it was the only thing that could solve their problems.

"I know your game," Rise told him plainly, the age of fawning over Cypriot and losing hours, days, to his bed now long past. "And I do not like your room. There's too many bugs there. Sometimes, I think your orchids are watching us."

"They probably are." Cypriot deflated as he spoke. Deep worry lines in his forehead aged his face. His brown eyes gazed at Rise; their depths held the history of their relationship across hundreds of years. When Cypriot yawned again, and more tears spilled over his cheeks.

"Do not beg me to fuck you, not with tears in your eyes," Rise warned. Because of what lay outside their walls, because of the revelations that the world teemed with his kind, the age of fawning over Cypriot was now long past. Rise told himself this again.

"I wasn't going to, Rise. I was just yawning."

"Cypriot. Everything's different now. Nobody can be selfish anymore, not if I have to try and have a clear head to talk to those monsters outside. You can't just expect me to lay—"

"I never knew you felt that way, Rise," Cypriot interrupted. He sounded too worn out to be angry. "I didn't know you hated my room. I'm sorry."

Rise expected snapping and bristling at anything that came close to criticizing Cypriot's plants. But his heart sank when Cypriot looked so defeated. "It's ... it's a beautiful room, though," Rise began. As the words left his lips, Rise realized he'd fallen back into the trap of placating Cypriot.

"No, I know." Cypriot shrugged and rubbed a tear-stained cheek with his sleeve.

"It's just all the bugs." Rise couldn't help it. This was the trap he loved.

"Sure," Cypriot nodded and then shrugged again. "But I don't know if I can do anything about them."

"I'm sure the bugs are needed." Rise scrambled to cobble together something to say. "Probably for the health of your plants?"

Cypriot kept his eyes downcast. He leaned against the barn pillar as if it was his job to keep it aloft. "I heard you talking to Iskar. You always forget. I've got such good hearing."

Rise watched him, really watched him. Even after all these years, Rise had no idea if Cypriot strove to manipulate him or not. Just as Cypriot turned to leave the barn without a further word, Rise crossed the distance between them and gently caught his elbow. Where Iskar had felt strong, meaty, Cypriot was pure bone.

"But—" Rise offered as he brushed his thumb over that warm joint. "There's always here?"

When Rise saw the beginning of a smile on Cypriot's lips, he let out a breath of relief. Over the past few weeks, Rise had forgotten the beauty of that rosebud smile.

"I suppose." Despite his clear exhaustion, Cypriot gave him that certain slanted gaze again, rich with even more promise.

"I was just ... I was just letting you know about your room." Rise could feel himself babbling. "That it really is crawling with bugs and that it makes me—"

"Shh." It was Cypriot's turn to catch his elbow.

Their mouths met over and over as they steered to the nearest bed: burlap sacks, empty and stacked high for the next harvest. As they toppled onto the makeshift bed, Rise tore the clothes from Cypriot with such hunger that he scratched deep, red welts across the swivel of his hips.

Afterwards, just as Rise was about to get back to his earlier idea of visiting the owls, Cypriot slid from their nest. The faint moonlight caught on his skin as he opened the nearest barn window. As he watched this little performance, enjoyed the view, a sudden idea seized Rise.

"Come with me?" He realized he'd never asked Cypriot this one question. "Come with me. Beyond the walls, into the world. You. Not Salter. Not Iskar. Not myself, alone, never again. You agreed with me, once, that I needed to leave. So, why doesn't Cypriot leave with me?"

"Leave?" Cypriot blinked over his bare shoulder. A cloud passed in front of the moon, until he was just another shadow against the dark window. "How can we possibly leave with all those people outside? And ... leave Salter behind? What would the coven do if something happened to me out there? Who would the coven feed upon?"

Rise did not answer. He didn't want to say aloud that he and Cypriot could make a new coven, together. A final chance for Cypriot to taste freedom, that thrilling freedom that Rise experienced whenever he set foot outside these walls. Sometimes, leaving Owl Court was the only thing that had made Rise feel alive. He idly rubbed his stomach, as if still nursing an old wound. He watched Cypriot's dark form until the need to explain his desire to leave nearly overwhelmed him.

"It's not as dangerous as you think, Cypriot, out there in the world. Once we get past the Warwolves outside, of course. I'd hoped that you would come adventuring with me, like the good old days? When we found Owl Court together? Being out in the world, it'd clear your head. Get you back in touch with everything, with life, outside these walls."

It took Cypriot a long time to answer, but eventually he shook his head. He returned to their bed of sacks, crawling close to Rise's body for warmth.

"I cannot," Cypriot said. "Don't—don't ever make me leave here, Rise. No matter what happens to us all under the thumb of those creatures out there. Don't ever order me to go, not in that tone of yours." Two huge tears rolled down his cheeks.

"Shh, no. Command you? I would never." Rise squeezed him. He hid, burying his nose in Cypriot's silken hair.

"Don't ... don't be disappointed in me," Cypriot gasped as he cried.

"Shush now," Rise lied and cuddled him close, stroked his long spill of hair. "How could I ever be disappointed in you? Everything you've ever done is for the benefit of the coven, isn't that right?"

Cypriot nodded and returned the embrace. "You know, you were right, Rise," he admitted, voice thick with tears. "I actually really do care about what you get up to with the newcomers. So, love me. Only me. That's all I ask."

Rise dried his tears and whispered sweet nothings. When Rise finally asked Cypriot to return the chronicle to Salter's desk without her knowing, Cypriot bent to the task gratefully, without question.

Rise got dressed and listened to Cypriot's footsteps patter across the courtyard. He heard something else, too. A low hum. A sound from the earth that Rise couldn't place. He found the barn's ladder again and hoisted himself into the loft. Then he took the smaller, rickety ladder that led into the rafters. Rarely would Rise enter the owl's space like this. He'd only done it recently when the outbreak became serious and brutes began to wander the world. The owls of Owl Court kept to themselves, and the coven respected that. Tom was their pet. The owls? Never.

"Ah, I should have brought a gift," Rise muttered as he shuffled from the last ladder and sat on the nearest rafter. He patted his pockets, but no dead mouse magically appeared. "I'm sorry—" he began, turning to apologize to what would surely be lines and lines of owls roosting in preparation for their hunt, later in the deep belly of the night.

But Rise stopped mid-sentence. The rafters were empty. The entire loft lay bare.

The owls of Owl Court were gone.

Chapter 20

Brute Force

Rise waited in the barn all night for the owls to return. He dozed in fits and starts, but that low hum kept him from fully falling asleep. Rise saw only the many-striped faces of yesterday's vampires, beautiful and powerful. When dawn threatened and not one feathered friend returned to roost, he wiped his eyes. Defeat hung in the air. They'd lived entirely separate lives over the coven's hundred years at Owl Court. The owls had always kept to themselves, fended for themselves. Rise thought he'd done them a favour by being so hands-off. They were wild birds of prey, after all. Not pets, not like their Tom. Still, Rise deeply missed the owls' presence, which was as constant to him as the red bricks of Owl Court.

He stayed in the loft for as long as he dared, wishing for, craving their return. Then, with the sun almost to the horizon, Rise hurried from the barn. As he crossed the yard, he caught sight of Iskar still sleeping on the floor of the lean-to. Inside, Cypriot curled up in Ogrim's armchair, a peaceful smile upon his face—a solitary relief for Rise. Annette slept on the drawing room couch. Rise could see her bundle of hair as he passed through the hall. Salter stood at the bottom of the stairs, already dressed in her floor-length cloaks.

"There you are. I was looking for you," she scolded as Rise pushed past and they raced to the roof.

"The owls, they're gone," he managed to say. The house passed them by in a blur of shuttered windows and freshly trimmed banisters.

"Gone?" Salter halted mid-step. "What does that mean?"

But Rise wouldn't let her stop; he caught her arm, goaded her ahead. They had to make it to the roof before dawn. "I thought a dream might come to me," Rise admitted, more to himself. "Last night. A dream that'd show me the way out. Or show a solution to how we make those bastards go away and we find peace once again. But. There was nothing. The owls are gone."

"What's Owl Court without its owls?" Salter asked in horror. She braced herself before opening the little wooden door to the roof. The moment she stepped outside, Salter tossed back her hood and revealed her face to the day. She grabbed for Rise's hands to form a circle.

Their fingers barely interlocked, his feet barely touched the flat patch of roofing, before Rise began the incantation. Louder this morning. Louder, so that it carried throughout every nook and cranny of their home and to every Warwolf camped outside. A declaration to anything and everything listening that the coven was still alive. Rise gave the prayer everything he had, and Salter's voice rose in support. But even Rise's recent reconciliation with Cypriot could not overcome a court with no owls, nor an incantation with no Ogrim. The Old

Language left his throat and Rise braced himself for the seal of protection to renew. Which it did. But no stronger than yesterday.

Rise flopped onto the water tank as bleakness overcame him. Answerless, he wanted to cry, but no tears came.

Salter tossed up her hood and stepped into the sliver of shade alongside the great chimney breast. "Rise?" she said simply, softly.

"What?" Rise muffled his face against his sleeve. He longed for sleep, like a soreness in his soul. He saw no way out. Nothing more that he could do to protect those he loved, all those souls under his care. Rise could do nothing.

"We need to leave," Salter stated. "We need to trade Owl Court, unsullied and undamaged, to the Warwolves for our safe passage."

"L-leave Owl Court?" he asked, mystified, lifting his head to look at her.

Salter stood as imperiously as a Warwolf. She was serious.

"The chronicle said, do you remember, Rise? I read back through the August entries of 1914. The chronicle said, quite clearly, that the original owner of Owl Court told you that we're merely keepers of this place. That this coven would one day pass it on to another. You should've asked her when this might happen, whether it was to come in hundreds of years or just a scant few. But, never mind. We can clearly see that the hour is upon us. Rise, you should've asked her too if there was anything the coven could've done to extend or deepen our hold or length of time here at Owl Court."

"Aye," Rise answered smartly as he sat up. He hauled his hood over his head against the rising sun. "Should've done a lot of things. Hindsight is great, isn't it?"

"Are we not going to fight at all, then?" Salter snapped. "Are we to hide in here until they decide to kill us, as if we are foxes caught in a den?"

"What should we do?" Rise snapped back with just as much venom. "What can we do? As long as the coven is inside these walls, we have invoked protection and—"

"That may not hold, Rise!"

He faltered. For the boundary to yield, that was a fate worse than an owl-less barn. "Of course it will," Rise said, but his voice crackled, came out weak.

"But, what if it doesn't?" Salter spoke in a light tone now, as if he were too simple to understand the true scale of their predicament. "We'll have stayed in here like literal sitting ducks. Instead of doing something. Instead of trying to barter with them out there. I get the impression they appreciate action, Rise. I don't think, from listening to Cantabar and Menelos yesterday, it's just us they want to conquer. They want *here*, Holly Hill itself."

"So we just give it to them?"

"Oh, Rise! Stop being so stupid!" Salter slammed her fist on the chimney breast. She advanced towards him, tall, commanding. They'd always led quite different lives, he and Salter. She was forever down in the cellar. Rise whiled away his hours with Cypriot. In truth, for a long time since they came here, Rise hadn't crossed Salter at all. From his low angle on the water tank, he saw beneath her hood. Black cloth covered her jaw and throat, but Salter's eyes glared at him.

"It's not stupid to want to save your home. To not want to give it away," Rise countered. "What do you expect me to do? Walk out onto the wall again and just give it to them? Those Warwolves, they won't keep any promise. They know no honour. If I were to drop the boundary's protection, they'd swarm inside and snuff us out." He took a shaky breath. "And if that's what they're going to do, they'll not have Owl Court without at least some whisper of resistance. Bargain with them, indeed," Rise snorted at the end, knowing her suggestion to be pure madness.

"You're not the boss here, Rise. No one is," Salter said, voice deep and serious. "There's not just you and your ego to think about. There are other people, too—"

"Annette?" he interrupted. "Is that it? You'd split from—"

"Oh shut up, Rise. I'm thinking about everybody. Not just what you couldn't possibly understand and only see to the end of your nose!"

Rise bridled and had opened his mouth to argue more when a great rumbling interrupted. The Warwolf camp burst into life. Horses saddled, dogs rallied, the scrabble of tents being dismantled.

"What on earth?" Salter hurried to the roof's corner to get a better look. "What're they doing down there?"

But Rise remained seated on the water tank. That low hum that had kept him from sleeping last night deepened, until it almost became too loud for his ears. It brought him right back to the autumn. He and Elaine and Marnie, being chased through the fields by the Dunsinann brutes. The day Rise first saw the Warwolves after the zombie plague was also the first time he'd seen the great brute river, worming its way towards Larnde.

He leapt to his feet. His hand locked over Salter's and, though unable to speak, Rise knew what was upon them. He tried to pull her back inside the house.

"Rise, what—?" Salter, surprisingly stronger, squirmed out of his grip. She grabbed him by the shoulders and shook him, hard. "Rise, what are you doing?"

"The brutes—" he could barely say.

"Yes? What about them? You've gone ghost-white, Rise. What about the brutes?"

Rather than leading the heroic dash through the house that he'd envisaged, collecting everybody in Owl Court together in one place so they could plan what to do next, Rise just slumped to the ground.

"Ow! Rise, what?" Salter complained as he landed awkwardly on her. But she knelt down with him, supported his head when his legs gave way.

"The brute river," he managed to say. His ears rang with the noises of the world.

"Yes, okay," Salter nodded frantically, trying to figure it out. "The horde of zombie brutes that you saw last autumn? When you brought back Elaine and her mother?"

Rise nodded, stars sparkling white in his vision. His ears throbbed to hear the shuffle of so many dead feet setting foot upon the base of Holly Hill.

"Yes, Rise," Salter shook him again. "What about it?"

But he couldn't answer. It was one thing to be surrounded by Warwolves. Quite another to hear your ultimate doom approach. He knew in his heart, as the one most knowledgeable about roots and boundaries, that the walls of Owl Court would not withstand such a mass of brutes. No incantation or protection or salted boundary could compete with the numbers he'd seen. Rise saw now why the leader Warwolves had camped at his walls: distracting the coven as the brute river was marshalled and directed to their gates.

Rise just pointed above their heads in answer.

Salter shoved him away. Stood to her full height and climbed onto the nearest slope of the orange-shingled roof.

"Oh no." Her whimper came to his ears above the deafening hum.

Hearing that terrible note of defeat in Salter's voice snapped something deep within Rise. He'd finally reconciled with Cypriot. He'd finally met his blood match in Iskar. With the owls gone, with Ogrim gone, many of the old shackles on his life had recently faded away. Replaced with good things.

The Judgement card stood in his mind.

"Well, if I'm going to be judged ..." Rise muttered to no one but himself. He struggled to his feet and opened the roof door. "Salter? Come quick," he called to her. She jumped down from the roof and they hurried inside.

"If I'm going to be judged, it'll not be because I didn't act."

"What?" Salter asked as they hurried downstairs.

Annette, carrying a huge kitchen knife, and Cypriot, holding his hedge clippers, met them on the second-floor landing, breathless and wide-eyed, barely able to speak through their terror. Iskar then met them in the hall, fresh from the lean-to, pale from seeing the approaching brute horde. He gripped something stripey and wriggling.

"Out there, they're herding thousands of brutes towards us." Iskar's voice trembled as he spoke. He shook his head, fists clenched. "Thousands."

"Oh!" Cypriot gasped when he saw that Iskar held Tom. Settling his hedge clippers under his elbow, Cypriot took the struggling tabby cat into his arms. He spun around to Rise. "What do we do?"

Rise looked at them all. His coven. They stood in an awkward huddle in the hall. Shambolic footsteps thrummed in his ears. It hit Rise then that, with everybody's eyes upon him and despite what Salter had said just now, he was the leader. And his next choice could be their last.

Rise dashed into the kitchen and scraped the armchair across the floor to keep the back door closed. His crowbar hung from a nearby nail, unused since that fateful night with Maxine. Rise grabbed it. Its metal chilled his palms, nearly transporting him back to earlier days.

"Into the root cellar," he told them.

"No, Rise, that'll be our tomb!" Salter gasped as the others sprang down into the darkness.

"We've nowhere else to go," Rise pointed out as he steered her towards the stairs. "At least underground, we're safe. You and I are at our strongest down in the depths. And didn't you always tell me that, when this door is closed, you'd barely know there's a root cellar down here at all? There's a good chance that anything that gets inside our walls will walk right past our hiding place. We'd just have to wait them out."

On and on, Rise cajoled Salter as he guided them all inside and shut the door, pressing the latch in that precise way that only a true resident of Owl Court knew how. He blinked as his eyes adjusted to the dark, until, knowing her way around the cellar best, Salter lit her lone candle and held it high for everyone to see. Iskar and Annette carried crates full of vegetables up the stairs to Rise. They brought up more and more, and stacked crates three, four rows deep behind the door.

"Either someone opens the door and sees nothing but potatoes and carrots," Rise panted as Iskar shoved Salter's chair onto the stairs to brace against the back of the crates. "Or they just won't be able to get inside, not through everything we've stacked here."

In a daze, sweat dripping from his brow, Rise nodded at Iskar. They'd done their best. He staggered down into the root cellar proper. It was tidier now than the last time he'd been down here, especially with most of the crates moved away. However, terrified faces looked at him. Ogrim's tall coffin stood in the corner. No time to wonder what the old fart would've made of all this.

"We shouldn't have trapped ourselves down here!" Cypriot flung himself into Rise's arms and tugged as if he could coax him back upstairs. "They'll bring the whole house down around our ears, Rise. And we're trapped in this cellar. We should've made for the barn, hidden high up in the rafters. Even if all the owls roosting in there would've given us away."

"Shh," Rise told him. "The owls are gone, Cypriot."

"What?" he gasped. Juggling the clippers and Tom under his elbow, Cypriot hugged Rise, crying harder now. "Then we really are forsaken. This cellar will be our tomb."

The brutes were so close against the walls of Owl Court that everybody could hear them. Rise cradled Cypriot against his shoulder and tried to think clearly. "You saw them?" Rise asked Iskar, just to say something, just to drown out the noises in his head. "You saw the brute river?"

"Brute river?" Iskar didn't understand at first. Then he nodded. "Yes, just as I said. The Warwolves goad them on so easily, like sheep. I couldn't see much from the lean-to, but I saw the ... river of them in the distance. Saw them approach. I lost sight when they came to the foot of Holly Hill. That's when I ran inside."

"When we were in the mines," Annette piped up as she clung to Salter's side, "any newcomers we found, most of them were refugees from the city. They told us about a great massing of zombies into one huge herd. I don't know if they're consciously coming together or not—"

Rise shook his head. "They're not. They're being herded."

"Well," Annette went on. Salter's candlelight gleamed like fire when it shone on her hair. "The refugees told us that the brutes swarmed whole buildings. Wherever people managed to set up shelter, it didn't matter. It was all decimated. The brutes work themselves into frenzies against stone, brick, concrete. They can bring down thick walls, if there's enough of them."

"Yes." Rise remembered Dunsinann bridge. "I've seen them do that."

"You knew this and didn't have us prepare?" Salter snapped at him.

But Rise waved her away. "Yes, just let me travel back in time—"

"Stop it, both of you!" Cypriot cried, his fist bunched deep in Rise's clothes. Tom struggled to be free.

Rise readied to counter Salter some more when the cellar shuddered. Something enormous gave way outside. The shuffling came louder. Tom flattened his ears against his furry little head and growled.

"This is a mistake." Salter carefully set her candle into Annette's hands and overturned her desk. From beneath her many layers, Salter pulled out a small pistol. She knelt and rested her elbows on the desk's edge, gun pointing up the stairs. With a nod, Annette and Iskar took cover behind the table, too.

Rise hadn't known that Salter kept a weapon. He stood in shock, staring at her pistol's elegant pearl handle. He hadn't known that she was just as devious as he.

Rise gathered his arguments, readied a rebuttal as to why hiding here was the correct course of action, when the house shook again. Footsteps of the dead thumped and crunched into the house, then higher overhead, as they spilled into the upper floors. Furniture crashed and smashed. How would the brutes fare in Cypriot's jungle of a bedroom? Rise took out his pistol and checked its full chamber. Then Rise knelt alongside Salter, keeping his crowbar close at hand, too. If the brutes tried to force the root cellar door, firing a gun would probably bring the whole stampede down upon their heads.

"The boundary's never been the same after Ogrim died," Salter said, glancing at the coffin in the corner. She took the safety off her gun. Rise did the same.

So, Salter had felt the boundary weakening. And she had not said anything to him.

"Rise," she whispered low, knowing he'd hear. "How could you not see that, from the moment the Warwolves crossed the holly yesterday, they were going to obliterate Owl Court off the face of the earth?"

Rise opened his mouth to argue. But he felt in his bones that Salter was right. The Warwolves wouldn't spend great effort dismantling a boundary by quenching its invocation. They were going to brute-force it. Boundary or not.

A bang at the cellar door jolted Rise out of his thoughts.

"Hide!" he told Cypriot, whose red, crumpled face dripped with tears and snot. Cypriot obeyed him for once and ran to Ogrim's coffin. With Iskar's aid, Cypriot hid in the tiny space behind, folding his limbs and hedge clippers so that he was out of sight. An odd yowl came from the hiding spot, but a jolt at the door turned Rise's attention to the stairs. He readied his gun. Waved to Salter to quench her candle.

It seemed everything wandering Owl Court now hammered and bashed at the door. Rise could put a spell of protection upon such a boundary, but he didn't know if he needed Salter's help, hand in hand, like the dawn invocation. He didn't know if he needed salt. Rise didn't know so many things about how his, their, powers worked. Sadness clawed at him as his ears pounded. The Warwolves knew so much, yet only sought destruction. Rise listened to the horde and massed Warwolves that circled their door, the floors of their home, and all throughout Owl Court. To Salter's shaking breath, to Iskar's, to Cypriot's. Tom's breath—tiny and furious—came from Cypriot's hiding place, too. Rise heard the clinking of sharp tools, from Cypriot's hands.

"Don't worry," Salter whispered, wincing at the terrible sounds reverberating throughout the root cellar. She smiled grimly and patted her side. "I have the chronicle. I thought I'd lost it, but I have it well hidden."

Rise nodded, even if he didn't care a whit about the book. "Can you shoot that thing?" he asked about Salter's gun as the cellar's door shook.

"It's ... been a while."

In the dark, beneath the noise, Rise began to count. First the minutes that passed, then the pounding beats of Cypriot's heart. To go to ground, like a knot of deep-drinking roots, Rise's choice was best. Not Salter's crazy plans of trying to barter with the Warwolves. Not Cypriot's crazy plan to flee to the barn. With Cypriot hidden, with Iskar leaning against his back as they crouched behind the table, Rise just closed his eyes. Minutes passed. Time spilled through their hiding place as they waited for it to be over, so they could experience the minutes and hours that lay on the other side of this moment. The faint sound of thin leather creaking as Salter squeezed the chronicle tight against her chest. Annette hid under her arm. Ogrim's coffin loomed obelisk-like in the dark.

Then, Rise heard Elaine's voice, bragging: "We command the greatest weapon of our time. Letting this load of brutes attack cities to deliberately bite any humans remaining. It's so easy to quell resistance against the Warwolves, so we can take over."

"Elaine?" Catabar barked, her head hooded against the daylight. "Come help."

"Huh? Oh yes, right away."

It was if their faraway voices found the single tone and pitch that carried right to Rise's ears. Elaine and Catabar, now joined by Menelos, sat on horses that impatiently pawed the earth. As brutes seeped out of Owl Court in bulges and dribbles, the trio observed the rest of the Warwolves that rode alongside and herded the shape of the great brute river. The Warwolves rode as one mind around the base of Holly Hill, keeping the horde contained.

"Those two that spoke to me. Catabar. Menelos. And Elaine. I can hear them," Rise said in shock.

"What?" Salter gasped.

"That should be enough damage done," Rise heard Menelos say.

Then Catabar fired into the air. The Warwolf riders changed to being rowdy, yipping shepherds and forced the brutes into a massed river once again. They led them away from Holly Hill and north over the countryside, away from Dunsinann and Larnde. Away from Owl Court.

"You can hear them?" Salter pressed in a hushed tone. The clamorous noise slowly drained from the house. "I can't hear anything; only the brutes above us."

"Why're they leaving?" Rise muttered, ignoring Salter and Cypriot. He'd thought the brutes would have stayed at Owl Court for days and days, until certain that the whole coven was wiped out.

It was like a hawk spotting something from a great height. Catabar snapped right into his ears again:

"They are great diggers, Rise. The brutes. Great destroyers of boundaries. And how do you, a sage of roots and groundworks and all deep things, not know what we were doing? How did you not realize what we are at?"

"Consider Catabar's words, Rise," Menelos said smugly. She kicked her horse and it broke into a canter. But she didn't enter Owl Court. Instead, Menelos sprang past the other Warwolf riders to the front of their line, to lead the brute horde away. Still, Menelos' voice carried to him. "Because you keep asking us why, acting as if you cannot comprehend why we might do any of this at all."

"But I don't—" Rise replied, then he blinked in the darkness of the cellar.

Crashing came from the top of the stairs. Wooden planks split and splintered as brutes forced their way inside. Some stacks of crates held upright, others toppled, spilling vegetables down the stairs. Pale daylight filtered in and lifted the gloom of the cellar. Rise and Salter sprinted upstairs, Iskar and Annette at their heels, scrabbling over potatoes and carrots.

"Don't shoot. It'll only attract more of them," Rise warned Salter as he put away his gun and took up his crowbar. The stench of rot caught in his throat. Angered that his home should be sullied with the brutes' mere presence, Rise thrust the crowbar through the narrow opening between the many crates and the hole in the door. On the far side, in Owl Court's hall, brutes snapped their jaws, curled their rotting fingernails into the wood. The brutes shimmied their shoulders, their whole bodies, against the doorframe. Just as Rise had seen at Dunsinann bridge.

Rise's crowbar plunged into something brittle and yielding. A brute dropped mid-shriek. A touch to his shoulder. Iskar and Annette held the cellar's huge broomstick. Rise stepped aside and let them jab it through the hole. Strengthening his grip on the crowbar for his next turn, Rise heard a crack from below in the cellar. Salter's foot was planted upon her desk as she wrenched off one of its legs. She rejoined them at the top of the stairs as, one by one, the four of them took turns stabbing their weapons through the gaping timbers. Iskar grunted at the brutes that they couldn't reach. Beyond, corpses piled up. The door's hole the only source of light.

"They're ... the Warwolves are leading the main horde of brutes away," Rise said to galvanize everybody, as his arms burned with exertion. "So ... these brutes here, these are just stragglers. We can do this." He didn't shout, lest he draw any more attention to the cellar. He spoke calmly. The four of them fell into an easy rhythm of step in, thrust, step back, wait your turn. Calm, collected, measured, never letting anyone get too tired; this was the coven's defence. Pride in their teamwork swelled through him. Rise didn't know what would happen next, what they'd have to do after this moment. Maybe make for the barn? He didn't know.

Menelos' voice came into his ears. "We have more than enough to feed on, Rise. And all of our fed-upons have more than enough food to sustain them. We've taken care of our sustenance far better than you, Rise. We don't even need to keep any of your rescued alive in order to pad our numbers. We can just erase you all. And we will. You ... who have done nothing."

Rise didn't let her words stay in his head. With the crowbar in his hands and the pistol at his hip, those two things assured everybody's escape. Choosing the right moment to act was just a matter of waiting and doing nothing. Something those Warwolves didn't seem to understand.

The door rattled. Shimmying zombies worried its hinges. With a great crash, it gave way.

Rise shoved Iskar and Annette aside as he and Salter braced the opening with the surrounding crates. As decaying arms reached inside, Rise and Salter flung the crates against the splintered doorframe. Some crates toppled through the gap, crashing into the brutes and corpses piled outside. That bought mere moments. Rise grabbed his gun. Salter did the same and stood side by side with Rise. They fired together.

The attacking brutes fell to the ground. Twitching, then still.

Rise braced for a hundred more brutes to appear after making such noise. But nothing happened after that for a long time. No more brutes came. Rise could hear them, but most were far away. Rise just stood, pistol drawn, watching black blood seep from holes in those rotting heads.

"There's nothing more we can do." Salter, her hands shaking, touched Rise's outstretched arm. He lowered his gun as she handed him his crowbar. "Only escape and save ourselves. That's all."

Rise nodded. The cold metal in his hands dragged him back to his senses. He turned around to check on Iskar and Annette, who huddled midway down the cellar stairs.

"Cypriot!" Rise cried in shock, as movement blurred around Ogrim's coffin and Cypriot sprang from his hiding place. A ball of something dark and furry shot across the root cellar as Tom leapt out, too.

"I can hear something!" Cypriot pointed, horrified, at the walls. "There's something in there! I can hear—"

From beneath Owl Court, in the depths of the earth, a deep explosion boomed.

"Dynamite!" Iskar gasped as the cellar crumbled and everything went dark.

Chapter 21

The Base Brute

Rise roared in pain as the explosion reverberated throughout the landscape, torturing his ears.

"Out, out!" Rise made the snap decision as his arms held aloft a great slab of ceiling. Better to die in fresh air at the hands of a brute than to suffocate beneath the earth. Salter knelt safe in the cellar doorframe, pushing crates and brute corpses out of the way. Annette coughing, hacking in the dust. Others crawled about in the cellar, knocking into debris and chunks of fallen ceiling. How the whole house hadn't collapsed around their ears, Rise would never know.

"Come to me!" Rise called as his arms shook. His wrists threatened to give. Rise dug deep, tapping that great well of strength. "Come to the stairs. The banisters saved us. There's a way out—crawl up the stairs. Hurry!"

Shadows passed by Rise. Annette. Iskar, with a deep gash above his eye. Then Cypriot, still clutching his hedge clippers. Everybody was coated in a thick layer of dust as they crouched low beside Salter, their filthy, bruised hands gripping the doorway as they crawled into the hall.

The house juddered and Rise nearly lost his grip.

"Come on!" he called for one more. Tom cat raced up the stairs and bolted out of the cellar door. Rise gave a last glance at Ogrim's coffin in the wreckage. He cursed that he was unable to give Ogrim a proper burial and said a silent prayer that he still might, one day.

Salter peeked in at Rise from the hall. He nodded at her, drew on his strength and pushed the ceiling upwards. That gave Rise a split second, before everything crashed down, to dive for the door. Thankfully, Rise had his vampire speed. Not even his feet were caught by the collapsing debris as he landed on his stomach in the hall.

"Thank—thank goodness," Cypriot whispered as he bent and helped Rise to his feet. Iskar and Annette leaned against one another, dazed.

"Is everybody okay?" Salter asked, gazing at the destroyed staircase alongside them that once led to the upper floors.

"Outside, outside," Rise herded them. "No time to stand around."

Normally, they had never used the house's front door. Too unlucky, Rise had always thought. As if his kind needed permission to enter their own home. That's why they preferred the back door. But, with a quick glance to the kitchen, Rise saw only piles of rubble from the floor above.

"My plants!" Cypriot whined at the sight of their kitchen, their home.

Rise took the lead as he guided everybody to the gaping hole that had once been their front door. Pistol lifted. He had no idea how many bullets were left.

"Where're we going, Rise?" Salter caught his elbow as Rise stepped through the hole first, carefully avoiding the splintered wood and broken glass on each side. Tom sprang past Rise's feet and ran into the courtyard. Their little cat fled through the destroyed walls and on until he disappeared into the countryside, ears flat against his head. A line of dark fur bristling down his back.

"Why did the protection not work?" Rise asked, as their little cat showed them exactly what to do. Run. Don't look back. The sun revealed a bright spring morning, nearing noon. At least the dust hanging in the air kept his skin from burning. "Why would any explosion damage what I've spoken?" Rise helped everybody through the door and cast his hearing abroad but heard only Warwolves yelling and hollering in triumph. Their horses struggled to direct the brute horde away from Holly Hill, but the Warwolves were loud in their victory.

A creak came from inside the house, then an upper floor gave way, crashing into the hall they'd just stood in.

Drawing everybody back from the rising cloud of dust, Rise led the way into the courtyard. Several straggling brutes stumbled towards them. He put away his gun and picked up a scythe discarded near the front doorstep. Rise halved the brutes' bodies, easily. Then the terrifying rattle of automatic weapons fire jolted through the air.

The courtyard lay filled with the trampled bodies of brutes, animals, even some Warwolves and horses that had been caught up in the herd. The cobblestones slick with blood and odd bumps and lumps of entrails. They'd brought fire, too, to the house and trees. Smoke trailed from the scattered bonfire; the hedge at the back door was now only charred twigs. Their barn and stables had been destroyed, either by the cascade of brutes or by the explosion. Their farm animals ran loose. Pigs waddled about, feeding alongside the odd brute, then squealing in terror when they in turn were fed upon, too. Salter hid her face in her hands as they crossed the yard. Cypriot kept both of his arms wrapped around her, hugging Salter tight as they made it to the huge gap blasted into Owl Court's wall.

A hand clasped his shoulder. Rise turned with the scythe to end the intruder.

"Rise, no!" Cypriot cried and shrank away in terror.

Salter's tall figure stood behind Cypriot. Rise barely had a moment to register either of them.

"This isn't our home, Rise. Not anymore," Salter told him sternly, as if he hadn't heard her properly before.

Rise lifted the scythe in his hands to indicate the destruction around them. "The Warwolves mean to obliterate not just us, but the house, the whole hill too," he told her grimly. A part of Rise wanted to hurry into the house's ruins, clamber to the topmost collapsed roof to invoke protection all over again.

Salter whimpered something. She tucked Cypriot under her arm. She tried to cover her head and face with her usual long clothes. Rise attempted to do the same, pulling up his hood.

"Are you both okay?" he asked Annette and Iskar.

"We're fine," Iskar answered. He held a scythe, too, although the wound at his eye bled down his face. Rise patted his pockets for a handkerchief and handed it to him. Annette held the rosary beads in her chalky white hands, the cross missing.

"Where are we going, Rise?" Salter asked again as they stood in the wall's opening, red bricks shattered and crumbled at their feet.

"I don't know," Rise growled through gritted teeth. Dynamite underground and dynamite at his walls. And enough brutes to overwhelm them all. The occasional shard of sunlight knifed his skin as he stepped outside the boundary of his home. His whole life narrowed. *Just put one foot in front of the other*, he told himself. *Just keep breathing. Keep Salter and Cypriot and Iskar and Annette safe.* He could think of more; Rise could allow himself to mourn for their home, long after these moments had passed. But right now, he took everything one literal moment at a time, like lining up delicate beads on the thread of a necklace. One spill, and they were all asunder. "What I do know is that we need to get ever so far away. And out of the sun."

"Okay," Salter nodded, terrified. "Okay."

"You still have the chronicle?" Rise asked as they passed through the ring of holly trees, or at least, what was left of their smoking trunks.

Salter nodded again as she clung to Cypriot.

Several brutes shuffled about the tall grasses. They straightened to attention when they saw the living. Rise stepped forward with his scythe and staved in their skulls, leaving them writhing, squawking messes upon the trampled earth, until the silence of the last blow. In the confusion, another brute reached for them, but Cypriot was too quick. He jumped from Salter and buried his pruning shears deep into the side of the creature's neck, then jumped back when the brute turned to hit him. Cypriot ducked and sprang up beneath its outstretched arm. Another blade plunged into its ribs. When Cypriot stepped out of reach again, the brute dropped dead.

"Be careful with these stragglers. Especially from behind." Rise caught Cypriot's elbow to keep him close. Rise ignored the terror around them, ignored the grisly blood spatters on everybody's faces and clothes. What the Warwolves would do when they discovered that they'd escaped—well, they'd destroyed Owl Court. But Rise knew that there was plenty else that the Warwolves could do to them.

A shriek and the thunder of hooves made Rise turn. A hooded Warwolf rode towards them, scythe high overhead. Rise instinctively threw Cypriot to the ground, using his own body as cover. The other three dove out of the way too, as Rise ducked his head and trampling hooves sped past. Rise braced for pain, for a blow that did not come.

When he opened his eyes, Rise pulled Cypriot to his feet. The rider sprang from the horse and ran at them, scythe aloft. It was no Warwolf at all, but Elaine, who had waited and watched as the ever-sentinel, under the burning holly trees. Rise, standing in front of Cypriot, frantically looked for Salter, for Iskar and Annette, but they were nowhere to be seen. Amid the dust, Rise gritted his teeth and swung his attention back to Elaine, gripping his scythe and feeling Cypriot's jagged breath in his ear. He didn't want to show his gun until the last moment. For interminable seconds, Elaine ran towards them as Rise bore Cypriot's fingers digging into his shoulders, bore the sharp sun, like acid in his eyes. He hoped Salter had fled and taken Iskar and Annette with her, somewhere.

"I wasn't dead, Rise," Elaine shouted, smirking, descending upon them like the shadows in his dreams. "I ran away that night when Cypriot butchered my mother. He let me escape, though. To live without her. Did he ever tell you that, I wonder?"

"Hey!" Iskar shouted. He jumped out from behind a nearby holly tree and flailed his arms, waving his bloodied handkerchief.

Taking advantage of the distraction, Rise reached for his gun. As Elaine's shadow fell across them, she lifted her scythe. Rise fired. *As I should have done since the moment I met her.* Rise lifted his crowbar above her crumpled body to finish her off. He felt no sorrow, no regret as she died.

"I should've killed her, along with her mother that night," Cypriot said and spat on Elaine's corpse, even as Rise pulled him away from the grisly scene. Rise looked around, about to thank Iskar and ask after the others. But Iskar had vanished.

"Where is he? Where's Salter?" Rise ran to the holly tree, but Iskar was nowhere to be seen. Brute tracks littered the ground, sure, but brute tracks were everywhere. Rise leaned against the charred, smoking trunk, as Cypriot tried to pull him away, to flee from the carnage.

"No, no, we can't stay here," Cypriot coaxed, terrified. "There's too many brutes, the stragglers. There's probably still Warwolves about. Let's get to somewhere quiet. Then you can listen for the others, yes? You can listen for them then, right, Rise? Come on."

Reluctantly, Rise saw the logic of Cypriot's words. He wiped his face with his sleeve, scythe still in his hands. Elaine's corpse lay just over there. Her horse stood there, too.

"Rise, come on!" Cypriot pleaded, nearly in hysterics, as he tried to draw Rise away from the holly tree. Eventually, Cypriot got his way and they made for Elaine's horse. The blade of her discarded scythe glinted in the harsh sun as the day passed into afternoon.

As they ran for the horse, shadows rose out of the surrounding clouds of dust and smoke. Something thumped Rise hard on the back. He fell, bringing Cypriot with him. Brutes rushed upon their bodies. Rise tried to get his scythe lifted in time. He tried to flip onto his back to protect Cypriot. Fight off the brutes.

Rise tried.

He screamed at a sudden pain in his neck. The fallen, mangled walls of Owl Court echoed him.

*

The next thing Rise knew, he and Cypriot were hurrying down the lane, away from Owl Court. Stinging pain radiated from Rise's neck. Rise wanted to stop and scratch it.

"No, no," Cypriot whimpered and struggled with Rise's arm, which he'd draped over his narrow shoulders. "No stopping."

"Hurts," Rise snarled and tried to shake him off. He wanted to turn around, to see how they'd managed to escape the brutes.

But Cypriot held on tight, with a vicious, stubborn strength. He hauled Rise along, bitterly weeping as they stumbled down the path. The destruction of Owl Court, the dust kicked up by the brutes, all hung in the air. Rise could barely see a few feet in front of them. His ears still rang from the explosion, but he could make out the Warwolf riders whooping and shouting in the distance. He tried to reach for Salter, for Iskar and Annette, to see where they were, but howling dogs interrupted his ears, setting his teeth on edge.

"Dogs." Rise jolted upright. "Didn't Maxine say, when we first came across her, that the Warwolves were training them?"

"W-what? I—I don't know," Cypriot sobbed. He shook his head and maneuvered the two of them off the lane, into the row of trees that ran alongside the path. It was darker here, shaded from the sun, with less dust and smoke. "I don't know why you're asking, Rise. I wasn't there with you and Ogrim, remember? I wasn't there when you found her. I don't know."

"Where's Iskar? Where's Salter? Where's my crowbar, my pistol?" Rise demanded when he realized that it was just the two of them. And Cypriot's hands were empty of weapons. But Cypriot just shook his head again. His dark eyes pointed forwards between the trees as they followed alongside the lane, as if life itself lay ahead.

Rise felt disconnected. He eased his struggling and let Cypriot drag him along through the softer grass beside the lane. He felt pain, though, beyond the deep pinch in his neck. Daylight strengthened as the sun gripped the land. But Rise, oddly, couldn't bring himself to care about anything. Even though a small corner of his mind screamed at him to care. Instead, he lifted out his free hand as the trees offered shade, strobing dark blobs and patches of shade across his arm. He sighed at the tiny relief.

Cypriot soon grew too tired. They collapsed into a thick crop of grassy bushes just before the lane met the wider road. Rise fell against something hard and hidden. He yelped and slowly turned to see what it was, as Cypriot pulled at the grasses to make it look like they were never there at all.

"Where did those owls ever go, Cypriot? Why would they leave us? Is it like when animals flee before an earthquake? I needed to gather ... gather ... so that I'm not alone. Oh, it's ... it's my bike." Rise had to smile at the recognizable handlebars and frame. So that's where it was. "That's right. I never had a chance or thought to retrieve it. I should have, but I didn't. No time for anything."

But Cypriot wasn't listening. Instead, he peeked out of the grasses and kept patting his pockets, as if looking for something.

Rise gently touched his arm. "Hey," he told him. It was so important for him to know. "It was round here that I found your flowers. Back in the spring. Do you remember?"

Cypriot gave up on making their nest look hidden. He sagged. When he turned back to Rise, he was still crying. In fact, Cypriot sat and wept for long minutes, muffling any sound by pressing his hands to his face. Then, wiping his nose on his sleeve, Cypriot reached into his shirt pocket and showed Rise a clump of pale and wrinkled purple flowers.

"Of course I remember, Rise. I've kept that helleborus with me. Always. Anything you've ever given me, I've always kept." Cypriot looked mournfully at the flowers. "They're supposed to be a cure for madness? I can only hope. At least I think we're safely hidden, for now."

They remained hidden and still for unknowable time. Whenever Rise opened his eyes, he felt as if hours passed, or sometimes only mere seconds. The ages and eras of his long life melted together. Months spent in one far-flung place felt as short as a mere breath, a blow of air to cool the morning's porridge. He should have felt such panic at his loss on the grip of time. But to let all such concerns go, to let the future go, it was actually a pleasant and relaxing thing. Rise had his Cypriot in this moment. The moments that would follow, the moments that had passed, the panic that should surely ignite fight and fury within him, it all coalesced into dim, dark waters.

With a sigh, a sad smile came to Cypriot's lips. "Do you know why I garden, Rise?" Cypriot spoke softly now, to the point where Rise felt that it was actually rather cosy for them to be tucked away in this little bore of springtime grass, shaded and cupped by nature.

"Because my grandfather always had dirty hands," Cypriot explained as he turned the delicate flowers between his dust and blood-caked fingers. "My brother told me that it was because he was a gravedigger. I was terrified of my grandfather after that, for the rest of his life. But it was only after his death that I realized something. Our grandfather just liked to garden." The sad smile pulled at the corner of Cypriot's chapped lips. "That's why I love plants so much now. To atone for that."

"You were only a child." Rise tried to lift his hand to touch those lips, but somehow that felt difficult, strained.

"Yes. But also old enough to know better." When Cypriot smiled again, another tear spilled down his splotched and bloodstained cheek. He took a shaky breath. "'Plants sacrifice themselves to the gaze of your enemies.' An old lady in Shanghai told me that, when any of my plants died, even if I had cared for them with all of my knowledge. So, now when my plants die, I thank them. They died protecting me. Like all those in the kitchen. You know what, Rise? I always thought it good for the coven to live so deeply in the countryside, in all this greenery. I always thought it protected us from the eye of our enemies. I guess not."

"Oh?" asked Rise, confused, "Why do you say that?"

"Oh Rise, you don't know?" Cypriot began, distraught, but a tremendous shudder rattled the earth beneath them. Cypriot gasped and peeked out of the grasses again. Then he flung himself back onto Rise as hoofbeats pounded the lane past their hiding place.

Rise tried to sit up, but the pain in his shoulder stabbed. He winced and grasped Cypriot's sleeve. Cypriot clung to him until Rise would lie back down. When Rise just stared at him, Cypriot burst into sobbing again and touched the crumpled collar of Rise's coat. "You're bitten, Rise. A brute bit your shoulder right after we tried to get Elaine's horse." His voice broke.

As Rise soaked this in, he tried to draw on that deep reserve of vampire strength that he knew—he knew!—he possessed. But nothing came. All wasted upon the cellar's ceiling. His mind leapt ahead to the next plan. Could he and Cypriot somehow take the bike and escape?

But the bike was rusty now. No use to anyone.

The wound in his shoulder would take him, just as it had taken Ogrim. He, too, would be no use to anyone.

"Then, you need to leave and get far away from here." Rise, without much further ceremony, opened his mouth to use the tone of command on Cypriot, to send him away, perhaps even to tell him to find Iskar. Safety with that one.

"No! Don't you dare!" Cypriot apparently knew what Rise was up to. He clapped his hands over his ears and curled his chin into his chest. He stayed ever so still. By the time Cypriot cracked open an eye to look at Rise, Rise had lost the strength to command, to do this to him. Rise shook his head in anger, tried to shove Cypriot away. But he was too weak and Cypriot was too stubborn.

"I can't hear them coming, the Warwolves, because they're vampires, Rise. I can only hear their dogs or horses. So, if you send me out there, if you send me away from you, I'll surely die, Rise. Either way, let me stay here. Let me have these moments. You've never commanded me; please don't start now." Cypriot gathered Rise against him and pushed away the bike frame.

"Watch over me." He clung to Cypriot. "I might come back, like Ogrim. You ... you always said you'd never do anything to hurt the coven. And look at you now—still here."

Rise remembered his Ogrim. His Iskar. His Salter. Rise couldn't even summon panic any more at the easing of his pulse, the stilling of his senses. He gripped Cypriot, but his fingers only gently lay above his heart. A familiar burn came as Rise's Blaschko lines rose across his face, down his body, like a firecracker streaking through a foggy night. All around looked so much greener than before. Rise tried to rub the old wound on his stomach, half-knowing it was not real, only a dream wound, half-rubbing it out of habit.

Rise remembered that Salter still had the chronicle. Then his vision was haunted by the many vampire faces he'd seen only yesterday, all of them striped and beautiful with Blaschko lines bared to the sun. What would such people make of his coven's written word? "The record of who we are. What we did. It must be saved, spared. Maybe that's what Marnie told me to gather, in order to cross the bridge?"

"I don't ... I don't understand," Cypriot whimpered, his chin on Rise's chest, as if they still lay in his jungle of a bedroom.

Tall, plush ferns and grasses encircled them. Dissolving into the green was a relief, an escape for Rise. "A countryside taking back its realms," he murmured as the pain in his neck spread down his spine, into his shoulders, like a rictus ruling his veins. Did Marnie wait on the other side, ready to taunt him again once he slipped from consciousness?

"We were all scared savages at Owl Court, huddled around a fire. Like a cluster of teepees, and they came to colonize us." Then, he managed to say, as his jaw froze in place, "I am sorry, Cypriot. I am sorry about ... about Iskar. You finding me drinking from him in the—"

"Shh!" Cypriot pressed their lips together insistently.

The kiss felt like nothing. He was unable to form proper words, no matter how hard he clung to life.

In the distance, Rise heard Warwolves approach their hiding spot. Dogs ran alongside. Rise worried that, when he woke up, he wouldn't be able to pray or invoke any protection for himself and Cypriot. He worried, in a dull, fading pinpoint-corner of his mind, that he should have tried invoking protection around their little green embrace long ago.

As the lights went out across his life, Rise trusted one thing: that there were always survivors after the collapse of great things. He, at least, would not be the last of his people. Zero times.

There was so much I should have done, Rise wanted to say aloud.

He held Cypriot as people approached. People that Cypriot could not hear.

"Keep watch," Rise wheezed as Cypriot bowed and kissed him. Would he ever resurface—anew—changed enough, so much, too much, that he would want to take his life as Ogrim had? His blood waned as everything darkened. The gentle scent of his Cypriot ... until the tenuous link between smell and memory eased into nothing.

A bridge rose in the gloom. Statues of horses reared. The host of shadows swept him to Marnie. One crack of his crowbar collapsed her skull, and Rise finally entered Dunsinann. The town disappeared into greenery as he crossed between the two pillars. A countryside taking back its realm.

The End

THE BLOOD BRUTE SERIES

Prequels:

1. On the Edge of Salt
2. Finding Home

Series:

1. Rise of One
2. Fall of Two
3. Ebb of Three
4. Strain of Four
5. Myth of Five

Find out more at Amazon or www.DixonReuel.com

PREQUEL SHORT STORY – *ON THE EDGE OF SALT*

On the Edge of Salt covers the early onslaught of the zombie apocalypse, when firebombs are first used to take out whole cities that are brute–infested. With a hidden home and smallholding shielded from the world, Rise is confident that his coven is safe behind the red brick walls of Owl Court. But as the night sky burns, a stranger with a terrible secret approaches his walls...

PREQUEL SHORT STORY – *FINDING HOME*

Set in the early days of World War I, *Finding Home* tells the story of how Rise procured the beautiful red brick house of Owl Court. While an old lady refuses to vacate her smallholding, a town drains of its young men with WWI on the horizon, and a vampire comes to town...

BLOOD BRUTE BOOK TWO

DIXON REUEL

BOOK TWO – *FALL OF TWO*

Capture. Old Dreams. New Powers.

On the verge of a lifetime of servitude under the evil Warwolves, The Vampire Rise hatches an escape plan. But when Rise fails to also rescue his imprisoned lover, Cypriot-- choosing revenge on their cultish captors over escape--Rise must find a new way out before Cypriot succumbs to the Warwolves' torture.

ABOUT THE AUTHOR

Irish award-winning and best-selling writer, Dixon Reuel is the author of the Dark Urban Fantasy series, **Blood Brute**. Dixon lives in Dublin, Ireland and holds a First in History & Early Irish Studies and another First in Creative Writing. She is a lifelong nerd and devoted hobbyist of cosplay, gaming, and other surely worthwhile pursuits.

www.DixonReuel.com

Rise of One by Dixon Reuel

missnatmack

BOOK DESIGN & ILLUSTRATION

"Every great design, begins with
an even better story."

t: +44 (0) 7487659299
missnatmack@gmail.com · missnatmack.com
@missnatmack

Made in the USA
Coppell, TX
08 October 2021

63671007R00167